7

Lindsey S. Frantz

THE UPWORLD Copyright ©2017
Line By Lion Publications
www.linebylion.com

ISBN: 978-1-940938-93-6

Cover Concept: Joe Stockton
Cover Art: TJ Brandt
Editing By: Enchanted Editing

Dedication

TO MY MOM AND DAD, BONNIE AND EDDY,
for encouraging me to always pursue my dreams
(even if they really wanted me to be a lawyer).

TO MY BROTHER, JOEY, AND MY COUSIN, SONDRA,
for their creative support and advice, and their loving
guidance through every word written and rewritten.

AND TO MY HUSBAND, VINCE,
for his unending, unshakable belief in me and his
willingness to talk about my stories day after day after day.

Prologue

Erilyn

Stones bounced off my body and laughter bounced off walls. My hands glowed with the iridescent blood of glowworms, my blood mixing with it.

Heat welled in my belly and burst forth from my hands, causing the earth to shake. Laughter turned to screams and ricocheted against the inside of my skull. All I could see was her face—terrified and white—as rocks fell all around.

I ran. Wind whipped through my hair. The cave thinned and thinned. A fiery, furry monster painted on the wall—a warning to stop. Just past it, white light so brilliant my eyes and heart ached.

I fell into the light, the earth trembling beneath me, and stared up into eternity.

Chapter One
Awake

Erilyn

Autumn air cooled the sweat on my skin as my heart pounded against my ribs painfully. I squeezed my eyes shut and pressed the heels of my hands into them so hard I saw a rainbow of stars. It was the same dream I'd had for weeks on end—a distorted memory of the night I left my home in the caves of Citadel and came upworld. It had been four years and I still wasn't sure if I had killed any of the children that had been with me. Through the starry rainbow exploding behind my closed eyes I could still see Aiyanna's face in the darkness, her mouth wide in terror as she screamed, rocks falling all around. I pressed my hands into my eyes harder until the image faded away.

I forced my eyes open and focused on the pine branches above me as the stars blinked out, focused on the holes in the grass mats I'd woven and tied to the branches to keep out the rain. I slowed my breathing like Rosemarie had taught me and tried to focus—the smell of the pine needles and sap, the feel of my large cat's belly pressing into my side as she took deep sleep breaths, the way the light filtered through the holes in the mat and trickled down to me. I exhaled slowly and closed my eyes.

My heart wasn't racing anymore. The echoes of their screams were nothing but a memory again.

Next to me, Luna, my serval cat, woke. She yawned and stretched, the muscles beneath her thick white fur rippling. Luna chirped at me—her voice both delicate and fierce—to say good morning. I sat up and she rubbed the side of her body against me, her tail curling around my neck as she slipped under the pine branches and disappeared into the woods.

I pushed myself to standing, the mat covered branches well above my head, and winced. My nails had almost bitten through the soft flesh of my palms as I slept. I stretched my hand, feeling the little crescent-shaped indentions ache.

I slipped between the pine branches and stretched into the cool morning air, working out the final kinks in my spine from my nightmare. The air was spicy with the smell of drying leaves. Uncovering the fire pit, I got a small fire going. Using a dented metal pan, I scooped water from the tiny stream that fed my pond, adding some broken needles from my pine tree for tea.

Rosemarie had always told me the longer you watched a pot the longer it would take to boil, so I sat, closed my eyes, and let the tiny flames dance across the backs of my eyelids. My hands curled into fists and I forced them to lie flat on my knees instead.

Some days were harder than others to outrun the ghosts of my past. I knew that the only way to move past it was to let myself really truly remember for a single moment—like intensely watching a shooting star as it streaked across the sky before it fizzled out.

I gripped my knees with my sore hands, took a breath, and let the shooting stars fly.

Memories played out on the backs of my eyelids, dancing with the flames and shadows. With each inhale came a single vivid memory and with each exhale I let it go for one more day.

The laughter and screams of children. Hands covered in glowing blue-green blood.

Lavender and mint—the feel of Rosemarie's cool, rough hand against my forehead.

The moon hanging bright white in a sea of infinite stars—blindingly bright.

Baby Luna resting in the palm of my hand. Rosemarie's house in flames.

Rosemarie, a halo of sunlight in her silver hair.

With my last exhale I opened my eyes. I was able to push the memories back into whatever dark corner of my brain they lived for another day, just as Rosemarie had taught me to do when I first started waking from night terrors.

My mind was clear. The scent of pine tea wafted toward me, and along with it, my name whispered on the wind. *Erilyn.* Muscles tensed to run or fight, I looked all around. This wasn't the first time I'd heard voices whispering from the trees. I let my awareness—a part of me that could sense the area around me without using my eyes or ears—search for anyone nearby who might have spoken, but there was no one. I shook my head.

I poured tea into a tin cup I'd found my first summer on my own. It had been half buried in the woods next to the foundation of an old cinder stone house. The exposed part of the cup had been bleached by sun and scratched clean by the elements, but the buried part still showed part of the picture that had been painted on it so many dozens of years before.

While the tea cooled, I examined the cup as I did every morning. I hated this cup. Next to the handle was a group of children holding hands, wearing rags and no shoes. I could never look at them very long without feeling that same anger and fear that caused the earthquake all those years ago, even though these children were nothing like the children in Citadel. Beside them sat a man holding a jug with XXX written across it. The man, with some kind of grass clenched between his gapped teeth, was smiling. Drunk. He looked stupid and I hated him most of all. Above the stupid, awful people were the letters LUEGRASS.

I turned the cup so that I could only see the scuffed, blank metal. The first sip burned my tongue, but the tea was rich and eased that gnawing ache of hunger that had started deep in my belly. I sighed as I mentally went over the food I had available for the day. It was time to start rationing for winter.

The sun was fully up now and shining through the tall oak and maple branches that reached over the top of my clearing like a tent. The leaves were starting to change — crimson and gold. I loved how they could look so soft and delicate and like they were on fire all at once. Even after being upworld for four years, I still wasn't used to all the color and how it changed day by day.

I finished my tea as Luna returned from her hunt. She tucked her large white and gray head under my hand and bumped my shoulder. She was brilliant white and speckled with gray spots. She was the most beautiful creature I'd ever seen and my only friend.

Rosemarie had given her to me the week after she was born. She had been solid white then. The rest of the litter had been gold and black, so her mother had refused to let her nurse. Instead, I fed her with goat's milk and a spoon. She was only a few weeks old when the Wylden killed Rosemarie and burned her house to the ground.

I stroked Luna's head, rubbing her large, soft ears between my fingers. She was content. Happy. Her aura a deep, satiated purple. When I petted her, I could feel what she felt, could see her mood, her aura, like a light around her. I'd been able to do that my whole life. It was how I knew no one in Citadel wanted me there. It was why leaving, even under duress, hadn't been a tough choice.

Citadel was a city of caverns and tunnels — some carved by us, some there already — that all led to a primary central cavern called the Village Square. I never understood why it was called a square when it was circular. There was a stone statue of the founder — a man whose face was stern but full of hope — carved from the earth itself right in the center. Stairs carved into the wall spiraled up from the floor all the way to the top. The wealthiest families lived on the top levels, away from the noise and commotion of the town center.

Beside me, Luna growled and pawed my hand, her claws retracted. Just like I could read her, she could read me. I ran my fingers through the thick coat around her neck and shoulders, grateful for her warmth and comfort.

I gazed down at my tan fingers lost in Luna's bright white fur. Her vivid whiteness reminded me of the people in Citadel. Everyone there had white blonde hair and skin that was nearly the same color, with eyes that were either icy blue or pink. Everyone except me. My eyes were closer to the color of stone, and though I'd been fair-skinned then, I had always been darker than anyone else below ground. Rosemarie told me later that my hair reminded her of honey.

Rosemarie, from my first day with her, had shown me that she loved me, something I'd never really experienced before or since. She'd found and rescued me after I left Citadel and almost died, because I didn't know how to live in the upworld. I was only a child.

I'd left because I'd made a mistake and let Aiyanna, who was the chief's daughter, know what I could do. I'd read her thoughts and it scared her, so she and the others chased me out.

I shook my head and stood. The past was gone and the present was here and waiting. I stretched and dumped soggy pine needles into the pond, then rinsed my cup— holding it under and watching the pictures of those awful people blur beneath the greenish water. Luna followed me, forever my lovely white shadow.

"Luna, what are we to do today?" The air gobbled up my words. It had been four years and I still half-expected to hear my words bounce back to me from stone.

She stared up at me and yawned, showing off her pink tongue and long, sharp teeth.

"No, it's not time to sleep." I walked to check the few plants I grew in my clearing. I looked back at her, because she often liked to dig and roll where I pruned, but she was already asleep in a shaft of sunlight next to the fire.

I gathered a few ripe peppers and greens and dug up sweet potatoes. There was something calming about digging my hands in the soil, even when it was cold. I felt less alone, almost like someone was holding my hand. Sometimes I would work my fingers into the earth and just sit there, listening, feeling. But it was already getting too cold for that. Now the cold earth made my fingers ache if I left them there too long.

After I finished I covered the ground around the plants with forest litter. My apple tree held fruit and I piled dried leaves near the base before climbing it. I crawled out onto the lowest, thickest branch. I tossed apples as gently as I could onto the leaf pile, wincing when I would hear one split. This had been a good fruit year thanks to a lot of rain.

From where I stood, I could see the upper part of my pine where I'd tied the grass mats. The mats were starting to wear holes between the needles. They needed to be redone if I were to stay hidden.

As I worked, Aiyanna's terrified face, and then Rosemarie's, flames behind her, popped into my head. I paused to squeeze the bridge of my nose. It was never this hard to separate myself from the past.

A breeze shifted my hair. Looking up at the sky, I sniffed the air. It was going to storm, or at least rain. I needed to go on a run for supplies before the rain hit and running always cleared my head.

I would cross the big field to see if any of the trees on the other side still held fruit. The Wylden had been camped across the field the last time I went a few weeks earlier. They would be gone now and would stay gone until the end of autumn. Hopefully they'd left something good behind—tools or clothes that had been forgotten or lost as they moved on.

I grabbed my pack, a discarded Wylden treasure, tied it around my shoulder so that it rested on my hip, and rubbed the rough cloth with my finger. I put an apple and some nuts in one of the pockets and drank deeply from my tiny stream. I covered the fire with a flat stone to keep any tendrils of smoke in and clucked for Luna. She was up and beside me so quickly I wondered if she'd only been faking sleep.

As I left the clearing, I was careful not to break any branches and to leave as few footprints as possible. Luna darted around me, climbing trees and jumping from branch to branch before rejoining me on the ground. She loved going on supply runs.

I kept an easy pace, warming up my muscles until I got to my first marker, a giant metal post that disappeared up into the foliage. Rosemarie had shown me things like this and other pre-war remnants. This one had once held a huge sign telling people where something was. Now it was just something that didn't belong, being slowly covered by vines. After we passed the post, we picked up speed, as if the earth and wind were propelling us along. When I was finally running, the thoughts that had been lurking behind my eyes started to melt away. I focused on the sounds of my feet hitting the earth, of the bright streaks of white as Luna moved quickly and silently all around me.

As the wind whipped by, so did an awareness of all the animals around me—darting points of yellow light were birds up in the canopy; still, warm, lavender bodies, startled by my passing were deer or rabbits, huddling with their young; the excited orange blurs in trees, only growing still as Luna got close, were chipmunks and squirrels. If it were warmer still, there would be more—the blue and green of snakes and frogs and the trees would be saturated with a greater number of birds. For a flash, I thought I felt the red presence of hunting coyotes or wolves somewhere behind me. But if they were there, they were gone quickly. I didn't know these animals like I knew Luna, but being able to find them had saved me from a run in with a big cat or wolf more than once. In some way, these points of light were like my friends, and seeing them as I ran felt like visiting family after a long time away.

Today was a good day for this, cool and crisp. To keep my past from catching me, I needed the present to be vivid and bright. I ran, bathing in the range of color and emotion I sensed all around as I made my way to the field, letting the sound of my steadily beating heart dictate the cadence of my feet.

Luna and I reached the edge of the woods and stopped almost at once. After being beneath the shadowed trees for so long, the golden grass of the field was like sunlight itself and difficult to look at directly. It was midday and the noon sun was intermittently covered by rapidly moving clouds as the storm got closer. I took a deep breath. It would be a few hours still before the rain. Luna took a moment to clean dirt from her paws while I caught my breath and pulled some dried fruit from my pack. Chewing it, I grimaced at how tough it had gotten.

Luna looked up and I patted the tree closest to me—an ancient silver maple that was my second landmark because it reminded me of the maple in my clearing. Luna chirped and darted up the trunk to hide near the top in sun-dappled shadows.

I followed her up and stopped on the tallest branch that would hold me, then stretched to pet her before turning my attention to the field. Clouds passed overhead and darkened the grass in shifting waves.

At its height, the grass in this particular field reached above my head. But before I could cross it to reach the fruit trees that waited on the other side, I needed to see the other side to make sure it was safe. The field was huge, the other side just a smudge on the horizon, though the trees there were just as big and old as the trees here. With my eyes closed, I took a deep breath, and focused on my heartbeat.

After a moment with my eyes closed, my vision sped across the field and traveled further than my eyes could see—an ability I hadn't discovered until I'd come upworld. It was hard to control. I had to find a spot to focus on, like an anchor, or it would keep moving, racing, darting around. I needed to make sure no one was there before I crossed to the fruit trees on that side.

No one lived there, but four times a year, near the solstice and equinox of each season, a caravan of Wylden came through and camped in the field for a week or so. They'd been here three weeks ago—right around the autumn equinox—so they should be gone, but with the Wylden I never took anything for granted.

I expected to see flattened grass and the litter they always left behind when my sight settled. Instead my stomach lurched and I clung to the tree I was in. My sight swung around, looking at Wylden children and adults, sleeping, fighting, and waiting for food from the fire. They had never stayed this long before. I could almost smell the putrid stink that followed them.

I tried to direct my vision, to see what was going on outside their camp, see if they were readying to leave, but I couldn't control what I saw once I anchored myself. Each time this happened, I had to stifle a surge of panic. I didn't like being out of control.

When I opened my eyes my vision returned to normal. The ground tilted and shifted for a moment before settling as I adjusted to being back in my own head. Above me, Luna chirped.

Erilyn.

My name on the wind again. I looked around, but still didn't see anyone. It was louder this time and that worried me. I'd been hearing that voice a lot over the last few weeks. It had started three years ago after Rosemarie died, but it was getting worse. Maybe I'd been alone too long.

Erilyn.

Shaking my head, I rubbed my shoulder up against my ear.

I looked back with just my eyes to where I now knew the Wylden were. Maybe, since the Wylden were there, the animals would leave the fruit trees alone. There were still a few weeks before snow.

I decided to wait a few hours to see if they moved out in the afternoon. If it looked like they were readying to leave, I'd come back in a day or two. I still had time. It wasn't cold enough to start worrying yet.

Leaning my head back against the tree, I closed my eyes to wait. My stomach growled and I dug my fingertips into my belly to distract myself from the feeling, saving my apple for the trip home. I let my mind wander to the animals around me—the yellow spots of light that were birds nesting, the darting orange squirrels. I focused on them, counting them like stars, until I fell asleep.

Chapter Two
The Wylden

Finn

Finn rushed to gather the best of the dark red lilies from beside the stream. It wasn't sunset yet, and while it was frowned upon to be outside the wall this late in the day, it wasn't illegal. He couldn't go back without the perfect flower. He found it nearly in the water, growing tall and proud from the rich soil on the bank, hidden away in tall coarse grass. He cut the stalk with his small, sharp carving knife and added it to the bouquet. Lilies were Morrigan's favorite—beautiful, but dangerous if you ate them.

He held the bouquet against his chest as he ran back toward Sunnybrook. He darted between the two ancient white Sycamores that served as gateposts and nearly collided with the sentry. Stumbling, he took off again with a wave of apology. Most people would have been stopped, but all the guards knew him, because Morrigan was their captain, though she'd only been captain a few months.

He slowed as he approached Morrigan's building—the Eagle, the one where all the town leaders lived. Finn still wasn't used to coming here to see her. Until she'd made captain, she'd lived in the Finch, a few doors down from him. He wanted to catch his breath before he knocked on her door. As he pushed his hair off his forehead, he reminded himself to get a haircut. Morrigan liked his hair short, because she said it showed off his jaw line.

By the time he made it to the bottom of her stairs it was nearly dark. He looked up toward the second story. Her door was right at the top of the stairs. He'd painted it dark red the summer before and it was starting to chip and fade. People were headed toward the commissary for dinner, but he knew she wouldn't have left yet. Morrigan said she liked to go late, to let everyone else get their fill first, but he also saw the way she smiled at the men who watched her as she walked in after everyone was seated.

He took the steps two at a time and knocked, three quick taps. He fidgeted. As he lifted his fist to knock again, the door opened.

"Hi." He tried to smile, but her cold gaze stopped him. He cleared his throat and offered her the bouquet, the perfect lily he'd found right in the center where she would notice it most. She appreciated perfection. His words tumbled out of his mouth. "I'm so sorry for last night. It was all my fault." He couldn't remember what they'd fought over, but he knew it was his fault.

Morrigan looked down at the waiting flowers in his hand and sighed. "What is this, Finley?" She was wearing one of her summer dresses—a purple one with white lace trim at the bottom and white flowers embroidered around the neck. He was already chilly in his long sleeves, but she always swore she didn't notice the cold and wore her summer dresses well into autumn and sometimes winter.

"It's my apology. For last night." He offered her the flowers again.

She took them. "*This* is your apology?" Her eyes flashed darkly, her long dark hair falling across one eye in a way that made his heart race, despite her anger. She shoved the flowers back. "This isn't even close to being enough."

"Can we just talk?" He took a step toward her and she held up her hand, forcing him back without ever touching him.

"We've talked, and we've talked, and we've *talked*. I can't do this anymore." Her voice was cold, but she looked at his face as it crumpled and sighed, her eyes softening. "Finley." She put her hand over her heart. "I just *can't* do this anymore. I *truly* believe this is what's best for both of us." She tilted her head to the side and gave him a smile that didn't reach her eyes. He'd seen her do that in conversations with people she thought very little of and he wilted. "We can still be friends."

When Finn was twelve, he'd fallen from a tree and for long moments after had lain on the ground, trying to breathe. That's what he felt like now. He could hear his heartbeat in his ears but couldn't find any air.

She put both hands over her heart, her look turning to pity. She wasn't wearing the ring he'd made for her—a wooden band with a lily painstakingly carved into it. "This is for the best." Without another word, Morrigan closed the door and Finn was left in the dark wake of sunset.

The flowers fell from his numb fingers. Red petals lay around his feet like puddles of blood. He stared down at them, then picked up the one he'd picked last and walked away.

In his own apartment he locked the door and put the flower in a chipped cup of water on the windowsill. In the basin of water beneath it, he scrubbed his hands.

If he didn't go to the commissary soon, he'd miss dinner. But he wasn't hungry. He fell back onto his small, hard cot and stared up into the dark.

Sunnybrook was a small town, but Finn had lived here his whole life and knew how to avoid seeing someone if he had to. The commissary was where everyone in town ate meals, so that would be his biggest hurdle. There was a bakery and a few food stalls where you could trade for food, but the commissary was the only place you could go to eat hearty meals free of charge. He'd have to wait until they were almost closed and hope food was left.

To avoid seeing Morrigan the next night, he waited until well past dark. Only Lucy, the mayor's adopted sister and one of Finn's closest friends, was behind the counter. She always stayed later than she had to.

She saw him and smiled, her eyes sad. Word got around fast. He put on his best smile and leaned against the wooden countertop.

"Hey, Lucy. What can I trade for an extra plate to take home tonight?" He looked at the food instead of her.

"It's on the house." He knew she was trying to sound chipper, but she'd always been a terrible liar. He looked up. Lucy's eyes were large and green. She tucked a brilliant orange curl behind her ear. "Really. Free of charge." She held up her hands, palm out, and pursed her lips.

"How much, Luce?" He sighed, all pretense gone.

"Oh, Finn." Tears welled up in her eyes, making them look like grass after a rainstorm. She'd always been like this—taking things that happened to her friends personally and trying to fix it or at least help. He'd always loved that about her. Until now.

He scrubbed his hands over his eyes. "I just want to buy some extra food so I can work through the day tomorrow." He looked back at her, expecting more pity and tears, but she wasn't looking at him, she was looking behind him. Her eyes quickly darted back to his and she shook her head, but it was too late.

Finn turned and saw Morrigan walking in, arm-in-arm with the mayor, Cillian. She was wearing another summer dress, a green one this time that made her hazel eyes seem greener than they were. Her hair was piled high on her head and tied back with the red scarf he'd given her for her birthday. It was finely woven and he'd had to trade a month's worth of carvings for it.

With hands that were suddenly fists and a chest that felt tight, he turned back to Lucy.

"Finn—" she whispered, her voice barely audible above the low din from the remaining diners.

Morrigan's sudden decision to end things suddenly made sense. Cillian was older. The mayor. He controlled Sunnybrook. Morrigan had always told him she was meant for big things. It was inevitable that once she made captain, she'd move on to better things in all areas of her life.

He needed to leave before she saw him. He walked toward the door, head bowed, but he couldn't help one last look back. Morrigan met his gaze, a brilliant smile still plastered on her face. She only looked at him a second before she turned away, back to Cillian, as if she didn't know Finn at all.

Finn's hands shook as he walked out of the commissary. He heard Lucy calling his name as she tried to follow him, but he didn't turn back.

He'd meant to head home, but his feet took him toward the sycamores, faster with each step. It was dark, well past nightfall, and the gates would most likely be closed, but he ran for them anyway. Torches flickered and burned, casting sharp shadows, but the gates were open. Once an hour, the guard left the gates ajar and walked outside with torches to scare off any big animals that had gotten brave enough to get close. Finn shoved through the gates, running now, followed by a single shout from somewhere near him in the darkness that quickly faded to silence.

Finn ran until his lungs and muscles burned—hours. He stumbled over roots. Tree branches snapped his face and tore at his clothes. He pushed himself until the world started to spin with exhaustion, until he left the trees and found himself in an immense field. The sun was peeking gold and pink over the horizon as it started to rise. He stared down at his shaking hands. His breaths came in sharp, rapid bursts. Leaning forward, he dug his fingers into the cold hard earth, squeezing what dirt and grass he could, and letting the hard pieces dig into the palms of his hands.

Until he'd seen her with Cillian, some part of him had believed that this was temporary, that he'd give her space and they'd be back together. It had happened a dozen times before. But seeing her with someone else, with the most powerful man in Sunnybrook, made it final. Morrigan had been his only family since his mother died from the malady some ten years ago. Now he was alone.

He rolled on to his back and looked up at the sky through the tall, waving grass. The stars were still bright, the morning sun still just a hint as it rose and he was taken back to a night just before fall. Morrigan had lain in the grass near the quarry with him, finding constellations and searching for shooting stars. Painful tears welled up, but even here, where no one would know or hear, he choked it back. He felt his vision blur, but his cheeks stayed dry. She'd always said he was too emotional. Instead, he closed his eyes and tried to force the empty feeling in his chest away.

Finn woke, curled on his side, nestled in grass that reached high above him. It was around midday, but dark clouds were rolling in and, in the distance, he heard rolling thunder. He pushed himself up to a sitting position and rested his pounding head in his hands. He'd slept through half a day. He took a deep breath and his stomach growled—he hadn't eaten since yesterday.

With legs that shook, he pushed himself off the ground. The grass tickled his chin and bent with the wind that the looming storm pushed ahead of it. In the distance, lightning forked.

He was in the middle of a massive field surrounded on all sides by trees turning red and yellow and he wasn't sure which direction he'd come from. He couldn't remember, he just knew he'd never traveled this far from home. He scanned all around until he saw the wagon train circled near the tree line closest to him. He dropped to the ground, heart in his throat, skin prickled with fear.

Finn had never worked a patrol, never been a scout, but he knew a Wylden caravan when he saw one. As children, everyone in Sunnybrook was taught what to look for.

Finn crouched, his heart beating a staccato rhythm against his ribs. The Wylden were monsters. As soon as children in Sunnybrook were old enough to talk, they were taught to hide if they ever saw a Wylden—savage beasts that looked like men. His breaths were shallow and quick. He didn't think he'd been seen, and hoped he could stay below the top of the grass and make it away from them so they'd never know he was there.

Even as he planned to get away, some part of him was telling him to go *toward* the camp. Morrigan had wanted him to join the patrol, to be brave. If he could kill a Wylden, he could win her back. And even if he died in the process, maybe she would hear about what he'd tried to do and would love him again.

Finley closed his eyes. He pictured her hazel eyes in the sunlight, her long, dark hair falling over her cheek just so he could brush it back. Then he pictured her on Cillian's arm and white-hot rage filled him up. His eyes opened and he felt himself snarl.

Crouched, Finn rushed toward the Wylden camp. He had to stay hidden until he could drag one away and kill it. Then he would return home the kind of man she'd always wanted him to be.

The storm clouds cast long, angry shadows across the Wylden caravan. The clouds made it seem later than it was, just past noon, and the lightning made Finn dizzy in the half-dark.

He watched the camped wagons through grass that waved in the wind. There were two Wylden men, posted near the front of the caravan, both asleep, leaning against a wagon. Finn had never seen an actual Wylden in person, only drawings. These Wylden looked like men, their bodies covered in dirt, rags, and animal skins. Their hair was long and hung in clumps. One was blonde, the other a redhead like Lucy. For some reason, he'd always pictured them with black hair.

Finn was glad he couldn't see their faces. Despite how wild they looked, they were more human than he'd thought they would be and it disturbed him more than if they'd had the faces of goats or dogs. He looked around for a rock or a sharp stick, anything he could use as a weapon, but there was nothing except tall, willowy grass. His only hope was to sneak into the camp, hope to find a weapon there, and somehow incapacitate one of the weaker ones. With a surge of adrenaline, Finn ducked and darted between two wagons near the unconscious guards.

He stood in a wagon's shadow, shoulder pressed against the wood and tarp to keep from being seen. In the middle of the caravan, a group of Wylden sat around a fire. The men were closest to the fire. Spears were jammed into the ground at an angle, each holding chunks of meat over the fire. Juice dripped and sizzled as it hit burning logs. The men ripped hot meat from the bones with their teeth and tossed the bones behind them where the women and children scrambled to scrape off what was left with their teeth. Finn watched as the women bit the ends of smaller bones and offered them to the children to suck out what marrow was leftover. Finn felt a surge of pity for the scrawny children, but then one turned and the firelight caught its eyes. They reflected light like an animal's and Finn's pity was replaced with a mixture of fear and repulsion.

A child climbed over a woman to grab leftovers that had fallen from a man's fingers. The man backhanded the child before it could reach the meat. One of the women hissed at the man and gathered the bleeding child to her. She offered it a bone. Stroking the child's matted hair, the woman crouched as if she might pounce on the man who'd hit it, though the male had already turned away.

The wind shifted and Finn was assaulted by the smell of rotting meat and unwashed bodies. He barely stopped himself from gagging. If the wind shifted again, they would smell him. He was sure their sense of smell was better than his.

Across from him, a Wylden man with red juice dripping down his chin picked up the woman nearest him. She screeched and clawed at his back, drawing blood. Shoulders hunched, he took her just past Finn's field of vision. From the sounds they were making, he was grateful he couldn't see anything that was happening. Finn's stomach turned as the woman's angry screams changed to sounds of pleasure.

The Wylden looked a lot like men, but they weren't people. It made the decision to kill one easier, though his hands still shook. He pictured Morrigan again, pictured her hanging on Cillian's arm, and let that anger fuel him. He looked around for a knife left unattended, a shovel, anything, but there was nothing except trampled grass and pebbles. Not even one of the bones had been tossed close enough for him to use. Maybe he could circle around, pick off a small one from the fringes where none of the others would see.

The nearest Wylden to him was a child, eating small scraps from the dirt. Finn could see the child's ribs and spine through his skin as he hunched over to eat, grunting with each bite—a weak Wylden, far from the others. This was his chance. He wouldn't even need a weapon to kill this one.

This child.

Finn broke out in a cold sweat. He was thinking of killing a child. It was a Wylden child, but a child nonetheless. He looked around as if waking from a nightmare. The smells and sounds accosted him and he felt suddenly sick. He shouldn't be here.

With steps as quiet as he could make them, he backed out the way he'd come. He kept his eyes on the people in front of him, still eating and growling, and no one saw him. The storm clouds rolling in offered more darkness than the wagon shadows alone and he hoped a sudden downpour or thunderclap would keep the Wylden distracted. He'd always hated storms, but today he was grateful for the thunder and the darkness. He felt along the edge of the wagon and peeked around it. The guards were still asleep. Relief washed over him like warm bath water. He was going to make it. He'd crawl back through the field, figure out which way home was, and head back to Sunnybrook where he could forget all of this.

Finn crouched and darted back into the field grass. He moved as quickly as could, staying low, hoping the wind would hide his movement once the grass covered him. He breathed easier as the grass welcomed him, but kept moving as fast as he could while staying below anyone's line of sight. As he was about to stop and catch his breath, barking broke out behind him. Finn broke out in a cold sweat as harsh, growling voices took up the call of the dogs.

Fear pushed Finn to run full out, to not worry about staying hidden. He ran as fast the dense grass would let him. It pulled at his pants and shirt like fingers. He glanced back and wished he hadn't.

Four Wylden men were after him, charging through the grass. He couldn't see the dogs, but there were at least two from the sounds of barking and growling. These dogs were trackers, held back only by leashes. The Wylden wouldn't let them go until they were right on him. The only reason Finn wasn't already dead was because Wylden enjoyed the hunt.

Chapter Three

Petrichor

Erilyn

The sound of rolling thunder pulled me from my impromptu nap. The storm I'd smelled earlier was close now, the dark clouds making the sky darker than it should be. Above me, Luna was sitting upright, sniffing the air. The smell of rain was thick and I sighed. One of the first books Rosemarie had given me was a picture book of archaic words. There was one word, petrichor, which meant the smell of the earth after a rain. I'd hated that page—remembering the smell of stagnant pools underground—until Rosemarie had taken me outside after a rainstorm and sat with me while I learned what petrichor smelled like. We spent many evenings after that sitting as she taught me this new world using my senses.

The thick, damp air hugged me like a chilled blanket. I closed my eyes, took a breath, and my vision sped across the dark golden grass, whipping in the wind from the coming storm. My vision settled faster than I expected it to and I gripped the tree for balance.

Looking, not toward the camp, but back toward the trees where I hid, I recognized the tree I was in—the only silver maple in the line. It felt like I was running—heart racing, breathing ragged. I was inside someone's head.

I wanted to pull away, but my vision swung toward the Wylden caravan. Wylden men were chasing me. They were so close, too close, and fear spiked through me, causing me—whoever's mind I was in, I mean—to trip.

I jerked myself back, reeling against the tree as my meager breakfast threatened to come up. Above me, Luna was staring out across the field, her eyes wide and her ears back. She was growling low and deep. With my eyes, I could barely see the heads and shoulders of Wylden parting the grass, racing toward where I hid.

"Luna." Her wide-eyed, icy blue gaze shot to mine. "Time to go."

She moved fluidly down the tree, remaining in the shadow as I made my much slower way down. I hit the earth and crouched next to her.

I put my hand on her, both my fear and hers a thick, acidic taste in my mouth. Her aura was a rippling silvery gray. "Go," I whispered. She chirped once then took off into the woods. Even though she was white, as bright as a full moon, she vanished in seconds into the shadows.

I was right behind her, moving as quickly as I could. Although I knew they wouldn't see me through the trees, somehow they'd known where I was. Maybe they could do what I could—see things they shouldn't be able to see. Find me. For the first time I was thankful for my childhood, growing up in the caves where I learned how to be neither seen nor heard. I ran, trying to stay on aerial roots and thick leaves to avoid leaving footprints. Clutching my bag to my side, I tried to keep it from snagging on anything and slowing me down.

I ran without stopping until I was back in my clearing. Luna chirped from beneath the maple tree. She was safe and part of the tightness in my chest lessened.

I hastily scuffed up the clearing with my feet, trying to hide any evidence of us. They may not make it this far, but if they did, I wanted them to pass by this area like they had the first time I'd run from them. I scattered my apples, hoping they looked like they'd just fallen. But if they had dogs with them, they'd find me no matter what I did. My scent was everywhere and I couldn't hide it. I knew my pine wasn't safe. So I had to hide under the giant aerial roots of my ancient silver maple. The night Rosemarie died the Wylden had been chasing me. I'd tripped in the rain and found this clearing, had hidden beneath these very roots holding tiny Luna to my chest while the Wylden chased my ghost through the woods. These roots had kept us safe then and they would keep us safe now. I had to believe that.

Just as I rolled under the roots, bag tossed in first, rain began to fall in big, fat drops.

I settled back into the shadow and sensed Luna curled in her own hidey-hole behind me. I couldn't see her, but I could feel her like a tiny golden sun in the darkness. I reached out my hand to press into her fur. If they had dogs, the rain would help wash away our scent. We had a chance, now. For the second time, this tree and a rainstorm were going to save us.

I'd built up the earth around the edge of the opening so that it wouldn't fill with water when it rained. That first night the rain had filled up the hole I was laying in and I'd been scared I would drown. I'd held little Luna above the water and made myself not panic for her sake. When the rain had stopped and I was sure the Wylden weren't coming back, I'd crawled from the hole, covered in mud, cuts, and bruises—just like the day Rosemarie had found me—and run back to what was left of her house, with Luna held tight in my hands.

Rosemarie had found me weeks after I'd fled Citadel, curled beneath a thorny bush. Sunburned and covered in cuts and bruises, I'd covered myself in mud to try and block out the sun. I couldn't imagine not being in pain. I'd crawled there so that I could fall asleep and never wake up.

Rosemarie said she found me because she could hear me crying, but I didn't remember crying. I remembered the way the mud felt as it dried, how it itched, how the tiny little ants had crawled over my fingers and bitten the exposed parts of my skin.

She'd carried me back to her home—a rough stone cottage hidden in overgrown woods—and nursed me back to health with gentle baths and a sweet herbal tea that helped me sleep through most of the pain. How I wished for her gentle, reassuring touch now as lightning flashed and the Wylden grew closer.

Over the sound of pounding rain, I could hear the Wylden's grunting calls. Luna was completely still beside me. I let my awareness expand. The Wylden were moving spots of pulsing, red and black, the colors like static. Their energy seeped into me like smoke. It felt like suffocating.

Heat grew in my belly, just as it had that last night in the caves, and I felt my panic start to take control. In an attempt to slow my racing heart, I took deep, slow breaths, but it wasn't working. I had to calm down, to be as still and invisible as Luna. If I lost control, I didn't know what would happen to the woods, the animals in them, to Luna and me, trapped beneath this tree.

Part of me also worried that if the Wylden could do what I could do, if they were tracking me without their eyes and ears, then I was already lost. If they could find me, like I had found them, then I knew they'd feel the roiling energy inside me and hear my heartbeat echoing through the earth.

Chapter Four
The Hunt

Finn

Finn broke through the tree line with a surge of pitiful relief, but it was short lived. He took a few running steps into the semi-darkness beneath the trees and tripped over a tree stump, landing hard on his side, his breath ripped from him.

Vision blurry, he pushed himself back to his feet just in time to feel a knife slam into his right shoulder.

Finn stared at the knife for a moment. He saw it, but it was as if it weren't really there. Behind him, the Wylden cried out victoriously. He pulled the knife from his shoulder with a pained grunt and threw it back toward the creatures behind him. It tumbled harmlessly into the underbrush. He pressed his hand over the shoulder—blood pumping through his fingers—and ran.

The dogs, still leashed, growled and whined. Finn's blood ran cold. These Wylden were enjoying their hunt.

As the storm covered them, the sunlight faded away, leaving the woods dark and full of shifting shadows. He plunged ahead, not knowing where he was going, just knowing he had to get as far from the field as he could.

The sounds of the Wylden faded as their larger bodies moving through the dense undergrowth slowed them. He could barely breathe, pain radiating through his shoulder and right side.

Thunder clapped overhead, immediately followed by fat drops of rain. Finn stumbled to a stop, confused, his thoughts growing fuzzy. Through the new roar of rain, he heard the Wylden growing closer, heard the dogs barking excitedly.

It was getting harder and harder to focus as lightning flashes disoriented him. He thought he heard Morrigan calling his name and he spun around, almost falling. She wasn't here. She was in Sunnybrook. Rain ran down his face, blurring his vision. He pushed himself up, leaving a smear of blood on the tree beside him, and stumbled off, unsure if he was heading toward or away from his pursuers.

His vision started to tunnel as lightning burned through the sky. He stumbled and looked up—there weren't any trees. Had he left the forest? Was he back in the field? He looked around, trying to see through the curtain of rain, and found that he was in a clearing. Just ahead, rain jumped across the surface of the pond like a million insects. He could hide there, but how long could he hold his breath? Would his blood float to the surface? He looked down at his shoulder and saw that his shirt was soaked black with blood. His legs shook and threatened to give out.

Finn swayed and fell into the tree next to him. As he reached for a low branch, fiery pain traveled down his arm. His hand was cold and he fought back nausea and reached up with his left.

He awkwardly made his way up the tree. Losing his footing, his left arm nearly buckled under his weight, but he made it onto a thick branch. Pain blossomed in his right shoulder as he fell against the tree. He scooted back and tucked himself in a groove made by where the large branch met the trunk in a V-shape.

Half a moment later, two dogs burst into the clearing, leashes trailing them. Despite the roar of the rain and claps of thunder, Finn kept his breathing shallow and tried not to move.

One dog ran straight for the tree he was in and sniffed the ground around the base. Finn swayed as the edges of his vision grew black. He pressed his shoulder into the rain-slicked trunk and welcomed the burning pain that cleared his head for a moment.

The second dog froze, hackles raised, as it stared beneath a tree nearby with huge aerial roots. From beneath the roots, Finn thought he saw a flash of white. But his vision started to swim, so he closed his eyes. He felt like he was on fire now, burning up, but rain that pelted him was freezing.

Even though the whole world tilted, Finn opened his eyes. The dogs were here; their masters wouldn't be far behind. He wished he'd held onto that knife instead of stupidly throwing it.

The rain was a roar, or maybe that was his heart still pumping his blood from the hole in his shoulder. The dog at his tree still sniffed. The dog at the other tree was still frozen. How long had they been here? It felt like only seconds, or maybe hours. Everything was getting fuzzy around the edges.

One moment the second dog was still, hackles raised, and the next it jumped, as if it had been kicked, and ran off with its tail between its legs. The dog at the base of his tree only hesitated a moment before taking off after the first.

A breath later, two Wylden men tore into the clearing after the dogs without even watching where they stepped. They didn't pause to look up or to the sides; they crashed headlong back into the woods, trusting their animals to find him.

Relief washed over Finn like a warm summer rain. Was this rain warm? Was it summer? He looked up into the branches above him. It was too dark to be day, too light to be night. He thought the rain should be cold, but he couldn't tell. Maybe it was summer. Morrigan loved summer.

Finn's eyes rolled back and he tried to grip the tree. A glimmer of white beneath the tree roots caused him to lean forward. Did he see eyes, reflected lightning strikes there?

He shook his head. A girl's face appeared from beneath the roots. The rain was so thick, his eyes so cloudy, he couldn't be sure, but he thought it was Morrigan, come to save him.

Finn smiled and reached his hand out to her. He needed to get to her. She'd forgiven him and come after him. He reached a little further and then he was falling. The ground rushed up, muddy and cold, and suddenly he couldn't breathe. He needed to call Morrigan, but he couldn't breathe. Rain poured into his mouth as he tried to get his lungs to work.

When air finally found its way inside his lungs, he opened his eyes and saw someone crawl from beneath the tree. He mouthed, "Morrigan," but saw quickly that it wasn't her. This was a girl, much smaller with lighter skin and hair. She ran to him and checked his pulse, her soaked, matted hair hiding her face, then she grabbed his feet and dragged him.

He opened his mouth to speak and rain filled it. He turned to the side and coughed. She looked back at him, gray-blue eyes flashing, before she took up dragging him again. He wanted to fight, but couldn't. He barely felt the hard ground, the sticks and stones grating against his skin, as he stared up into the falling rain and lightning forked across the sky. Just before she pulled him under a giant, dark tree, Finn took a sharp breath and everything went black.

Chapter Five
Auras

Erilyn

As soon as the Wylden were gone, I pulled myself from beneath the tree and ran to the man who'd fallen. He should be dead, but his aura was still there, light green and faint. I knelt beside him, my hands hovering uselessly above his blood soaked shoulder.

Grabbing the man by his feet, I dragged him toward my pine. He moaned and I spun around. His eyes—a more vivid blue than even Luna's—were large and glassy as he stared at me before his eyes rolled back in his head and he was out again.

The man's body left a muddy trail toward the pine. If he weren't bleeding so badly, I would hide it as I went. I was going to have to take the chance that the Wylden wouldn't come back and see it. The rain would wash away his blood soon enough.

I dragged the man under my tree, making sure his head was under the branches and that the grass cover I'd woven as a door was pulled tight.

The storm had blocked out the last bit of fading evening light, and though my eyesight was exceptional from growing up in the dark caves of Citadel, I needed more light to care for him.

From my supply box, I pulled a lantern and some herbs. I cupped the lantern in my hands and focused on the wick, waiting for lightning to strike nearby. As I closed my eyes I let that part of me that was always on the edge of my control loose. Time slowed and suddenly the rain, the wind, and the lightning, they were all part of me. I traveled in the wind through the trees until I felt my skin prickle as electricity built up around me. As the lightning forked from the clouds, I pushed those electric sparks through my hands and into the wick. Time sped back up as the lantern flared to life and the injured man was suddenly illuminated.

I put a tin cup beneath the tree to collect water and sat the lantern near the man's head, then moved to check his wound.

I'd always hated touching other people's skin, because when I did I usually saw something I didn't want to see. But I had no choice. At least he was unconscious.

I rested my fingers lightly on his forehead. He was burning up. Carefully opening up a sachet of herbs, I dumped it in the cup. With my eyes closed, I held the cup tightly and directed the heat from the lantern's small flame through my hands and into the water. The water disappeared as the herbs swelled.

From my wooden box, I pulled a rusted pair of metal scissors and cut the shirt so that it fell away. The wound was angry, red, and smelled. Unless he'd been running for days, infection shouldn't have set in yet. I leaned down and sniffed—both sweet and rotten. Wylden poison. I had to move fast. At least the poison slowed the bleeding.

With the poultice I'd made, I packed the wound. The man groaned, but didn't wake.

I made sure to spread the poultice across the infected area. Where the slow-acting poison had penetrated, the veins were darker and I covered them with the thick paste.

As I worked, I whispered. When Rosemarie had found me and tended to my sunburned skin and injuries, she'd whispered over me. It was half prayer, half a wish that I would live. I did that for this man now, knowing that Rosemarie would want me to. Using every bit of the poultice, I then tied a scrap of cloth around the shoulder.

I pulled out one of my blankets and covered the man up to his chin. Reaching my hand out, I rinsed the cup in rainwater, then filled it to try and get him to drink. I wet a scrap of cloth and draped it over his forehead. I was chilled to the bone with sopping wet hair and clothes in the cool autumn night, but his skin was still on fire.

Now that I'd done all I could, I wrapped my second blanket around my shoulders. Luna curled beneath it and fit as much of her body on or around me as she could. With nothing else to do, I sat back and really looked at him in the flickering lantern light.

He looked about my age, maybe seventeen or eighteen. His hair was shaggy, dark brown, and curled at the ends. His long nose was covered with a smattering of freckles, but otherwise his skin was fair. Beneath closed eyelids, his eyes darted around—dreaming—but I'd seen them in the rain, and they were bright blue like the clearest summer sky. Though his expression, even in sleep, was strained, he was handsome. The only men I'd ever seen were from Citadel. It was strange seeing a man with color in his cheeks and his hair. I found myself wanting to reach out and touch his face, to see what his stubble felt like. Even in his strained state of sleep, his mouth turned up a little at the corners and made him look inherently kind. I'd never seen a man that looked kind.

My hand moved toward a wet strand of hair that was stuck to his forehead and I pulled it back. I wasn't Rosemarie. Even asleep, I might still see something in his mind, learn something I didn't need or want to know.

My stomach growled and I felt suddenly tired. I repacked my box of supplies and pulled out some roasted nuts. I ate them without tasting them and sank against the tree to wait and see if he got better or worse.

Hours later, long after the rain had stopped and the moon had risen, I felt his mind begin to stir. Luna had stretched out between the man and me, her head in my lap. I'd been watching him, carefully cataloguing his features. His clothes were nice with few patches. He had to be from a town where they could afford such luxuries as sturdy boots. If we were standing, he would be taller than me, but that wasn't surprising—all people from the caves were small, though I had been taller than the other children my age. Though I didn't dare, his dark hair had dried some and curled around his ears in a way that made me want to touch it.

He woke but didn't open his eyes. I took a quiet, deep breath. This was what I'd been dreading. After a long moment, he blinked his eyes open and stared straight up into the woven grass tied to pine branches, hazy in the meager lantern light.

He took a breath and winced, his face screwing up in pain. It had been three years since I'd spoken to another being. I opened my mouth, knowing I should say something, reassure him, but nothing came out. He looked over at me, his eyes glassy and bloodshot.

I had no words, so I moved so that I was seated near his wound. With deft, delicate fingers, I pulled the blanket back. The redness was starting to dissipate, but it was still swollen and angry. I picked up my cup, still filled with rainwater, and tried to figure out how to get him to drink without touching him. I could just ask him to, tell him to. My hands were shaking a little.

I prepared myself to talk to him like Rosemarie had talked to me—to tell him it would all be all right, to tell him I would take care of him, but he spoke first.

"Kill me." His voice was barely a whisper, but his words hung suspended in the air.

I looked down into his eyes. He was still feverish, his lips dry, and his skin was pale and yellowed. As I dipped a relatively clean cloth in the cup of water, I let the cloth drip water onto his lips. He turned his head away and I stopped.

As he turned back to me, the intense blue of his eyes, ringed in red, startled me with their vividness.

"*Please*, kill me." A tear leaked from the corner of his eye, but his mouth was firm. His pain surrounded me. It felt like being pulled underwater.

"I'm not a Wylden." My voice was barely a whisper. My heart raced.

"I know." He closed his eyes and took a deep breath, wincing again. "It just—" he shuddered. "It hurts. Everything."

His breathing was shallow and labored. His skin was flushed. He'd lost a lot of blood, though not as much as he should have. And there was a chance I didn't get to the poison in time.

His eyes—wide and scared—searched my face. They were so intensely blue I couldn't look away.

His weak hand pushed out from under the blanket and grabbed my fingers. I pulled away and scooted to the tree trunk. Luna was still asleep, so I knew I wasn't in danger. He tried to sit up, but couldn't. He started to fight with the blanket, his breaths becoming labored.

I dug back into my supplies, not caring if he saw where I kept it hidden. There I had berries that would help with the pain and make him sleep. If he slept, I could figure things out.

There was plenty of water left in the cup. He'd barely had any. I found the dried berries near the bottom of the box—I didn't use them, but I'd given some to Luna once after she injured her leg. Grinding them between my fingers, they stained my fingertips purple like a bruise. I stirred them into the water with my fingers, not caring that I should mix it better then pulled some more energy from the lantern flame to warm the cup. I was nervous and pulled too hard. The flame flickered.

He was still trying to sit and I saw fresh blood oozing into the blanket on his shoulder. I realized I'd have to help him sit to drink the medicine and fought back a sudden, irrational panic. It had taken months for me to touch Rosemarie voluntarily, but she'd taught me that to put my own needs after the needs of someone or some animal in need was how I should be.

Taking a deep breath, I sat at the man's head. I helped him up enough to lean his head against my shoulder. He was breathing heavily and his head sagged against me.

"Drink this," I whispered. He tried to turn his head away. "It'll do what you need it to." I felt a surge of guilt, but it would save his life, so I pushed that guilt away. I told myself he didn't need to die, he just needed to sleep, so it wasn't a lie. Not really.

I put the bowl to his mouth and he drank it greedily, swallowing the largest pieces of berry that hadn't had time to soften yet without flinching. Watching him, I remembered the sweetness of the cocktail. The berries were like honey and their relief was almost instant.

When the draught was gone, I gently laid the man's head back down and scooted away.

"Who are you?" he asked, the lines of pain and tension already melting from his face.

"Erilyn." I pushed my hair behind my ear.

His eyes were starting to close, but he kept forcing them open. "Erilyn." He breathed.

Just before he passed out, he reached over and his fingers brushed my hand as he tried to hold it again. In the second that his skin touched mine, I saw the face of a beautiful girl, heard his voice calling her name as if it were the last words he'd say—Morrigan—and felt the hollowness inside of him that made him want so badly to die.

As the man slept, the image of the girl named Morrigan stayed stuck in my mind. This is what I'd been hoping wouldn't happen.

I knew I would remember that girl's face for the rest of my life just as if I *had* known her. I sat down next to the man and looked into his face. Although I didn't know his name, seeing in someone's head made me feel connected to them. His pain was mine, at least for a time, and it was almost too much to bear.

Shaking my head, I tried to get Morrigan out of there. It was stuck worse than my own memories, my own ghosts, chasing me.

I peeked out of the tree. It had been dark for a few hours. I never stayed awake at night and it felt strange to look up at the bright white moon, the earth all around us asleep.

Luna woke as I stood. I rubbed between her ears and the sound of her purring filled me up, warming me from the inside out and pushing away some of the borrowed heartache.

"Guard him?"

She licked my palm before curling up next to him. She didn't touch him, but she put herself between him and outside.

I kept most of my rations hidden underneath the aerial roots that had now saved my life twice. I crawled beneath them, proud that my reinforcements had kept it mostly dry. Inside my tiny cave, I grabbed dried fruit, nuts, and a few sweet potatoes. I could boil the potatoes in the morning and the fruit and nuts would be my dinner. I grabbed enough for him, too, in case he woke, though I knew the draught I'd given him should keep him out 'til morning.

When I returned, Luna chirped, stretched, and darted out into the night to find her own dinner.

The cold night air had helped water down Morrigan's face in my mind, but as soon as I was back beneath the pine, near the man, she was back. It was as if she were there, in the space with us. She had full red lips, dimples, and eyes that crinkled in the corners when she smiled. Her nose was long and her hair fell around her face in dark waves.

Shaking my head, I turned the lantern wick down until it snuffed out. Outside the tree, though the earth slept, the night animals had come to life. I closed my eyes and *looked* as I did every night in case a wolf or bear was close. I could feel Luna, close now, returning from her hunt. It must have been successful, because she felt sleepy and content—a swirl of ivory and sunset orange.

This helped me sleep, *seeing* and *feeling* the plants and animals all around. Luna's aura color changed depending on her mood, which meant it changed a lot. The other animals were mostly steady, and the plants never changed—they were soft and glowing and still.

I looked toward the man. His aura had been light, watery green when I found him, but it was a little stronger now, darker like a pine in deep summer, soaked with sunlight.

As Luna came slinking back under the tree, I tore my sight away and opened my eyes. I adjusted his blanket back under his chin, careful to only touch the fabric. She skirted the man, and rubbed her head under my chin before draping part of her long, lean body along mine. I held her and turned so that I could lay down, her weight pressing down on me like a warm blanket. As I grabbed my blanket and pulled it over the two of us, I buried my face into her fur and let the sound of soft purring lull me to sleep.

Chapter Six

Nightmares

Finn

Morrigan. Just across the field. Surrounded by wagons. He had to save her. Tried to run, but his feet were stuck in thick mud that walked its way up to his knees.

She was so far. He reached out his hands. And there she was, just close enough to touch. The mud covered his hands and arms, holding him.

She smiled and leaned toward him, arms outstretched.

A Wylden ran toward her. Finn tried to yell, but sticky sweet mud filled his mouth.

Morrigan spun toward the Wylden and it vanished. She turned back to him, blood dripping from her lips, and lunged.

Finn jerked awake. He was inside a small, dark space. His head and shoulder both throbbed angrily and his right arm ached down into his fingertips. His mouth was thick and sticky with something sweet that had gone slightly sour. The green scent of pine needles and tree sap permeated his senses.

His head hurt so badly it was hard to think straight. Wylden had chased him. A girl had saved him. And he thought he remembered seeing a strange-looking white cat.

The girl. Thinking of her helped his head clear some. Her hair had been wet, dark blonde, and very long. Her eyes—he remembered them the most vividly—had been large and round. They'd reminded him of an animal's eyes with how they reflected the light.

He remembered talking to her and asking her to kill him. Grateful she hadn't listened, he winced, thinking he'd have to thank her for that.

He pushed himself up with his left arm, his right shoulder aching. Gently touching his bandaged shoulder, he remembered how it felt to have a knife lodged there.

Holding his throbbing head with his good hand, he glanced at his shoulder. It was wrapped up, but there were spots where something dark had leaked through. He looked around. A torn, dirty blanket fell from him. A cup that was half-full sat near the wall of pine branches. He looked up and took a deep breath. He was beneath a tree. The trunk soared high into the sky. The branches had been cleared away about six feet up, and some kind of grass tarp had been tied to form a ceiling and wall. Looking up made him dizzy and he lowered his head quickly.

A deep growl caused him to jerk his head to the side. A big, white cat—the odd looking one that he'd seen with the girl—crouched near the edge of the tree branches, ears flattened against its head. The cat was scrunched up, but he could tell it was big. Or rather, long. He'd seen savannah cats, except they weren't bright white like this one and they didn't have icy blue eyes.

He held his good hand up. "Easy there." The cat hissed at him, but its growl lessened. Finn slowly reached for it. It hissed again and swatted at him with its very large paw then darted out from under the tree. It hadn't hurt him, which was a little surprising.

Finn let his head fall back against the tree trunk. Was this the girl's home? Was he in some strange village? People didn't live alone out in the wilds.

He listened outside for signs of other people, but it was quiet except for the sound of someone, the girl—she'd said her name was Erilyn, he thought—moving around outside. He heard a fire crackle and twigs snap. Light filtered in through the grass mats she'd tied up and he noticed some holes that needed mending. He thought thin, cured bark might be more durable and decided he'd offer to make those for her as a thank you for saving him.

He jumped as she parted the branches. She tied them back as she came in and sunlight poured over him. Squinting, he tried to shield his eyes, grimacing when he lifted his bad arm.

She stood in the doorway and looked down at him. "Luna told me you were awake." Her voice was soft and light. She cleared her throat, her head down. He tried to see her eyes, but all he could see was her silhouette. "I have food for you." He leaned forward, trying to see her face.

With a breath that sounded like a sigh, she came and sat next to him, offering him a bowl. Her hair was long and tangled and hung over her face like a curtain of vines.

"Boiled potatoes." She motioned toward the bowl in his hand. "I need to check your shoulder."

She moved to his other side, still hiding her face. He shoveled the tiny, hot potatoes into his mouth, barely chewing them. They burned his tongue, but he didn't care. He hadn't realized how hungry he'd been. Erilyn pulled the fabric away from his wound, but didn't touch him. He winced as the fabric tugged the edges of his wound and jerked way.

"Sorry," she whispered as she leaned down and smelled him. He could see her face clearly for a moment. Her eyes were a deep, gray blue—a color he'd never seen. She glanced up at him, took a quick breath, then gently touched the swollen skin and sighed.

"It needs to be repacked. But the infection is gone. No signs of poison." He felt her breath brush the sensitive skin and shivered.

He looked at her, startled. "Poison?"

"Wylden poison." She seemed unaffected as she unearthed a wooden box and pulled things he couldn't see from it. "It's gone now. Caught it in time."

"I was poisoned?"

Erilyn rolled her eyes and looked up at him through her hair then went back to work. She darted out from beneath the tree, and returned just as quickly with a bowl. She mixed some things together and sat down again. She moved as fluidly as the cat, who Finn realized with a start was back beneath the tree, flat to the ground, staring at him through squinted eyes. He hadn't heard it come in, hadn't seen it.

"This might hurt a little." She used a damp, ripped piece of cloth to wipe away blood and the remnants of whatever she'd packed it with before. He winced and clenched his fist. He felt her put something cool and wet against the wound, then wrap the bandage back around it. "There."

"Wasn't so bad," he said through teeth still clenched. Where the poultice sat burned for a moment before it grew cool. The pain that had been throbbing down through his elbow and into his wrist slowly faded. He sighed and sagged back. "Thanks." He looked at her, relief clear on his face. She looked at him sideways through her hair, like an animal about to bolt at any moment. "Thanks for everything." He tried to make his voice soft to match hers.

She gave him a small smile and then ducked her head to replace everything she'd taken from her little cubby in the dirt.

When everything had been put back in the little basket she kept buried near the base of the tree between some roots, she turned to him. Her forehead was all scrunched up and her lips were pursed.

She reached toward his face, then stopped. "May I?" she asked in her quiet way. He nodded and she took a deep breath then pressed the back of her hand against his forehead. "Fever's down." She nodded to herself as she almost jerked her hand away. Clearing her throat, she looked at him for the first time dead on. "I don't know your name."

"Finley." He shook his head. "Well, Finn. I'm called Finn." She looked away and he leaned to try and catch her eyes again. They were the color of the morning sky before the fog had lifted. "And you're Erilyn, right?"

She looked up at him, a piece of long, dirty hair falling across her face. She nodded. The cat growled low in its chest and Erilyn scratched between its ears absently.

"And this is?" He motioned toward the cat. He didn't really care about the animal's name, he just wanted to hear her voice again. It was quiet and calming and had a certain music to it.

"Luna." She smiled when she said the cat's name and Luna's growl subsided into a purr. "Like the moon." She looked down at the cat, her features softening, and Finn felt his breath catch.

"Beautiful."

Her cheeks reddened and it grew quiet again, the only sound was Luna's loud purr.

"Do you still want to die?" Erilyn's question came out of the silence like a Wylden spear, sudden and startling.

"No." He shook his head and pushed himself up so that he was sitting a little taller. "No." He wanted to tell her that he hadn't wanted to die the night before either, that he'd just been hurt and delirious. But part of him *had* wanted to die. Now it seemed ridiculous, but at the time he'd been in so much pain, physically and emotionally, it had seemed the best course.

"Do you—" she hesitated, cleared her throat, and looked him right in the eye. "Do you want to talk about it?" Her jaw was squared, defiant almost.

"It's not important." He shook his head. "I was just hurt, I think. And hurting. I mean—" he shrugged, then winced as his shoulder ached. "This is going to sound really idiotic, but I went after the Wylden—"

"You attacked them?" Her face brightened with a smile and he smiled back.

"Sort of. I mean, yes. I went into their camp and got caught trying to sneak back out." Saying it out loud made it all seem even more ridiculous.

"You went in their camp? On purpose?" She cocked an eyebrow and tilted her head to the side like a curious little bird.

"I wasn't exactly in my right mind." He sighed, embarrassed. "My girlfriend dumped me."

"Morrigan." Erilyn whispered, but hearing her name caused Finn to sit up straight and lean forward.

"How do you know her name?" His voice was sharper than he'd intended. His heart raced.

Erilyn stood, eyes wide, all traces of that small, playful smile gone. "You said it. In your sleep." She set her jaw and turned away from him. "A girl is a stupid reason to try and kill yourself."

"Who said I was trying to kill myself?" He tried to push himself up to standing, but collapsed back against the tree.

"Why else would you go *into* a Wylden camp?" She spat the words at him and then strode outside. He heard her moving around out there, but couldn't see what she was doing. She whistled once and Luna jumped up and darted after her, leaving Finn alone.

Why had he gotten so angry with her? He must have been mumbling Morrigan's name as he slept. He'd dreamed about her all night. He dropped his head into his good hand and rubbed his forehead. He should apologize to Erilyn, but seeing as how he couldn't even stand on his own, he'd have to wait until she came back.

If he leaned to the right enough, he could see her. She was tending a small, smokeless fire. Luna was stretched nearby, watching Erilyn with her head on her paws. She was incredibly long and bright white and Finn was amazed she'd survived to adulthood. Her coloring would have made her easy prey as a kitten. But the way they moved around each other, he thought Erilyn must have cared for her and protected her.

Erilyn was boiling something—he could see an old, dented pot. She squatted by the fire, feet wide and knees bent. He'd only ever seen men and children sit that way. She had a tin cup that she'd put something in. He couldn't see what she was doing, but he couldn't take his eyes away from her. Her hair reached her waist and was tangled like a birds nest. In the open sunlight, it looked like warm honey. She looked so small out there—smaller than she did in the tight space beneath the tree—and her clothes hung from her body as if they'd originally been made for someone else.

As she looked over at Luna, Finn could see the gentle slope of her small nose. Even beneath all the dirt she wore like a second skin, she was lovely.

Her head jerked toward him and he quickly looked away, overcome with embarrassment. He made it a point not to look at her until she came back.

Erilyn crouched next to him and held out the cup. He took it cautiously and sniffed it. It was warm and smelled sweet. She'd given him the same thing the night before and he'd fallen asleep.

"You're trying to knock me out?" He raised his eyebrows and waggled the cup at her a little. "Tired of me already?" He smiled with one side of his mouth, hoping he could repair whatever damage he'd done by being short with her moments before.

Erilyn's tight stance loosened and she smiled that small smile she'd worn earlier. "It'll make you sleep, but it'll also make your shoulder heal faster." She touched her lips. "Drink it and lie back."

"How long will I be asleep?" Some part of his brain didn't want to sleep. He might see Morrigan again, or worse, he wouldn't see her at all. He was also a little bit worried that he would wake up and Erilyn would be gone. He was getting the impression they were alone out here.

"A while." She cocked her head to the side, as if she were trying to figure him out. "Don't worry." She gently placed her hand on his shoulder, on the top of his bandage. "We'll protect you."

Her hand on the fabric over his shoulder was warm and it felt like being immersed in a warm bath. He trusted her. It was something in the way she spoke, something in her eyes.

Finn brought the cup to his lips and sipped. It was sweet and spicy. She'd added something to it that hadn't been there the night before. Clove or cinnamon, maybe. He drank it quickly then did as she'd asked and laid back. By the time his head rested on the earth, the tree above him was spinning.

"Close your eyes, Finn." Erilyn pulled the thin blanket he wore up to his chin and carefully tucked it under his shoulders. "We'll be here when you wake up."

Finn smiled as he closed his eyes and fell down into the oblivion of a deep, dreamless sleep.

Chapter Seven
Enthralled

Erilyn

I'd planned to gather food and water while Finn slept, but more often than not, I found myself standing in my little doorway, watching his chest rise and fall. I told myself it was to make sure his infection didn't return suddenly, but really, I was just curious. He was the first man I'd ever had the chance to just observe without fear.

I eventually pulled myself away, angry with myself. Luna followed me, nervous. She chirped at me in quick succession and pranced around my feet as I went to my pile of apples. Some had been nibbled or taken by wild life since I'd tossed them down from the tree the day before. I tossed the apples that had started to rot into the woods, and took the rest into the hem of my worn tunic to the pond. As I washed them, I tried to think of anything except Finn sleeping close by.

As I washed, I let my mind and awareness of my surroundings wander. This was a common way for me to pass the time, checking in on the birds and squirrels nearby. I did this now, but somehow my mind always found its way back beneath the pine, back to Finn's evergreen light.

The apples wouldn't keep long unless they were dried. Rosemarie had taught me how to cook them over a low flame for hours to preserve them, but I'd learned, after she died, that I could do it much more quickly.

I sliced all the apples and piled them on a piece of thick bark. I checked in on Finn, quickly—still out cold. Sitting beside the apples, I wiggled my fingers into the pile and then closed my eyes.

I had to be careful not to dry them too much—once they'd burst into flame. As I took deep, slow breaths, I pictured the cool, wet apples around my hands. Once the image was clear and crisp in my head, I started to imagine the water, the juice, heating and evaporating like fog. I felt the apples warm and soften. I had to go slowly, make sure I left just enough moisture—barely any at all—to keep them from catching fire.

When I was done, I removed my hands and opened my eyes. The apple slices were dried. The pile much smaller than I'd hoped for, but better than nothing.

I stood, my hips popping, and stretched a kink from my neck as I moved quickly beneath the pine. Finn was pushing himself to sit and I froze, heart racing.

"Is it morning?" He yawned and I noticed he didn't hold his injured arm quite as carefully as he had that morning.

"No. The sun's setting, not rising." Had he seen? My hands shook, so I balled them into fists and held them tight against my legs.

"Oh." He yawned again.

I stepped past him and pulled the bag from the little compartment where I kept the things I wanted to hide. Without an explanation, I left to gather the dried apples and my thoughts. If he'd seen, what would I do? Maybe he would just leave and never come back.

I layered the apples in the bag, my mind a mess, took a deep breath, and turned to go back inside. Finn was standing in the pine's entrance, a little too tall for it, watching me.

"Were those dried apples?" he looked from the bag of apples to the coals of the morning's fire, still smoldering softly.

I nodded, waiting for a question, an accusation, some barbed comment. Instead, I heard his stomach growl, and he self-consciously ran his hand through his hair.

"They look really good." He laughed a little. "Can I help you put those up or anything?"

The tension in my shoulders and neck lessened a little, but only a little. I reached into the bag, grabbed a handful, and handed them to him as I ducked back under the tree to store the rest.

"Thank you," he said as I turned to face him. He'd eaten the whole handful.

"It's almost dark," I said. The sleepy time tea should have kept him asleep 'til past sundown. I needed to adjust its strength for Finn's size. He was bigger than he'd seemed, taller. My head would come to just below his chin. "But I was going to do a quick walk around, see if the animals have left any greens." He looked at me hopefully, and I resisted the urge to try and read what he was feeling. "Would you like to help?"

Finn broke out in a huge grin. "I'd love to." He went to raise his right arm and winced, then held it against his body.

"You need a new shirt." I looked at the bandage and exposed skin of his arm. "And a sling." Shaking my head, I realized I should have done that first thing. I had lots of scrap cloth—bits of clothing I'd scavenged that weren't worth wearing unless it got nasty-cold and a shirt that was too big for me, but that I sometimes used to stuff around my body during the coldest nights.

I held the shirt out toward him and he took it, the shirt he was wearing hanging off his body from where I'd torn it to get to the wound. He looked down at it in his one good hand then back up to me and I flushed.

"Can you sit? Or kneel? I'll help you." He knelt in front of me and, after a deep breath, I gently pulled the torn, bloody fabric from his shirt over his head and then slipped it off his good arm. I tried not to look at his body, but couldn't help it. He wasn't a large man, but his muscles were well defined and freckles dotted his shoulders. His face and arms were tan, but his torso was pale and I had the brief instantaneous desire to reach out and feel the paler skin.

He offered me the shirt I'd given him and I slipped it over his head, letting him settle his uninjured arm in the sleeve, and then carefully guiding his injured one where it needed to be. When I touched his forearm, I felt the tight, lean muscle there, and blushed.

"You'll need a sling, too," I mumbled and turned to grab another old shirt that was too worn to wear. "Just bend your arm at the elbow." I helped him bend it and hold it away from his body just enough that I could thread the fabric between his chest and arm. I reached around his head, my hand brushing the warm skin at the back of his neck, and tied the shirt's sleeves there. His breath tickled my cheek as I tied the knot and I felt a flush of nervousness that wasn't entirely my own. I stepped away to make sure the shirt was holding his forearm securely then tried to hide my red cheeks behind my hair. "Better?"

He moved his arm a little and smiled. "Much. Thank you."

Luna, who'd been my silent shadow since Finn woke, walked between us. She reared up onto her hind legs, balanced for a moment, and then put both paws on Finn's uninjured shoulder. She was my height and reached Finn's shoulders easily.

Finn froze and looked at me with wide, scared eyes. I couldn't help but smile and hold my tongue. Luna's energy was calm and warm. He didn't have anything to worry about, but I often forgot that many people would be afraid of her—her sharp teeth and long claws.

She looked at him, leaned in close, and pressed her nose to his. His eyes were nearly crossed, but I saw the moment the fear left his eyes and he smiled. Once he did, she chirped and jumped back to the ground, letting her long, white tail curl around his leg as she walked away.

"She likes you." I smiled as I watched her slink into the forest to find her dinner.

"As long as she doesn't think she'll like the way I taste." He laughed.

I peered at him from behind my hair. "She's too small to eat you."

"Not from where I was standing." His smile stretched across his face and up into his bright blue eyes. The smile was open and honest and I was smiling back before I realized it and felt my stomach flutter. I ducked out of the tree and trusted that he would follow. I didn't know how to talk to this person. It wasn't like talking with Rosemarie at all. I hadn't been good at talking to her at first either, but this was different. He made me nervous and I wasn't sure I didn't like it.

The light was fading, but we had an hour or so left. Once the first frost hit, all the wild plantains would die. I'd forgotten a sack or basket to carry them in, but I didn't want to seem distracted so I kept walking. Finn's steps behind me were loud and I cringed.

"This is what you're looking for." I found a grassy spot and plucked a handful of old, tough plantains to show Finn. Most of the young, tender ones would already be gone, but these would keep our bellies full. He nodded and started searching, bent over, looking through the shadow in the dim light.

As I gathered the broad, green leaves in the hem of my shirt, I watched him from the corner of my eye. Wherever he was from, he wasn't used to gardening. He kept standing and stretching his back. By the time we'd finished, he'd made a small pile. I added it to the bunch in my shirt and led us back home in the near dark.

"How do you know where to go?" he asked as we walked. He stumbled even though there was still sunlight trickling down, and there would be a full moon out soon.

"I've walked this way countless times." I also could see better in the dark than any upworlder.

"You haven't tripped over a single root." He tripped as he said that and cursed under his breath.

"Where you're from, what do you do?" I asked, trying to change the topic.

He reached out and put his hand on my shoulder. I tensed, but kept walking. We were almost back, and he wasn't touching skin, so all that happened was a heightened sense of his feelings, which were annoyed. But I'd known that already.

"I'm a carpenter." He stumbled but his hand on my shoulder stabilized him. "Well, sort of. I apprenticed under the carpenter, but he died, so I do my best to figure out what he didn't teach me." He tripped again and nearly fell into me. "I build furniture and carve things to trade.

His hand on my shoulder was warm—warmer than it should be. He told me more about his trade as we walked, but his words were starting to slur.

When we reached the clearing, I led Finn to the pine. The leafy plantains I put in a pile, out of the way, and I guided him to a seat. He was still talking about his craft, how to join joints so that they were seamless and how to measure. He mentioned dovetails and I thought he was delirious.

I sat him down and felt his forehead with my bare palm—he was burning up.

"Stay here." Heart racing with sudden worry, I went out to the fire pit and quickly got a fire going. I helped the embers that were still warm spring to life with a single, panicked thought, blocking what I was doing with my body. I put water on to warm then went back to Finn.

"I'm not hungry," he said. I turned his face so that the firelight could catch his eyes. They were glassy. I shouldn't have let him walk all that way with me. "Are we eating?" His cheeks were pink beneath his few days' growth of beard and his lips were cracked. I hadn't given him water all day. Rosemarie wouldn't have made those mistakes.

"I'm getting you something right now." I darted out to get the water and made up a cup of sleepy time tea. It was all I knew to do to get the fever down. Rosemarie hadn't had time to teach me more than that.

When I came back he was slumped against the tree, cheeks red, his lips pale. "Drink this."

"Is that the stuff that knocks me out?" His words were slurred now and his head lolled to the side as he spoke.

"No. Drink it." I put the cup to his mouth and tilted it, not caring if it burned him, only caring that he drank it. He coughed a little, but drank.

I adjusted his frame against the tree as his eyelids started to flutter.

"Liar." He smiled and his head fell toward his chest, then he jerked it back up. "You're so nice." He reached for my face, but his hand fell back to his lap before he touched me. "So pretty."

His eyes closed then. I propped him up against the tree with a bucket that had a hole in the bottom and the words "Lake Cumberland" etched into the side and rusted over. I pulled the blanket over him and sat back, heart racing.

I'd touched his skin and seen into his head again—Morrigan, shining bright like a goddess. And I'd also seen myself through his fevered eyes—gray eyes shining, skin golden, hair long and bright like summer wheat. I had seen my reflection in the water, and I didn't look like that. I reached up and felt my hair. It hung in heavy clumps from my scalp. I tried to see my reflection in my old, dented tin cup, on the side without faded pictures, but it was too warped and old.

I looked outside. The sun had nearly set, but light still trickled through the trees—enough light to see by. Careful not to disturb Finn's form, I pulled the winter clothes I had stored from one of my earthen compartments and my blanket. I gently draped Finn's blanket over him and resisted the urge to push his shaggy hair from his forehead. Rosemarie had done that for me. I told myself that's why I wanted to do it, not because I wanted to see if it was soft or coarse.

Outside, I stoked the fire. Luna joined me from her nightly hunt and I rubbed between her ears, noticing for the first time how dirty my fingernails were in her bright white fur.

"Watch him." I nodded my head toward the tree. She stretched, rubbed her body against my legs, and then ducked under the pine.

The water in the pond would be cold this time of year, but it didn't matter. It had been too long since I'd last taken the time to scrub. I'd been negligent with myself.

With one last quick look back toward the pine, I put my winter clothes and blanket next to the pond. The water reflected the rainbow colors of sunset up at me.

I pulled my clothes off. They were dirtier than I realized—Wylden dirty. I stepped into the water and shivered. With a deep breath I drew a bit of warmth from the fire into my body. As I let myself fall beneath the water's surface, I felt the water seep through the layer of dirt and kiss my skin. Using my fingertips, I began to scrub my scalp, feeling tangles start to dislodge, wondering how dirty the water would be when I got out. I surfaced to breathe, then dove under again, swimming toward the very bottom where there would be some sandy earth. I grabbed a handful and used it to scrub the layer of dirt off my arms, legs, and torso. It stung and I had to swim for air a few times before I felt clean enough.

I floated in the water a moment longer, staring up at the sky as stars started to sprinkle here and there. When the water started to feel chilly again, I pulled myself back to shore, wrapped my blanket around myself, and went to stand by the fire to dry.

My mind kept going back to Finn—to the way he'd seen me in his head. I knew it was his fever, but I'd caught a whisper of his emotion. And though I couldn't be sure if it had been about me—Morrigan had been in his mind, too—I'd thought it was. Admiration. Attraction. Intrigue.

Just thinking about it, remembering what it had felt like, caused my cheeks and belly to grow warm. I closed my eyes and for less than a moment, I let myself *feel* what he'd felt. I let myself experience what it might feel like to feel such things for another person, what it might feel like to be someone normal, someone who wasn't me.

Chapter Eight

Firelight

Finn

Finn was swimming through fog. His eyes didn't want to focus, couldn't focus. He saw light up ahead and struggled to swim toward it. A person was there, surrounded in light. No, creating the light. It was hard to see past the light to see who it was, hard to see the person's face, but he felt drawn there. Felt like he had to get to them.

The closer he got to the person, the easier it was to move. His mouth was sickly sweet. The light was warm and soothed an ache in his shoulder he hadn't noticed. It washed over him like warm water and made him feel more awake.

He could see a silhouette now. A woman. *Morrigan.* He swam harder, faster.

The light-filled figure became clear and Finn stopped. The light faded and he saw—

"Erilyn."

She turned, the fire flaring, her hair and eyes flashing in the reflected light.

Finn's eyes cleared and he realized he was clinging to the pine branches that hung as the doorway, looking at Erilyn standing next to the fire. She was wrapped in a blanket, her hair hanging in a wavy sheet down her back.

He felt woozy, but the longer he looked at Erilyn, at the fire behind her, the clearer his head became.

"You should be asleep." Her cheeks were flushed and her eyes were wild.

"I heard something." Except he hadn't. He cleared his throat and shook his head, confused. "I think."

"You should still be asleep." She tucked the blanket more tightly around herself, as if trying to hide in it.

As Finn's head cleared completely, as he realized that Erilyn only wore a blanket, no clothes, his cheeks warmed and he looked away.

"You had a fever again." She held the blanket tightly. "You should go back to sleep."

"I feel fine." His gaze kept darting back to her and away. He couldn't help it. She looked different, and not just because of her dress. In the firelight, her skin glowed like it was absorbing the light from the fire. Her hair was wild and long. She was small, and looked smaller still in a blanket, but something about the way the firelight made her glow made her seem powerful.

Erilyn turned away from him and opened the blanket. Finn flushed as he imagined what was beneath it. She held the blanket under each arm and tucked it in securely by her collarbone. She picked up the pile of clothes next to her and walked over to him with her head held high.

The closer she got, the clearer his head became, until she was right next to him. As she looked up at him, his heart sped up. She shifted her clothes to one arm and used her free hand to feel his forehead and then his cheek. Even though she was away from the fire, she still glowed. Her hand on his skin was so warm he wanted to lean into it.

"Fever's gone." She jerked her hand back as if he'd hurt her. He almost sighed at the loss of contact.

"I told you I felt fine." His heart was thudding rapidly in his chest and his mouth was dry.

She nodded and then looked uncomfortably into the pine and back to him. "Will you wait by the fire?" She tugged her blanket dress a little higher. "I need to change."

Finn nodded and waited for her to walk past him. Even with the space between them, he felt heat as if she were bringing the fire with her. He slowly walked to the fire.

While he waited, Finn kept his back to the tree. It was hard, because he felt drawn to her like a moth to a flame. Luna rubbed against his legs and he knelt to pet her with his good hand.

"Are you hungry?"

Her voice directly behind him startled him into standing. Luna chirped in irritation and head butted his hand. She looked different still. Her hair was golden in the firelight. She wore a sweater with rolled up sleeves and fitted wool pants that had clearly been made for someone else.

"You changed." Finn felt nervous, though he wasn't sure why. Now that she was back, he couldn't help but imagine her hand on his cheek. Her warmth.

"Winter clothes."

They stood in silence and for a moment and Finn fidgeted, feeling as nervous as he had on his first date with

Morrigan. He'd taken to her a tall hill beneath an apple tree and given her sweet buns—her favorite. The silence then had been awkward too, thick with tension.

Remembering that day, remembering Morrigan, seemed to clear Finn's head. Looking down at her, he felt guilty for having such thoughts. He was lonely and still sick. He shook his head to clear it.

Erilyn was staring at him, her brow furrowed, a confused expression on her face.

"I'll make food." Erilyn walked away abruptly and Finn sat down and curled in on himself. He absently stroked Luna and tried to ignore the fog building in his head.

Erilyn quickly put together some of the remaining dried vegetables and apples and they ate in silence, Luna purring contentedly between them.

With night fully present, the sounds of the forest had come to life. Finn watched Erilyn out of the corner of his eye. She seemed to be listening to every sound, her head subtly turning this way and that when a new insect or frog would start up. She smiled softly as she listened.

"It's beautiful," he said, breaking the silence. Her smile vanished as she turned to him. "The forest sounds. We don't hear sounds like this in Sunnybrook."

"They only sing when it's safe." She looked up again as if she could see the tiny frog that sang so loudly. "They'll be quiet soon, when it gets too cold. But for now, they let me know there are no predators around." Her smile was back and he felt himself want to lean over just to see it more clearly.

To keep from doing so, he looked up into the dark trees where she looked, trying to see whatever it was she saw. All he saw were the dark canopies of trees topped by the beginnings of the night's stars.

"Can I ask you—" her voice startled him and he turned toward her. She was looking at him with her big, blue-gray eyes open wide.

"Anything." And he meant it. He would tell her anything she wanted to know. She was still glowing and he wondered how the firelight played so beautifully on her skin.

"Why did you go into that Wylden camp?" she almost whispered.

He looked away from her, back toward the fire. Luna, awake now, pressed into him and laid her head in his lap. Her weight was a comfort.

"To kill one of them." His tone was flat as he remembered with shame the child he'd considered killing. The scrawny, dirty, wild child that he'd thought would be the easiest Wylden to kill. He felt sick all over. He continued before she could ask why. "I was angry for a stupid reason and needed to hurt something as badly as I hurt."

"Because of Morrigan."

His head whipped toward her, but after a moment he nodded. Realizing he'd been talking in his sleep again, he turned back to the flames. "We were supposed to be married. I mean, I hadn't asked her yet, but she knew. And she left me because of one stupid fight. So I was angry and stupid." He quit petting Luna to rub his eyes. "It seems petty now."

"Heartbreak makes us do strange things." Her voice was a whisper, but he could hear the deep sadness there. He wondered who'd broken her heart that she would understand so well.

"You must think I'm a real moron." He looked at her and she smiled, still gazing into the dancing fire.

"No." She held Luna's tail and stroked it, running it between her fingers. "I think anyone who loves that big, that much, must be doing something right."

Her words released a knot in Finn's chest, and with it a flood of emotions, both good and bad. It was as if her acknowledgement had freed him to really feel the pain of losing Morrigan, as well as the joy of having loved so deeply. He felt tears, but held them back.

They sat in silence for a while after that. Until the flames started to die. Until the stars overhead were the brightest points in the sky, except for the nearly full moon.

"We should get some sleep," Erilyn said as she stood. Luna followed her, stretching toward the tree, looking like a beam of moonlight.

Finn followed her as if in a dream. What had his life become? Just a few days ago he'd been planning how to propose to Morrigan, the love of his life. And now he was sleeping beneath a pine tree with a wild forest girl and her jungle cat.

Despite it all, he followed her. He settled in next to the trunk, more tired than he thought he'd be, and covered himself with his blood-stained blanket and watched her as she drew the pine branches closed and tied them shut. He could barely see her outline as she lay down less than a foot away.

He could feel how close she was. All he'd have to do would be to scoot over just a little and they'd be touching. He shivered in the cool night and wondered if the cold would be enough of an excuse. He told himself he just needed some human contact. And then he thought of Morrigan again and guilt made him go cold.

In the darkness, Erilyn sighed and he felt Luna slink between them and lay down. After a few more tortured moments of battling his desire to touch her, even just the tips of her fingers, to feel her reassuring presence while also battling the guilt he felt at betraying Morrigan, he fell asleep.

Chapter Nine
Sparks

Erilyn

I woke feeling more relaxed than I had in a long time. Luna was a warm, reassuring presence at my side, and the sun was just beginning to peak beneath the pine branches where they brushed the dirt. I looked up to where the branches met the trunk and smiled as a chipmunk peeked out at me before darting back around to the untouched side of the tree.

I wondered why I felt so rested, then realized I hadn't had the nightmare. No running through the caves. No dead glowworms. No fire burning. I sighed and stretched, my muscles and joints releasing as if it were a warm spring day.

Then I felt Finn's foot move against mine and I froze. How long had we been asleep like that, our feet pressed together. I hadn't noticed at first, because we were both still wearing our shoes. He was waking and I jerked my foot away, wondering how long it had been there, wondering how we'd gotten close enough to touch. At least our shoes had kept me from getting any flashes.

My heart was racing. I tucked my foot back under the blanket and pretended to be asleep.

Next to me, Finn slowly sat. I kept my eyes nearly closed and watched him through my eyelashes. He rolled his neck and massaged his bad shoulder gently. He was healing quickly—more quickly than he should. He looked back at me over his shoulder, his expression soft.

"Erilyn?" he whispered, but I stayed still. He turned away and I tried to slow my breathing down.

He sat there, head in his hands, until Luna moved. When she moved, I allowed myself to as well, pretending she woke me.

He turned to look at me, his expression guarded. Pained. I wanted to touch him to see what was going through his head, but didn't.

"Good morning." I tried to smile, but the memory of his foot touching mine, of how relaxed and peaceful I'd felt, made me blush instead. I couldn't meet his eye.

"Are you ok?" he asked and I looked up at him, his expression sad.

"Fine." I pushed my own feelings aside and carefully slipped the mask I'd developed as a child in place. If the other kids thought their words hadn't hurt me, they had left me alone. It had served me then and it would serve me now.

"I just wanted to apologize—" he trailed off, breaking his gaze from mine, his cheeks growing pink.

"For?" Again, I had the desperate urge to look into his head.

"Maybe you didn't notice—" he cleared his throat, clearly uncomfortable. He met my eyes then looked away.

"Our feet, last night. While we slept." He shrugged, his face going redder beneath the beard growing in slowly. "I didn't mean to. I shouldn't have, I mean." He shrugged again and coughed.

"I didn't know anything happened with our feet." I tried to sound nonchalant, even irritated, but my heart sped up. Being in such a confined space, I could feel what he felt. Our auras were close enough to touch. He was embarrassed. Ashamed. And beneath those feelings was something else—desire.

"Why does it matter if our feet touched while we were asleep?" I asked, my voice soft. Morning light filtered through the pine branches and the birds were beginning to sing.

He sighed and put his head in his hands. "It shouldn't." His voice was muffled in his fingers, and I noticed that he was using his bad arm as much as his good. He shouldn't be healing this fast, even with the herbs I was giving him. "But it does." He looked up at me, his face stricken. "Because I wanted to be close to you, to be close to another person. Even though I love someone else." His head dropped back into his hands, and Luna, who'd been silently watching the exchange, leaned against him and rested her large head on his shoulder. "It was wrong because of how I felt about it."

Something inside me quivered. His emotions rolled off him like fog. He was deeply ashamed, and he wasn't telling me everything. He'd said he just wanted to be close to another person, but he'd wanted specifically to be close to me. To touch me. My mouth went dry.

"We all sometimes need comfort." I was surprised that my voice was steady. His desire pooled in my belly and I felt my own desire spring to life. It was a brand new feeling for me and more than a little uncomfortable. "That's what friends are for." The word *friend* felt alien on my tongue. I'd known him barely a day, but he felt like a friend. I hadn't had many.

His eyes met mine—electric blue—and I felt a surge of intense sadness. He opened his mouth, then shut it with a shrug. "I guess I over reacted." His voice was deadpan. He didn't believe what he was saying.

"No harm." The air in the room lost its charge. His emotions gradually slipped away.

After a long silence, Finn said, "How can I help you today?" His expression was eager.

I chose my words carefully. Today would be hard. "I have to go on a run. Across the field."

He blanched and sat back slightly.

"You can stay here," I offered, but he immediately shook his head.

"If I can help, I want to." He rubbed his shoulder. "I owe you."

I sighed and nodded. "Let me check your shoulder first. We can make it there and back before dark." I sat up on my knees, the blanket falling away, and reached for him. He didn't shy away as I pulled the neck of his shirt down and peeled away the bandage. He shivered as my cold hands prodded the tender skin. The wound was nothing more than a young, puffy pink scar. It shouldn't have healed so fast.

"I'll be right back." Hands shaking, I slipped out of the pine holding the dirty bandage. Had I done that? Or did upworlders heal faster than my people?

I rinsed his bandage in the pond and returned to the pine. Luna had slunk out after me and chirped from a nearby tree.

Finn sat where I'd left him, the neck of his shirt still pulled open. Careful to keep our skin from touching as much as possible, I gently wiped his skin with the cold water. He jumped.

"Sorry," I whispered as I kept working, trying to get all the herbs and dried blood off.

He shivered again. "It's fine."

Once the area was clean, it was clear that he was nearly completely healed. With a sigh, I sat back and watched as he pulled his shirt aside and looked himself.

"What was in that stuff you gave me?" He was smiling and he rolled his arm around. "It's healed!"

"You're a fast healer." My heart was thudding painfully. It hadn't been his upworld heritage. I'd done it, somehow. "Ready to go?"

I stood before he could answer and ducked outside, letting the cool morning air soak into my skin and cool the heat of my panic. This was something new. Useful and terrifying.

Finn followed me, still rolling his arm around. He winced and rubbed at the scar. "Still hurts some, but I'm ready. Lead the way."

As I imitated Luna's chirp, she dropped from a nearby tree branch. Making sure my fire pit was covered, I grabbed my good knife, sliding it into the makeshift loop sewed into all my pants. I could hear Finn behind me as I walked back the way Finn had come from initially and decided that I needed to help him learn to be quiet if he was going to stay here much longer. Every animal for a mile would hear him clomping through the trees.

Looking up through branches with leaves nearly half gone, I saw the wispy clouds of coming winter. No snow clouds yet, but they wouldn't be far off. I needed to get Finn home before then, I couldn't keep us both alive through a bad winter and I had a feeling this would be the worst yet.

We walked in silence, stopping at the spring for water. I showed Finn which leafy greens were safe to eat and we nibbled on them as we walked. He grimaced as he chewed the thick, bitter leaves, but he didn't complain.

We reached the edge of the field more slowly than we would have had I been alone, but I didn't mind. It was kind of nice, walking in the cool sunlight with another person. It made the woods feel warmer and smaller.

He started to step out into the field, but I grabbed his good arm and stopped him. The brightly lit field looked warm and inviting, but I knew better than to rush headlong out there.

"We have to make sure it's safe," I said, barely above a whisper. He'd discarded his sling, but I didn't think he could climb yet. "Stay here."

He opened his mouth to respond but I was already making my way up the tree, Luna climbing swiftly beside me. When I reached a high enough branch, I stopped, instinct keeping me next to the trunk even though the branch was sturdy enough for my weight. I looked down and saw Finn's open mouthed gaze. I gave him a little wave.

Luna chirped above me and I turned my attention toward the field. The grass was golden yellow and barely moved in the gentle breeze. With the high sun and wispy clouds, it was beautiful.

But the sunlight kept me from seeing cleanly to the other side with just my eyes. With a hand on the trunk to steady myself, I closed my eyes and let my vision soar across the golden grass to the trees that were no more than a dark smudge on the horizon.

Sometimes—like when I saw Finn for the first time running from the Wylden—my vision was clear and I could see things crisply. Other times, like now, it was hazy, as if I were looking through water or a small hole. I closed my eyes and pulled my vision back. The scene had been hazy, hard to see, but empty except for some litter. There was no trace of the Wylden.

It was always like that. If my expanded vision was clear, there were Wylden. If it wasn't, there weren't. I didn't let myself think about that too much as I climbed down the tree and back to Finn.

"They're gone," I said a little more loudly than before, and I saw him slump in relief. "Do you want to rest a bit before we cross? Once we're there, we'll need to work fast and get back." I didn't want to tell him that there were more big predators on that side of the field.

"I'm good to go," he said, rolling his shoulder and wincing slightly. "I can move fast."

I nodded and chirped for Luna to scout ahead. It was cool, so we didn't have to worry about the big snakes that liked to sun in the grass, but the mountain lions might be out in it instead of in the trees. Luna couldn't fight one, but she was fast and could warn us before we stumbled on one.

As soon as we stepped out into the sunlight I felt warmer. We were hunched over slightly to avoid being seen above the waving grass tops, but we moved quickly and it helped me retain that warmth. The longer the sun was directly on my skin, the faster I felt I was able to move.

Crossing the field only took about an hour. We stopped and crouched down just outside the perimeter of where the wagons had been camped. Finn was breathing heavily, and I felt bad for having run the whole way. I hadn't thought about him as I ran free in the open sun and air and guilt tugged at me.

I closed my eyes and quickly scanned the area, looking for any auras or emotions that didn't belong to the local wildlife. There were some bears, deep in the woods, and the usual smattering of birds and small tree creatures, but no Wylden or big cats that I could tell.

"Erilyn?" I opened my eyes and turned. Finn looked at me with a creased forehead. "You OK?"

I blushed, and nodded. "Just resting and enjoying the sun." The lie fell from my lips, but he nodded.

Sure that we were safe, I stood and made a point of looking around carefully—though I didn't need to—before walking directly into the trampled grass and litter that was the imprint the Wylden always left in their wake.

Chapter Ten
Scavengers

Finn

Erilyn walked into the open space left by the Wylden caravan. Finn watched her, still crouched in the weeds, and tried to calm his suddenly racing heart. The wagons were gone, but he reimagined the scene—the wagons, the child he'd thought about killing, the rotten smells and grotesque sounds.

He was shaking, even though there was nothing there except the remnants of a fire and a bunch of trash. It felt hard to breathe and his shoulder started to throb.

Luna head butted his back, nearly knocking him over. She then rubbed along his injured arm before letting her tail twitch against his face as she left the safety of the grass to join Erilyn.

He watched them as they sorted through the litter—Luna batting around things that Erilyn discarded. The way she'd closed her eyes before, he didn't think she'd been enjoying the sun. She'd looked intense and beautiful.

He shook his head and pushed himself up and over the threshold of trampled grass. "What are we looking for?" he asked, after clearing his throat. Erilyn smiled at him and returned to searching.

"Anything we can use." She didn't comment on his hesitation to come out here, which helped him relax.

Morrigan hated when he was at all indecisive. Once, they'd gone swimming in the pool near the bottom of the cliffs that surrounded one side of Sunnybrook. Morrigan convinced him to climb to a high ledge and jump off. She'd jumped straight away, screaming in joy as she splashed into the water, but he hadn't. He'd thought about it for a long time before he jumped. He jumped after a while, but she hadn't talked to him the rest of the day.

As he searched the debris, he realized he didn't know what to look for. Everything was broken or old. He watched her pick up a metal bowl—dented and burned in the fire—and hold onto it and knew he would have passed it up.

He started looking more closely, picking up scraps of wood, discarding bones and kicking aside scraps of rotting meat. He found some torn cloth that was thick and warm. Looking at Erilyn in her thin sweater, he thought of her threadbare blankets, and held onto it.

They worked in silence and his mind kept wandering to Erilyn. To the way it had felt to lean his foot against hers as they slept, how comfortable and warm he'd felt.

He snuck glances at her as he moved. Who was this girl? She was small but there was no doubting her strength. She'd saved his life, not knowing him in the least, and had asking nothing in return. She was beautiful and wild, but seemed sad in a way that made him want to make her smile. He felt drawn to her in a very gentle way and realized, suddenly, that he'd closed the distance between them without meaning to.

"I think that's all we'll find," she said, straightening from her bent posture. In her dented, fire blackened bowl was a horribly bent spoon, a knife that was missing the tip, and a handful of sharp rocks. He offered her the thick bit of cloth and the chipped wooden plate that had been half buried and she smiled, adding them to her bowl. "Thank you." She turned then toward the trees with her hands above her eyes to block out the sun. "We can use this cloth to carry any fruit left."

He followed her into the trees and shivered as the shadows stole the sun's heat. The leaves on this side were thicker than in Erilyn's woods, as if autumn hadn't quite reached here yet.

Erilyn led them straight to a group of trees just inside the tree line. She looked up into them and her face fell. "Not much to pick," she said as she put down her bowl and started to climb. "Keep an eye out."

Luna was up the tree beside her faster than Finn could track with his eyes. He watched her, dizzy, as she crawled out on the first branch with apples still hanging. The lowest branches were bare.

Shivering, he spun to face the woods. It was still full day, but he felt eyes on him. He'd been told stories as a kid—stories that were meant to scare him into staying inside the wall—about monstrously giant cats with tusks and claws longer than a man's hand and vicious wolves that could see in the dark. He'd disregarded those as stories years ago, but now as he stood in the shadows of trees he didn't know, he wondered if there was some truth in them. Luna was harmless enough, but he didn't know what animals lived in these woods so far from home.

He couldn't hear Erilyn and Luna above him, but he kept his eyes on the trees around them.

A few leaves fell from above and he glanced up to see Erilyn peering down at him through the branches with a small smile. He smiled back, suddenly warm. She disappeared further up into the branches and he turned back to the trees as a cool breeze blew through. He still felt eyes on him, but didn't see anything, so he held his tongue.

He strained his ears, but there was no sound. Nothing except the air in the trees.

Finn jumped when Erilyn's feet hit the ground softly beside him, her eyes wide. She put her hand on his arm, her fingers tight. "Follow me," she whispered harshly.

His heart rate spiked as he followed her, not toward the field as he'd thought, but deeper into the woods. She stopped twice, her head swinging around each time, before she took off in a slightly new direction. They walked so long the sun had started its descent. Finn was starting to get frustrated when he heard the sounds of crunching leaves behind them. Erilyn's head whipped around, her gray blue eyes shining bright. She grabbed his hand and started to run.

Behind them, something large crashed after them. Finn gripped Erilyn's hand tighter as they ran.

Erilyn ducked into the hollow center of a very old tree, pulling him after her. He crashed into her and she pressed her hand to his mouth and her body against his. His chest was heaving and he could feel her heart pounding as she looked through the tree trunk's split side, her eye wide in fear. She closed her eyes and a sudden wind gust blew a dead branch hard enough to make it fall in front of the split in the trunk that they'd come through. She took her hand from his mouth and leaned so close her lips nearly touched his ear.

"Try to be quiet." Her whisper was barely there. He nodded and tried to slow his panting.

She leaned back and looked into his eyes, her own widening as the sound of ragged breaths came from outside.

"Go away," she breathed, gripping his shirt with hands that shook. "Go. Away."

Finn suddenly felt calmer, less afraid. He looked down into her face in the near dark and wanted nothing more than to keep her safe. He pulled her against him to steady her.

Erilyn fell against him, gripping his shirt, still barely whispering, "Please, go away."

Finn held her close, his own breath moving her hair as he watched the crack in the tree trunk, now covered by a branch thick with evergreen needles. In his mind, he prayed for the animal to leave, too.

And then, out of the near darkness, came Luna's growling cry and the animal outside took off into the woods. Finn worried about Luna, but Erilyn relaxed against him.

After long moments, Erilyn pulled away. Light trickled in through cracks in the tree, so he could make out her shape, but the sun had lowered so that it was quite dark.

"We should probably stay here for the rest of the night. In case it circles back." Erilyn's voice, always soft, sounded shy.

The space wasn't large, but it was large enough for them to both sit across from each other with their knees folded. It was cramped and Finn wished they were shoulder to shoulder instead.

"What was that?" he asked in a whisper, wishing he could see her face.

"Wylden," she said, a little louder. "I think." Her voice was tight, and he couldn't help but remember the fear on her face before they'd crashed into this trunk or the way her hands had shaken as she gripped his shirt; the way her heart had beat a staccato cadence against his chest.

Finn tensed, a burst of adrenaline causing his heart to hammer wildly for a moment before it tapered off. It was gone—a delayed reaction to a delayed event. He looked at her now, eyes wide, body coiled tightly like a spring.

"You've—" he scooted a little, trying not to put so much pressure on her knees with this. "You've been chased before?"

She took a shaky breath and nodded. "Once." The pain in her voice called to him. He scooted awkwardly until he was beside her, his legs releasing from their growing cramp. She was still and quiet.

"What happened?" He wasn't asking to know so much as to help her get whatever it was out. He knew that feeling, of having something festering in your soul.

She stiffened next to him, but rather than pull back he shifted so that he could put his arm around her shoulders. He could tell she wanted to pull away with her rigid posture, but she didn't. He rubbed small circles into her shoulder with his thumb and after a moment, she softened.

"Erilyn, what happened?"

She hugged her knees closer and his arm around her shoulders tightened the smallest bit. With a sigh that sounded almost like a whimper, she told him.

Chapter Eleven
Hollow

Erilyn

He wanted me to tell him what had happened the night Rosemarie died. I'd never talked about it—never had anyone to talk about it with. A battle waged inside—my need for release quickly overpowering my need for privacy.

"They killed Rosemarie." I caught a sob in my throat and pressed my forehead into my knees, holding my legs so tight they hurt. Saying it out loud made it immediately real in a way it hadn't been a few moments before. Hot tears spilled down my face and soaked into the fabric across my knees. "Rosemarie. The woman who—" I sniffled. "Who cared for me. They killed her and burned our house."

I hugged my knees tighter and his arm over my shoulder tightened comfortingly. Something inside me broke and I leaned into his warmth as words poured from my mouth like water.

"I was only fourteen. She told me to run." My tears were too thick to see through. The world was made up of watery shadow. "I ran and they chased me. All I had was Luna." I looked up, suddenly, remembering that she wasn't there. I sent my second sight out until I found her, two trees over, falling asleep as she stood guard and I relaxed. "She was so small," I said, looking up as if I could see her watching over us. The top of the hollowed trunk showed a smattering of stars through half empty tree limbs from neighboring trees. Now they were nothing but bright blurry spots. "I could hold her in my hands." I cupped my hands and remembered her being there, so tiny and weak.

I looked over at Finn, but had to look away. His eyes were full of sadness.

"It was raining and I kept falling in the mud. They were behind me. With dogs." I shivered as I remembered how cold and afraid I'd been. He let out a sound, a soft sigh, and pulled even closer so that I was leaning against his chest. His lips pressed against my hair. "They would have found me if I hadn't found my clearing. I slipped in the mud and saw big aerial roots and crawled beneath them. The rain hid my tracks and my scent. The clearing saved me."

I had lain in the cold mud as I waited for them to leave, Luna dirty and shivering against my chest where I held her.

"What happened after they left?" His voice was quiet, but I felt his words brush my skin where his cheek now rested against the top of my head. My heart broke as I made myself remember.

"I went back." My voice cracked. "There was smoke. Fire. She had animals and they'd all run." The tears were hot and fresh and it was getting hard to breath. "Rosemarie. She—" I hiccupped a sob and no more words would come.

Finn turned and wrapped both arms around me. He pulled me so that I was leaning against his chest, so that he was holding me completely. It reminded me of how Rosemarie had held me in the night after my nightmares and the last bit of restraint I had vanished.

I gripped his shirt in iron fingers and cried, my tears hot and angry. I'd never found her body. Never been able to bury her. The fire would have spread far if it hadn't been for the rain, but the rubble was too dense for me to search for her. I cried until my energy was spent, and then I cried some more.

After a time, I could hear him whispering. His lips were pressed to my hair and each whisper sent warm air across my skin.

"I'm sorry, Eri. I'm so sorry." He kissed my head. "I just—" He kissed me again. "I'm so sorry."

I loosened my grip on his shirt, but didn't move away. I knew I should move away, but I didn't want to. It felt good to be this close to someone again. To not feel so alone.

When I finally managed to stop my tears, his whispers stopped. I waited for him to pull away—the thought of Morrigan ever present at the edge of my awareness—but he didn't. He was touching me, my skin, our auras mixing, but I didn't *see* anything. I just *felt*—felt his desire for me to be OK, felt his heart breaking for me. He also was feeling desire, a desire he was ashamed of, and even in my pain, I flushed.

I'd felt desire for me before—from the Wylden men who'd chased me, from a few of the older, nastier men in

Citadel—but this was different. It was a soft desire that pulled at me even as it calmed me. It wasn't full of dangerous fire and anger. I settled myself against his chest, content to bask in this moment of caring as the ache I'd carried in my chest since Rosemarie died started to ease just a little.

Finn resettled his arms around me, less intensely, and sighed into my hair. "All it took for you to open up a little was mortal peril and being stuck in a tree stump with me."

I smiled. I'd been closed off with him because it was the only way I knew to be. Being like this, being close to someone, felt nice. He sighed again and his contentment washed over me.

I leaned back slightly to thank him, to tell him how much he'd helped me, but before I could he leaned forward and pressed his lips against mine.

As I froze, he pulled back, his eyes wide, his contentment turned to panic.

"Oh. I didn't mean. Eri. I—" he trailed off. I could feel him scrambling to get his desire in check, though it was surging like a wave. I could feel his heart racing beneath my hand. His lips against mine, as chaste as they had been, had ignited something deep in my belly.

I put my hands on his chest, all thoughts of Morrigan forgotten by both of us, and leaned forward. As soon as I moved, he did, his lips pressing warmly against mine with a gentle release of breath. I'd never kissed a boy before and had a fleeting worry that I wouldn't know what to do, but his lips moved against mine and my worry vanished.

He pulled me closer and I melted against him. My fingers moved up to the warm skin of his neck and then back down to his chest. He held me tighter. Tiny lightning bolts raced through my body when his tongue barely dipped into my mouth.

I never thought I'd be in this position, be with anyone, but it felt good. Felt right. We moved together, trying to find a more comfortable position, but he never let me go and his mouth against mine never stopped.

Every inch of my skin tingled with pent up need. His kiss was soft and slow, but it stoked a fire in my belly. I moaned against his mouth. His hands rubbed my back and my sides. One hand went into my hair and ran down its length. Everywhere his fingers touched, my skin came alive.

My heart was racing as I realized what might happen, but I didn't stop it. Even if he left to go back to Sunnybrook tomorrow, I wanted this—a shining, warm memory of togetherness, to help with the loneliness in the days to come. I pressed my body against his, wanting to be closer. This time he moaned and gripped me harder.

Luna, perched on one of the branches still intact in the dead tree, jumped in through the split and landed next to our feet, startling us apart.

We clung to each other, both breathing heavily as if we'd just run. My mouth felt pleasantly swollen and my cheeks were burning. Luna glowed with contentment and curled up as well as she could on our feet. Side by side, we would almost be able to straighten our legs if we weren't tangled around each other.

Finn adjusted his grip on me, but didn't let go like I half expected he would. It was hard to read him like this when my own emotions were so volatile. Settling me against him, he placed another kiss in my hair. He grew silent as our hearts slowed and skin cooled. As I calmed down I could separate our feelings again. His desire had pooled beneath the surface, tinged by the same guilt that he'd felt when our feet had touched as we slept.

"Finn?" I whispered and he sighed. His grip on me never loosened as he held me to him gently and it made me feel brave. He kissed my hair again, his lips lingering there for a moment longer than was necessary.

"Yeah?" His guilt was still there, but it was being lost in a deeper feeling of contentment. I settled against him and let my hand rest just above his heart.

"Goodnight." My cheek was against his chest and his hand gently stroked my hair. Absently I was glad I'd gotten the dirt and tangles out.

"Goodnight, Eri." He tucked me against him and kissed the crown of my head. In just a few minutes, he was asleep. For a moment, I allowed myself to sit in the dark with him and listen to his feelings. With his consciousness went his guilt and as he slept, all he felt was happy. It was like being wrapped in a sun-warmed blanket, and I let that feeling lull me into sleep as well, Luna a heavy warmth across our legs.

I woke with the sun. Finn was still holding me, his arms having fallen to my waist during the night. I let myself bask in this moment before he woke and everything changed, as I knew it would. He must have felt me stir, because his hands clumsily snaked around my waist and held me as he sighed in his sleep. My cheek was still against his chest, my arm draped over his slim waist, and part of me never wanted this day to get started, because I knew things would never be like this again.

No matter what had happened between us, I knew his heart belonged to Morrigan. I knew he belonged in a town, not out in the wild like me. But I smiled anyway, because his calm acceptance of my fear the night before, his desire to comfort me and his desire for me, had pulled something from me that I hadn't even realized was there—a lonely, hurt girl who needed to *feel*. Even if he left today and I never saw him again, I would have that. I would have these memories.

I sighed as I felt his breathing change as he really woke. He stiffened for a moment when he felt me against him, but he relaxed in a breath and gentled his hands around me. Slowly, my hand on his chest, I pushed myself up, needing to see his face.

His eyes were heavy with sleep as he smiled at me. Taking an arm from my waist, he pushed a heavy strand of hair behind my ear. With the feel of his fingers on my cheek, I felt a flash—guilt, barely on the edge of his emotional range, almost overwhelmed by contentment.

As he looked at my lips, still swollen, I remembered the feel of his mouth on mine. I blushed and ducked my head. He pulled me back to his chest, gently rearranging his body to ease his cramped muscles. He rubbed my back with his thumb, each movement causing a wave of tingles.

Luna, who was now curled protectively in front of the cracked tree trunk, stretched with a chirp and headed out. We should follow, but I couldn't make myself leave this spot. Not yet. I'd resigned myself to being alone and I wanted soak in every second of this before I had to let it go.

"Morning," he said, his voice gruff with sleep. He pressed his lips against my temple again and I felt his stubble against my skin.

"Good morning." My voice was quiet, timid, and I wished I had more to say.

"Are you OK?" The gentle motion of his thumb against my back didn't stop, but I felt his sudden worry and doubt. Last night had been born of his need to comfort me, just as my foot pressed against his as we slept had comforted him.

"I'm fine." With a deep breath and a pain deep in my chest, I pushed away from him. His arms fell away and I shivered with more than just the loss of their warmth. "We should get going."

My hair fell to cover my face and I let my awareness go out for just a moment to make sure nothing was there before I pushed the evergreen branch aside and stepped out into the cold morning. I knew if I looked back I'd see his hurt expression and I couldn't handle that.

I heard him get up to follow, but I wanted to put some distance between us. Although I held the memory of feeling desired fiercely, pain was rapidly closing in. I wouldn't call it heartbreak, but it was edging that way. He'd kissed me because he, too, was lonely. Because he knew I was hurting. I'd thought I'd accepted that, that I'd made my choice knowing this would happen, but now that it was, I found I wasn't prepared for how badly it hurt. I knew the depth to which Finn could love—I'd felt that depth when he thought about Morrigan. And while we didn't know each other to love one another, I knew that what we'd shard was a shadow of it, and I felt the loss of that love as if it had been my own.

"Eri?" Finn's voice behind me was soft. I'd been staring into the trees. My fists were clenched at my sides and I forced my hands to loosen. "I'm sorry."

"Why?" I was proud my voice was level even as a tear fought its way down my cheek in the cold morning air.

"For kissing you. I shouldn't have made you kiss me." His voice broke and confusion swam through me like fog. I took a deep breath as a new, desperate hope blossomed in my chest.

"What?" I thought he'd kissed me for me, for comfort.

"I shouldn't have made you kiss me." His voice was gruff, broken, and I turned slowly. His shoulders were hunched. "I thought—" he shrugged then his expression crumpled as he saw my tears. "I held you because you were so sad." He took a deep breath. "And then I started to feel—I just needed to kiss you. I'm sorry. I just—" His head fell forward and he scrubbed his face with his hands.

He'd wanted to kiss me because he'd wanted to. Not because he thought it would make me feel better. I knew this wouldn't last, but it didn't have to end now. Closing the distance between us, I gently pulled his hands away from his face. His emotions washed over me—desire tempered with shame, as he believed he'd forced me to do something against my will.

I stepped against him, circling his waist with my arms. He sighed and wrapped himself around me.

"You didn't make me do anything," I whispered, loud enough for him to hear and he held me tighter. "I wanted to. I needed to."

He held me tightly then pulled away to look down into my face, hope as bright there as if it were the sun itself. Hugging me to him again, he leaned forward and kissed my forehead. Luna chirped as she returned from her hunt and I gently pulled away.

"We should see if our supplies are still OK," I said, and he nodded. He let me go, but I could still feel him, his energy beside me, as if he were still holding me. His hand found mine and squeezed, and with a small smile, I led him back through the woods toward the field.

Chapter Twelve
Dawn

Finn

Finn trailed behind Erilyn, watching Luna attack stray leaves blown by the wind. His mind kept wandering back to that hollowed out tree, to the way it had felt to hold Erilyn, to kiss her. Even with the guilt he carried, kissing her had felt right. Morrigan had moved on quickly, maybe he should, too.

They reached the trampled grass and Erilyn found her burned bowl right where she'd left it. The apples were gone, but the other supplies were still there, and she smiled, relieved.

Her smile caught at him—that she would be relieved to have such broken things made him angry for her, but he held his tongue.

"Animals got the food," she said, her smile falling.

"We can find more." He said it with conviction, though he didn't know how or where to even look. She looked at him from the corner of her eye, unsure.

"Maybe," she said. "We'll figure out how to make due."

He heard her say "we" and grinned.

She looked at the clouds starting to roll across the sky. The sun was bright in the early morning, but it was cold and Finn shivered as wind cut through his thin sweater.

"We should get back. If we move fast, we can get back before noon." Her face was unreadable again as she surveyed the area. "Luna." Luna chirped and took off. With a small smile for Finn, Erilyn headed after her, careful this time not to move so fast that Finn had to struggle to keep up.

They made better time than they had the day before. Finn saw the trees and sped up, ready to straighten his back and rest in the shade the woods offered, but before he could, Erilyn stopped him with a hand on his arm. Luna had stopped too, her ears perked. Finn listened and looked all around, but didn't see or hear anything unusual.

Erilyn crouched lower, pulling Finn with her. She whispered against his ear, "Big cats in the woods." His heart rate spiked and his eyes shot forward to the tall grass just in front of them. She squeezed his arm gently. "We just have to wait."

He watched her close her eyes, face toward the woods. Her hair blew in her face but she didn't move to brush it away. She was perfectly still.

Finn was just about to reach over and push it behind her ear when her eyes shot to him, open in panic. "Go!" she hissed, grabbing his arm and pulling him up, her bowl of found goods spilling from her hands. "Go!" she said again, pushing him toward the trees.

He stumbled from the grass, Erilyn right behind him.

"The trees!" Luna, behind them, was growling. "Go and don't look back," she said. He ran, heart racing, putting tree after tree between him and danger. He glanced back when he didn't hear her, and stumbled to a stop. She wasn't with him. Fear rose in him—for her and at the thought of going back.

And then Luna screamed in pain and he was running back before he even realized what he was doing.

Finn burst back through the tree line. Luna was standing by Erilyn, a huge gash on her front leg. Her fur was fluffed out, making her seem bigger. Erilyn was turning in a circle, keeping herself always between Luna and the two giant cats circling her. He'd never seen animals so big—not in person. They were gold like the field grass and seemed too big. They looked like the mountain lions they'd learned about in their survival classes, except so much larger. They didn't seem to have noticed him yet, but Erilyn had. Her eyes widened and she shook her head.

He didn't know what to do. He didn't have anything to fight them with, but Erilyn had a knife. And there was another—the one with the broken tip—dropped somewhere in the grass when they ran. He thought could see where they'd pushed through in their hasty exit, but Erilyn and the cats were between him and there.

He didn't have time to worry. The cats lunged toward Erilyn and Luna as if moving with a single thought as they lunged toward them. But just as quickly, they fell back as if they'd struck a wall. The beasts stood and shook their heads. With a growl, they tried again, and again they were knocked backward. In front of them, Erilyn was holding up her hands, as if she could hold them back with sheer force of will.

One of the cats fell back hard the next time it pounced. It stood, shook its head, and its eyes found Finn. It growled and crouched. Finn looked to Erilyn. "No," she mouthed, her head shaking frantically.

He didn't see what happened as the cat lunged, only that one moment it was ready to rip out his throat, and the next it was howling, lying on its back a few feet away. Finn had covered his head as if that would help. He met Erilyn's panicked gaze again. The cats were both shaking their heads as if they were disoriented.

Erilyn turned toward the cat nearest Finn and screamed, fingers outstretched. It had been ready to attack again, but went flying backward instead as if it had been thrown. Erilyn looked at him, tears on her cheeks, and collapsed. Finn ran to her, the disoriented animals momentarily forgotten, and gathered her in his arms. Luna stood alert, her leg no longer bleeding.

"Erilyn?" Finn asked, looking into her pale face. "Erilyn!" She looked up at him, her face contorted in pain. "You're ok." She looked past his shoulder and her face crumpled in sadness.

"Go away!" she yelled, her voice hoarse. The cats, who'd been sneaking toward them, cried out as if in pain. This time they ran, tails tucked.

Finn looked down at her. She was leaning against his body, eyes closed, shaking.

"I'm sorry," she whispered. He pulled her more firmly against him. "I don't mean to be like this." Her voice was barely a whisper.

"Come on," he said. "We need to get you home." He stood and helped her stand with him. She swayed, but he held her up, head on his shoulder, his arm around her waist.

"I don't know the way." He hadn't been talking to either of them, but Luna, who'd been cleaning the cut on her leg, looked up at him. She chirped and took off into the woods a little slower than usual. He followed while holding Erilyn up.

They stopped at the stream and Finn found plantain leaves for them to eat. Erilyn wouldn't meet his eyes, but she perked up a little.

They made it back to the clearing and Erilyn pulled away from his supporting arm. Without a word, she built up a fire from small sticks and a flint stone. He stood off to the side, confused. He couldn't figure out what he'd seen. She'd gotten those big cats to leave somehow, but he couldn't figure out how.

Erilyn built the fire and put water on to boil with a handful of pine needles for tea. She sat by the small fire and hugged her knees while she waited. Luna looked at her and cried mournfully before limping back out into the trees.

Finn sat beside her and she stiffened. Just like in the hollowed trunk the night before, he pulled her to him. She tried to pull away, but he didn't let her.

"Talk to me," he said quietly, leaning his cheek against her head, and she crumpled a little.

"You don't know me." Her voice was sharp, angry, even as she leaned into him.

"I know you risked your life for me." He kissed her hair and she sighed. "More than once. I know you've been sharing your food with me even though you don't have enough for winter." He kissed her hair again and felt her fingers gently grip his shirt. "I know you're brave. Selfless."

"You don't know what I am." Her voice was a hoarse whisper and her grip tightened. He held her closer.

"I know you're the kindest person I've ever known."

She buried her face in his shirt as the tea started to boil. He used one arm to lift the wood-wrapped wired handle from the flames.

He looked back to her and saw tears in her large, gray eyes. He decided he didn't need to know how or why she'd been able to scare the cats away. He trusted her. He leaned down and kissed her and felt fresh, hot tears where their skin met.

He pulled back and pressed his forehead against hers. "I know who you are. I feel like I know you better than I've ever known anyone." His eyes were closed, but he felt her nod.

They sat that way for a long moment, the fire warming them even though the sun was still high in the sky. He opened his eyes when she pulled away, but she was only pouring tea for them into a small clay mug, which she handed to him, and an ugly metal cup for herself.

Her hands gripped the metal cup and he could just see a painting of what he thought might be children on one side, between her fingers.

"Thank you," she said before taking a sip. "Just—" she closed her eyes for one moment before meeting his eyes. "Just, thank you."

He took a sip from his smaller, clay mug and his eyes closed in bliss as the warm liquid eased the gnawing ache of hunger he'd been successfully ignoring.

"My mother used to make tea like this," he said, taking another sip. "Yours is *almost* as good." He looked at her out of the corner of his eye and saw her small smile.

"Rosemarie taught me." She smiled again as she stared into the fire. "I could never make mine taste like hers, either." She looked over at him, tears caught in the corners of her eyes.

"Rosemarie," he said hesitantly, "she wasn't your mother. Who was she?" He knew asking her was tricky, that she might get sad, but he wanted to know more about her past, though he'd told her little of his own.

She stared at him for a long moment, as if figuring out a puzzle, before nodding.

"She's the woman who found me." Her chin was high and her fingers around her cup had gone white.

"Found you?" He tried to keep his voice soft. "Were you lost?" He sipped his tea and leaned his knee against her, which seemed to take some of her edge off. She sat her cup down and held her hands up toward the fire.

"Yes and no." She sighed and rested her head on her knees, the flames turning her gray eyes almost orange. "I ran away."

"From where?" He knew he was pushing, but he suddenly felt that he needed to know where she came from.

She sighed and closed her eyes. When she answered, she was whispering again. "The cave city. Underground."

For a moment, Finn was shocked, but that quickly dissipated as things started to fall into place. Her isolation. Her small size. Even the strange things she could do. He'd never met a nightcrawler—what the people of Sunnybrook called the near mythic people who lived in the caves. He didn't know anyone who'd met one, but he'd imagined something very different than Erilyn. He'd been told they were pure white with red eyes and only came upworld at night to steal food and sometimes children. He shook his head.

"Oh." He didn't know what else to say and she stayed still. "I've never met a Ni—" he snapped his mouth shut. *Nightcrawler* was what children called cave people, like the slimy earthworms that only earthed at night. "A cave dweller before."

Erilyn sighed and looked at him, resting her cheek on her knees. "You wouldn't have. We don't come upworld."

"But you did," he said, setting his own mug down and nudging her knee with his playfully. He smiled and draped his arm over her shoulder. "So you ran away from the caves, huh? Why?"

Erilyn was quiet for a long while. "I got in a fight with some kids, a girl named Aiyanna." She shivered beneath his arm. "It got serious, so I ran. Found my way upworld and then Rosemarie found me."

Something in her tone told him she was finished talking about it, and he kissed her hair. Immediately after, his stomach growled and he laughed in embarrassment.

"Let's get something to eat," she said as she pulled away.

He worried she would pull away—today had been a whirlwind of ups and downs and he wasn't sure what to expect, but she held out her hand to pull him up, and he took it.

Erilyn crawled beneath the maple tree with giant aerial roots—the tree that had saved her life—and returned with dried food. Luna rejoined them as they sat with their cool tea and stretched beside the fire.

As they ate, Finn felt a contentment like he'd never known seep into him. He looked toward the pine, the branches tied open, and then toward Erilyn who lazily petted Luna's long belly as she ate. She met his gaze and smiled. With a sigh, Finn finished his meal, feeling for the first time in a long time like he was home.

Chapter Thirteen
Evanescent

Erilyn

I put the fire out well after dark. Finn had gone inside earlier, but I'd waited. Scared. This was uncharted territory.

Inside, he had my small lantern lit and burning low. Luna lay on her back while Finn rubbed her belly. He smiled at me as I walked in, pulling the branches closed and tying them behind me. With a gentle shove, he moved Luna and shifted the blankets over him. He'd doubled them for us to share, his bloodstain near the bottom. I'd have to try to scrub it out tomorrow. My heart racing like a rabbit, I crawled beneath the blankets with him.

Lying down next to him, once I'd done it, was as easy as breathing. We curled around one another—my cheek on his shoulder, his arm around me—and Luna curled just behind my back. With his free hand, Finn turned the lantern knob until the flame went out, then he resettled himself around me. Never in my life, even in my year with Rosemarie, had I felt like I belonged as completely as I did now.

After that first night back, we settled into a routine. We worked together as fluidly as Luna and me. I got used to being touched while he spoke, found myself touching him without fear—I didn't get anymore Morrigan flashes. I got used to *feeling* his feelings without prying. He learned how to help around the clearing without me having to show him. He dug for roots and greens and my life became so much easier.

Once he asked why I never hunted, never fished. I wanted to be able to tell him that when the animal died, I *felt* it. When those cats that attacked us hit the ground, hit their heads, I felt their pain and that alone was so disorienting I could barely see straight. But I didn't tell him. He'd accepted what he'd seen of me—something that was more than I ever dreamed possible—and I didn't want to push it and ruin whatever it was we had. So instead, I just said I wouldn't eat an animal, and he accepted that. We both settled in to our new routine and for the first time, I knew what it was like to not try to hide.

Two weeks went by, but in that time, I felt like we had known each other for years.

I woke on a particularly chilly morning with my head on Finn's arm and his other arm around my waist. I smiled into the dawn light and turned so that I was facing him. He sighed and pulled me close then turned his lower body away slightly. He buried his face in my hair and my cheeks burned. There were some bridges we had yet to cross.

"What's the plan for today?" His voice was gruff and I was content to lie next to him for a few more minutes before we went out into the cold. We'd gone every day to search for food and supplies and we'd come up short.

"We have to go and just—" I yawned, "look for whatever we've missed." I rolled away from him, his arm loosening with hesitation, and pushed myself up. I always felt a dull ache in my chest when we weren't touching, but I was trying not to worry about it. "I'm sorry." It was my job to feed us. With the food stores we had, we would barely survive the winter. If it was just me, I could make it work, but for both of us, I wasn't sure.

Finn sat and pulled me to him. He smelled like the earth. "We'll figure it out."

He didn't know what he was saying. He was used to the comforts of a town, a society. He didn't have to stay here for the winter, he had a home to go to, and this shortage of food was nagging at me. I hated it, but knew he had to go back to his town so that we would both survive the snow.

I hugged him to me, suddenly terrified. Just over two weeks and already I was afraid to be alone again. Except that wasn't entirely true. I wasn't afraid to be alone, I was afraid to be without Finn.

As bitterly cold wind pushed in under the pine branches, smelling almost like snow, I knew I'd have to start accepting what needed to happen. I held him tightly for a moment, his arms around me warm and safe, and then I let him go. A few minutes ago I'd woken feeling safe and content and now I'd planned how, immediately, all of that would end. My heart broke.

To save his life, and mine, it had to happen. Today, we would travel out, away from the clearing, toward Sunnybrook—I had a general idea of where it might be— and I would tell him he had to leave. I would remind him of Morrigan—just the thought of her made bile rise up in my throat—and make him understand that we wouldn't make it out here together.

Outside, I loaded my shoulder bag with food—we had so little—and slipped my knife into the loop on my pants. "I think we should head back toward the field," I said, loading a few bites of dried apples in last. He stiffened. The field held nothing but painful memories for him, and I knew today would add another. "Then we can work our way back." I wanted to keep my expression neutral, but when I tried to smile I fell short and he looked at me curiously. His beard had grown in and the dark hair made his eyes look even bluer. I hitched the bag higher on my shoulder. "Ready?"

He nodded, still wearing that curious expression, and followed me. His hand slipped into mine and his emotions slipped into me just as easily. He was curious, and uneasy, but also happy. It just made what I knew had to happen all the more difficult.

We walked slowly. His hand in mine was a warm pressure that was both reassuring and painful, because I knew when we let go, it would be forever.

We reached the stream near my clearing and he pulled me to a stop. I let go of his hand, my fingers and chest aching with the loss, and stooped to drink some water next to Luna. I looked up at him when he didn't join me. He was looking at me strangely, and I felt more confusion from him now. I stood and took his hands but he pulled his away, which he never did.

"Finn?" I looked up into his eyes and was surprised to find tears there. "What's wrong?"

"I don't know," he said, shaking his head. "It's like—" he scrunched up his face and raked his hands through his hair. "It's like I'm feeling things that aren't mine." He shook his head. "Are *you* ok?"

We'd never talked about what I did with the cats, but he'd stopped acting surprised when I took us inside minutes before rain or when we hid moments before wolves came near. I just stared at him, shocked.

He took my hands and a tear slipped from his eye. "I think I'm feeling what you're feeling." I tried to pull away and he didn't let me. "I need to know why you're hurting. Why—" he struggled for the words. "Why your heart feels broken." His words cracked and he squeezed my hands.

I was broadcasting. Somehow, I was sharing my feelings with him as easily as I could read his. I tried to pull my hands away, but he just held on. He wasn't scared or angry about what was happening, he was just worried. I fell against him and he wrapped me in his arms.

"Tell me," he said into my hair. "Please."

"You can't stay with me anymore." My words were a bare whisper, but he jerked away as if I'd hit him.

"Why?" He kept his hands on my arms, but held me there, an arm's length away.

"Because—" I'd planned to hurt him to get him to leave, anything to insure that he went and that we'd both have a chance to survive. But his grip on my arms was gentle and while the tears were gone from his eyes, they were still filled hurt. "Because if you don't, we won't survive the winter. We don't have enough food."

He dropped his head, his fingers on my arms tightening. "There has to be a way." He stepped closer, his eyes bright. "I can't—" He took a deep breath. "I need to be with you."

"We've looked everywhere it's safe to look." I stepped away from him. "We have enough for one," which was a stretch, "but I can't keep us both alive." I looked up at him, the sunlight coming through the trees hitting him just right. "And you have a place, a *safe* place, to go." All I wanted was to go to him, to figure out a way, but I had to do what was best. I had to be strong. It was the lesson Rosemarie had taught me when she made me run away from her. I had to be strong for Luna then, to keep her safe, and I would be strong for Finn now.

"I won't go without you." His hands were in fists at his sides. He was stubborn and petulant and I grew angry.

"You don't understand!" I said, anger coloring my cheeks. "We will *die*. Winter is hard out here. The cold is hard, and without food—" I looked away from him, my anger quickly dwindling. "Without food, it's easiest just to lay down and go to sleep." I spun back to him, tears in my eyes now. "I will not let that happen to you."

"But you—"

"I can take care of myself," I snapped. Beside me, Luna chirped, but I ignored her.

"I know," he said gently, his hands finding my arms again, weakening my resolve. "I know you can, Eri. I was going to say, you don't have to do this alone."

I opened my mouth to argue and he stopped me with a soft kiss.

"You can come back with me." His voice was a whisper against my mouth and I jerked back.

"Finn—" The thought of living around so many people, so many emotions and thoughts, made me grit my teeth. It had been difficult as a child, but now that my abilities had gotten stronger, it would be unbearable.

"I can't," I said, my voice breaking. "I just—" I wanted to tell him everything, but I couldn't. "I just *can't.*"

He looked at me for a long time before a look of determination took over his face. "OK." He said and I felt something in me shatter, too distressed to notice what he was feeling. He was going to go. I was going to lose him. It was what needed to happen, but that didn't make it easy. "OK." He said again. He looked up at me, his eyes wild and bright again. "We'll go to Sunnybrook and I'll sneak in to get food."

I opened my mouth to protest again, and he met my silent cry with another kiss. He pulled me to him, one hand on my back, the other in my hair, and I felt his desire to stay with me in every fiber of my being. When he pulled back he held my face in his hands.

"I have a friend there. Lucy. She works in the commissary. She'll give us what we need. I know it." His eyes were full of hope and I let myself feel his hope, his assurance.

"But you have a home—" my voice broke as he kissed me again.

"You," he said, placing his hand on my collarbone even as he held me close with the other. "*You* are my home." He pulled me to him and I rested my cheek on his chest, wondering how in a few short weeks my life had changed so much, how I'd become this whole other person. "Please say we'll at least try." I felt his voice vibrate through his chest and I nodded.

His relief blended with mine, and even in the cold autumn air, I felt warm.

As the cloud of our emotions started to drift away, something poked at my awareness. Beside me, Luna was completely still, a growl deep in her throat. She'd been chirping earlier and I thought it was because of our agitation, but now I knew it was something else.

I followed her gaze. Above the stream was blue sky, and coming from the direction of my clearing was dense, black smoke.

Without a thought I took off through the woods. Finn yelled my name, but it was lost on the wind as I tore through the trees. As I ran, I let my second sight speed along before me. It burst into my clearing long before I would and I saw, in a haze of smoke, people. It was hard to see who—Wylden, maybe. They were wearing black, I thought, but that could be the smoke. I felt disoriented in the smoke, and it was hard to see.

Suddenly I wasn't running anymore. Two strong arms were holding me and I fought against them. I turned, ready to throw whoever it was off of me, but Finn's startled eyes—bright with adrenaline—stopped me as my vision returned.

"Someone's in my clearing," I said, breathless.

"I know," he said, pulling me back, away from the clearing, though we weren't close enough to be heard or seen yet.

"We have to go," I pulled against him, but he held me tighter. "We have to go!"

"If it's Wylden, we wouldn't stand a chance." His eyes were hard.

"We have to *try*," I said, needing to run, to save what I could.

"Erilyn!" his voice was a harsh sound and I looked at him in shock. He'd never talked to me like that. "You are more important than your clearing. Your life is more important." He let go of me and grabbed my face, his hands cold. "Please. If they're still there, they'll kill us. We need to wait."

I nodded into his hands, seeing the logic of what he said even as my heart thundered in my chest and begged to take off. The only thing keeping me here were his strong hands on my face and Luna's mewling cry from behind him.

He leaned down and kissed me. My hands shook where they rested on his chest as my own heart thundered. He looked down into my eyes and I saw that he, too, was afraid.

We'd only taken a few steps when the noise of something exploding filled the air. I'd heard it once before—the night they'd taken Rosemarie's house and burned it to the ground.

Pure, primal need coursed through my body. I pushed Finn away and took off, running again. I had to stop them, to try. Not even Finn would stop me this time.

Chapter Fourteen
Cremation

Finn

Erilyn was fast. She ran as if possessed, tearing through the woods, and Finn couldn't catch her. Even Luna was having trouble catching up as Erilyn ran like a woman possessed.

He tried. He ran as hard as he could, but she only moved faster. They would be in the clearing any second, and then it would be too late. If there were Wylden there, they would have them. Finn couldn't let them have Erilyn. He'd heard the stories of what they did to women. Men they killed, women they kept a while for their bodies.

It was the boost he needed. He lunged at her, his hands gripping the fabric around her waist, and she went down hard. He scrambled to cover his body with hers, cover her mouth. Her eyes were wild when she looked up at him and she was fighting. Her eyes lost focus and he knew she might do to him what she'd done to the cats, but he didn't care. He couldn't let her get hurt.

Her vision suddenly cleared and tears spilled down her face. He took his hand off her mouth and just lay there on top of her, holding her as she cried silently into his chest, her body shaking. Luna, next to them, chirped in warning, and this time they listened.

Finn stood and pulled Erilyn with him. She had leaves in her hair and her skin was flushed from running, like some wild nature spirit.

Luna darted up a tree and Erilyn followed, Finn just behind them. It was a large tree and would hold them all, but the leaves were nearly gone.

Erilyn disappeared into a large V-shaped crook and she pulled Finn in after her. They both fit, almost completely hidden, and Finn released the breath he'd been holding as he imagined the Wylden knocking them down from tree branches with rocks, like squirrels.

They ducked low and tried to keep their breaths slow as they heard the first sounds of approaching men.

Luna was above them, stretched on a wide branch, barely visible unless you knew just where to look.

Beside him, Erilyn was shaking from head to toe. Her fear of the Wylden was back, the anger that had fueled her run was spent.

He took her cold hands and shame colored her face crimson. He wanted to tell her that he was scared too, but that they would be OK, but he just squeezed her hands and rubbed her knuckles with his thumbs. Their hands were dirty from their tussle on the ground and he felt the dirt grit beneath his thumb.

Erilyn nodded at him, squeezing his hands in return, before her eyes went wide and she pressed herself against the tree trunk. If they were at the right angle, they'd be able to see the tops of their heads. Erilyn and Finn held completely still.

The sounds the Wylden made were more like animals on the hunt than people, but Finn could hear what almost sounded like words, garbled by grunts and heavy breathing.

Erilyn gripped his hands harder, her eyes squeezed closed. Her lips were moving, as they had in the hollowed trunk so many nights before. "Go away. Go away."

After a few moments, the sounds of the Wylden grew further and further away. When the sounds were gone, they still waited without moving for a while. Finn listened to the wind whistling through the empty branches and watched Luna above them. Luna stirred and he looked back to Erilyn. Her eyes were out of focus again, but she came back to him quickly, blinking until they were clear.

"They're gone." She said, her voice hoarse. "I need to see—" she trailed off and he nodded. They awkwardly climbed out of the scoop in the tree, Erilyn first. His feet hit the earth and Erilyn was still just standing, looking toward her clearing. Black smoke was filtering through the trees.

"Eri—" he put a hand on her shoulder.

"I have to see if there's anything I can save." Her voice was hard, but he could hear her brokenness. He squeezed her shoulder and followed her and Luna toward the smoke.

They reached the clearing in a few minutes and Erilyn stumbled. Her pine, her home, was half burned, small flames still burning. It was where the black smoke was coming from—the green wood burning. Whatever had caused that explosion had been hot enough to catch a living tree on fire without kindling. The pond was littered with ash and pieces of the pine that had flown when it caught fire so violently. The fire pit was destroyed.

Erilyn stood in the center of it all. He took her hand, to comfort her, but she just squeezed his hand and released it. She was staring at the burning tree and so was he.

The wind shifted and fear for their safety, for the whole forest, bloomed in his chest. He turned to Erilyn, but her eyes were closed. Her breaths were slow and steady.

He opened his mouth to say something, but the wind shifted, and he looked toward the burning pine, afraid the sudden wind shift would cause the fire to spread. Erilyn was breathing slowly and deeply, tears running down her dirty cheeks. The tree creaked and he jerked toward it, ready to pull her out of the way, but instead of falling, he watched as the flames still burning started to grow smaller and smaller. Erilyn's lips were moving, but he couldn't hear what she was saying. He watched her now instead of the flames. Her hands slowly extended toward the fire and he felt the fire's heat diminish as her skin grew pink as if she were too warm. He heard an almost inaudible pop and looked back. The tree was no longer burning. The smoke had turned white. Half of it still stood, tall and evergreen, the other side a blackened skeleton.

Erilyn passed him as she walked into the tree. He wanted to warn her to be careful, that it might be hot, but somehow he knew it wasn't.

Inside the half that was still intact, Erilyn gathered what she could. Their blankets hadn't burned, so she carefully rolled them and put them in the bag over her shoulder. They were thin and fit nicely. The tin cup with children had burned, but still looked usable. She held it for a moment as if trying to see through the char to the image beneath, then stuck it, too, in her bag. She had her knife and found the few remaining sachets of herbs she'd buried in her box.

Finn followed Erilyn quietly as she moved through her once peaceful home. Leaving the bag with him, she crawled beneath the maple tree's aerial roots. He heard her whimper and come out, empty handed.

"They must have found it," she said, taking the bag back. Her tears had ceased, but had left trails through the dirt on her cheeks.

Luna walled the clearing, mewing softly, sniffing the dirt here and there. Erilyn walked to the pond and used her hand to push the debris away from the surface of the water before scooping a handful to drink. Her reflection was distorted in the ripples.

"We should go," she said, her voice flat. She stood and shifted the bag's strap on her shoulder. He wanted to carry it for her, but it was all she had left. She took a deep breath and looked up at him. "I'll travel with you," she said, a catch in her throat, "but I don't think I can stay in your town." She met his gaze levelly, but he could see behind her mask. She tried to come across as someone without emotion, but he knew it was the opposite. She felt everything, and right now, she was afraid.

He took her hand, cold from the water, and nodded. "Let's just get there, and we can decide what we're going to do." He wouldn't leave her, of that he was absolutely certain. "Together." She nodded.

"We should—" her head spun around, toward the direction they'd come from and her grip turned into a vice. "Luna!" she whispered, and the cat mewled and was off into the woods in the other direction. "We have to run," she said.

But it was too late. A single Wylden walked into the clearing. He looked startled to see them, but recovered quickly and ran toward them. Finn knew Erilyn could do what she did to him, to the cats—throw him or scare him away—but her face was full of fear.

Finn, seeing Erilyn frozen, pulled the knife from the sheath in her pants and pointed it toward the Wylden as he fell on them. It pierced the Wylden's side as he fell away, grasping the bleeding wound. Finn hadn't let go of the knife and it slid from the wound as he scrambled to stand. He'd pushed Erilyn out of the way without realizing it and she now stood, horrified, a few feet away.

"We need to go." He pulled her hand and she looked at him as if not seeing him. "Erilyn," he said, dragging her away as the bleeding Wylden tried to stand. "We need to go *now*."

She nodded, taking the lead as they darted off into the woods, the Wylden howling behind them in anger and pain. The Wylden were never in her woods this time of year. Something had changed, something big. And where there was one, there were many.

They ran, hands stuck together, until Finn sagged with exhaustion. The sun was high in the sky and they hadn't seen any sign of being followed. Luna was up ahead, panting, favoring the leg she'd injured weeks earlier. She'd stopped at the stream—a section Erilyn never used—and was drinking heavily from the clear, cold water.

After drinking some water, Erilyn picked shriveled plantain leaves—tough and chewed already—for them to eat with the few dried apple slices she'd packed that morning. It wasn't enough.

"Luna, go eat." The cat chirped at Erilyn, a sad sound, then darted off into the woods. Finn watched her go, always surprised at her ability to blend in with shadows so quickly. "You should clean that," she said, gesturing to the knife, now covered in a dry, rusty blood. "And, thank you."

He hadn't killed the Wylden, at least he hadn't been dead when they left, but it didn't make Finn feel any less sick. He shuddered as he grabbed dried leaves and dipped them in water to scrub the blade, not wanting to pollute the stream by putting it in directly. He'd never stabbed anything, and he couldn't forget the way it had felt to force the blade through skin and muscle. He wanted to throw up.

Erilyn sat beside him and helped. The blood came off quickly, but Finn kept scrubbing. Erilyn, kneeling before him, gently took the knife away from him and dried it on her pants, then took his hands in hers. She used her cupped hands to pour clean water over his before drying them with the hem of her shirt.

Without a word, she pulled him to her and he buried his face in her chest with a deep, shaky breath.

"You saved us," she whispered, rubbing his hair. "I'm sorry you had to."

His arms went around her and he held her close. Just a few weeks ago, his biggest problem was that a girl had broken up with him. He'd had food, water, clothes, and a job. After that, his whole life had been turned upside down.

He pulled back when she took a shuddered breath. He wiped her new tears away with cold thumbs and pulled her face toward his for a slow kiss. "There's nowhere I'd rather be than right here, beside you." He'd lost everything he thought mattered and dealt with hardships he'd never imagined, but he knew he meant it. This was where he belonged—next to Erilyn.

Erilyn nodded and looked into his eyes for a long moment.

Before Erilyn, he'd loved Morrigan. He'd loved her fiercely, almost violently. What he felt for Erilyn was softer than that and ran deeper.

"Ready?" she asked. He wove his fingers into hers and together they stood.

"Ready."

Luna rejoined them and they continued on, going through woods he'd never traveled. Each step took him closer to his old life, to Morrigan, and while he knew nothing in the world could pull him from Erilyn, worry settled itself like a weight in his stomach.

Chapter Fifteen
Fringe

Erilyn

I wasn't exactly sure where Sunnybrook was, but there had been people patrolling through here. I could see their trails as easily as if they'd been painted. They were older, though—a few weeks—so I thought we might have a little way to go.

Finn's hand was in mine, but I felt numb. As we'd walked, he'd grown quiet; his thoughts—which weren't clear to me, but were growing more and more present—kept straying and making his aura cloudy with worry. I thought I knew what he was thinking about, but wasn't sure until Morrigan's face—angry and then joyful and then angry again—popped into my head.

When I saw her I gasped and dropped his hand. I hadn't seen her since before our night in the hollow tree.

"What's wrong?" he asked, going to grab me in case I was ill or hurt.

"Nothing," I said, then looked up at him and rubbed out a pretend cramp in my leg. "Muscle cramp."

He looked at me quizzically, but nodded. "Do you need to rest?"

"No. Let's keep going."

He took my hand again, and I shied away. I was afraid again of who or what I might see. The closer we got to Sunnybrook the further away he seemed, as if the closeness we'd developed over the last two weeks had been contained to the clearing, and now that it was gone, so was our bond.

We walked until the cold started to seep through our clothes and we both started to shiver. It wasn't safe out in the open to build a fire. I whistled to Luna, three short bursts, and she darted off to find a place for us to sleep.

I stopped, crouched, and waited.

"We're close, aren't we?" he asked. We circumvented the field, so the trip was taking longer than it would have if we'd taken a straighter route.

"A few hours away, maybe." I stood and resisted the urge to lean into him. I resisted the urge to slip my arms around his waist and share in his warmth. Instead, I turned to look for Luna.

"I'm glad we won't make it tonight," he said quietly and my heart skipped.

One more night. That's what we had. Some part of me knew it, knew that as soon as we reached Sunnybrook whatever it was we had would be gone.

The smart thing would be to start letting go now, to get myself used to being near him, but not with him. It would hurt less to start now. It was the smart thing to do.

"Eri?" his voice was quiet in the falling dark and I knew that I wouldn't be able to do the smart thing until I had to.

"Yes?" I said, still facing away, wanting to turn into him and hold him.

His arms went around me then, as if he'd heard my silent desire, and I turned into him, my cheek against his chest as his lips pressed into my hair.

"It's going to be OK," he said, and I thought it was more to convince himself than me.

"I know." Sometimes we told lies to protect the ones we loved, like when Rosemarie told me it would be OK before she told me to run.

Luna chirped from the darkness—she was a white specter in the coming moonlight and we moved to follow. I let go of him and he captured my hand. I wove my fingers through his, trying to memorize what it felt like—his longer fingers and broad palm.

Luna led us to a small cave set in one of the many hills we'd traversed on our way here. It went back about eight feet and was just as wide—just enough space for us to lie down. It was covered with overgrown brush. It was clear that no animals had been here for a long time.

I gathered handfuls of fallen, dried leaves from the maples and oaks all around. Finn followed suit. With them I made a crunchy, itchy place for us to lie down that would be warmer than earth and stone.

Finn lay with his back against the wall, and he held his arms out to me. With our blankets in hand, I went to him and covered us both. I relished the feel of the length of his body against mine, knowing that this would be the last time I felt it.

"It's all going to be OK," he said again, and I nodded against him. He didn't believe it anymore than I did. I didn't have to hear his thoughts to know that, I could hear it in his voice.

My heart was thudding dully and I felt tears start to prick the corners of my eyes. He pulled me closer and I gripped him tightly. I had only known him a few weeks. I was used to being alone.

"Erilyn." His voice was gruff and I could hear his need. I lifted my face, even though I couldn't see him in the pitch black of the cave, and met his lips. This kiss was unlike any before it. It was hungry. Desperate. He rolled so that he was over me and I pulled his face to mine and wrapped my arms around his neck. His weight on me made me breathless and I wrapped one leg over him, trying to pull him closer.

We were clunky and awkward, still wearing our shoes, the blankets tangled around us, seeing nothing but dark and having to feel our way to each other. His cold hand slipped beneath by sweater and rested on the hot skin of my back and I gasped into his mouth. I tangled my fingers in his hair as he rubbed my side, his hands quickly warming. I let my hands travel down to where his sweater met his pants and felt the skin of his strong back there warm like a fire.

I wanted this. I needed this.

Then suddenly his hands were hesitant. His thoughts were hesitant. Our kiss started to cool and whatever momentum we'd gained dwindled away until we were kissing softly, the fire gone.

He rolled so that he was beside me again and pulled my head onto his chest, rearranging the blankets so that we were both covered again. Next to me, Luna chirped as if to chastise me for keeping her awake.

I felt disoriented, my heart still racing and my body still screaming for him to touch me, to let me touch him, but his thoughts were a dark cloud and that quickly dampened my own desire.

I lay with my head on his chest and his arms around me, but in that moment I felt us start to separate.

Luna woke us with the sun, the light barely making its way through the shrubbery covering the cave. We gathered our things in silence and dusted bits of dried leaves from our clothes.

Finn followed me out, his hand finding mine. I slipped my fingers between his, but it wasn't the same as it had been. I couldn't feel him as clearly, like there was something between us.

We walked in silence, stopping one last time when we found a stream. It was just before noon, hours later, when we heard the first sounds of civilization.

I half expected Finn to speed up, to head straight into town, back to his life, back to Morrigan. But instead he tensed, and pulled me back, away from the sound, away from Sunnybrook.

"What are you doing?" I asked, jerking my hand away. "We're nearly there."

His eyes were bright, almost like when he'd had his fever. He took my hands and for a brief moment, the distance was gone. His hands around mine were warm and fierce and I felt all of him. But then it was gone, and his panic increased.

"We're not going unless you say you'll come, too. Come to stay." His voice trembled and his hands in mine shook.

I opened my mouth to protest, tried to pull my hands away, but he held on.

"At least through the winter. Through the snow." I'd worried he would die in the winter, and he worried the same for me. He thought I'd refuse the safety of the city.

And that had been my plan—to make sure he made it home and to leave, to find a new place before the snow hit. I knew I could do it. It would be hard, but I could do it. I'd survived worse.

But looking into his panicked eyes, feeling his worry roll off him in waves, I wasn't sure I could leave *him*. Part of it was because I knew he might follow me out into the dangerous world, possibly to our deaths, but most of it was because I felt selfish and I wasn't ready to let go completely. Not yet.

"I'm afraid," I said, shocking myself with the truth. "Of being around so many people."

Finn pulled me to him and held me, and for a moment I was reminded of being thirteen, held by Rosemarie as I told her about my awful life in the caves.

"I know," he said as he kissed my hair. "But I'll be there. We'll be there together." He pulled back and looked at me, his hands gripping my shoulders almost painfully. "Please say you'll stay."

I looked up into his eyes—still so incredibly blue they seemed unreal—and saw his desperation. I knew that things would be different and that, even surrounded by people, I would be alone again, but I would do whatever I could to take this pain away and that meant staying.

"OK." My voice was barely there and he crushed me in a hug as soon as the air passed my lips.

"Thank you," he said, sighing heavily. I didn't put my arms around him and he let me go after a moment. "We can go now." His voice was dripped with sadness, but I walked away and he followed, Luna between us.

"We shouldn't go in the main gate," he said as we walked. His hand swung by his side so close to me but he didn't try to take mine. "We need to sneak in. I don't want M—" he ducked his head and cleared his throat. "I don't want to cause a stir. We can sneak in the back, near the quarry, and make our way to Lucy's. You'll like her. She's younger than us. Talks a lot. But really nice. You'll like her. She'll like you."

He was talking faster than I'd ever heard, rambling. I'd never see him like this. He was brimming with nervous energy. His aura almost sparked with it—a neon green I'd only seen in nature once, when the sky lit up at night with what Rosemarie called the aurora.

"She's nice," he said when I didn't answer. "Loud, but nice."

"Whatever you say," I said into the silence that followed.

Around noon we came to a wall. The bottom of the wall was made of stone, and the top of logs and wood. It was at least three times as tall as me and leaned out just enough that it would be almost impossible to scale. To the left the wall stretched in a large arc through the trees. To the right, the wall cut off where it met the edge of a cliff. After peering down the wall for a moment, toward the arc that would surely lead us to the main gates, Finn motioned for me to follow him as he disappeared over the edge of the cliff.

I followed, Luna darting ahead and almost disappearing on the light gray stone. There wasn't a path, but the rocks offered handholds enough. Below us the rocks continued down for quite a while. I could see out into the distance—piles of rock and scraggly trees scattered here and there. I saw the glint of a large body of water—a strange teal-green—and heard the wind as it whistled through the nearly desolate landscape. We went down a little ways, angling past the wall, and then turned back up, Finn offering me his hand to pull me up the taller rocks.

As we turned up to go inside the wall, something pricked at my senses—something familiar—and I stopped as my eyes darted around.

"What is it?" Finn asked, crouching slightly and looked around for danger.

"I thought I heard something." I looked behind me, then to the right, away from the wall. I still felt it—a tingling at the edge of my awareness that felt familiar, though it was so faint I couldn't place it.

Finn offered me his arm again and I took it as he helped me up over the edge of the cliff.

Once we were back on even land, I turned and looked out over the quarry.

"They used to mine for rock and metals here," Finn said, catching his breath. "Then they found some vitium and started blowing holes all over the mountain." I looked at him and he shrugged. "They didn't build a wall on this side because the Wylden stay away from the quarry."

We stood in silence for a moment, staring out over the gray landscape.

Finn took my hand after a moment, and even though his fingers fit in mine as they had for the last few weeks, whatever we'd had wasn't there. I let his hand drop away and took a few steps toward the trees.

"How do we find Lucy?" I asked, hiking my bag higher on my shoulder. He sighed.

"We just follow the wall a ways," he said, hands now in his pockets.

I nodded and followed him, the distance between us growing by miles. Luna was a comforting presence at my side—my faithful, white shadow—but the closer we got to Finn's town, to Sunnybrook, the more the sadness in my belly grew.

Chapter Sixteen
Sunnybrook

Finn

Finley walked with his head down. There weren't any people in these back alleyways during the lunch hour, so he wasn't worried about being spotted, but he was worried about Erilyn. She was acting so strangely, so distant. It was hard to focus on that, though, because ever since they'd gotten close to Sunnybrook, he'd felt weird. His head ached and he thought he heard buzzing, like bees just out of sight.

He wanted to reach back to Erilyn where she walked behind him, reassure her, because he knew she was scared, but he didn't. It was like he physically couldn't and whenever he thought about it too hard the pain in his head flared, making it impossible to think about anything.

Finn looked down an alley and could just make out the clock tower. 12:53. People would be leaving the commissary soon. They needed to be in Lucy's apartment before anyone saw them.

Pushing past the pain in his head and the buzzing in his ears, Finn grabbed Erilyn's hand and pulled her into a faster walk toward the faded blue building on the corner—The Hummingbird. As soon as he touched her, the buzzing quieted and the pain behind his eyes lessened. He pulled her up the stairs—Lucy was on level 3—and pulled Lucy's spare key from where she kept it wedged between the door frame and the wall.

He tugged Erilyn inside, Luna darting in just before the door closed. People would eat until one, and Lucy would stay a little later to clean up before going back in a few hours to prep for dinner.

As soon as they were inside, Erilyn pulled away and the buzzing returned so loudly that he winced. He could almost feel it like a vibration against his skin. He was just stressed. He didn't want to be back.

The clocked struck 1:00 and he peeked out the window. People were starting to mill about the streets, heading for their shops and homes. The town worked like a single organism. Everyone had a job to do, though most of those jobs were for the benefit of others.

Some people made goods to trade, like Finn, but that was on top of whatever job they had that benefited the town. Finn worked as a carpenter, repairing and rebuilding furniture mostly, but he also was asked to make jewelry and figurines that he traded for things like blankets or special foods. In Sunnybrook, everything was free as long as you worked. The only thing you owed was a little extra of whatever you did for the mayor and patrol each month. It had always seemed like the only way to live, but after living in complete freedom for the last few weeks, watching the townspeople following the same paths they took every day made Finn sad.

"Here she comes." Finn cracked the curtain to let the light in and to let Lucy know that he was inside. He looked to Erilyn, standing stock still in the middle of the room, eyes wide and arms around her middle. "She's nice," he said, unsure of what to do. If they'd been back in the woods, he would have wrapped his arms around her and kissed her hair. He wanted to do that now, but he couldn't. "It's all going to be fine." He didn't believe his own tone.

She nodded and forced her arms down to her side, lifting her chin.

Finn went to the door and waited for Lucy's footsteps up the wooden stairs. When he heard them he took a deep breath and opened the door. Lucy jumped, but then smiled. Finn grabbed her hand and pulled her into the room before she could make any noise.

"Finn!" she yelled, throwing her arms around him. "You're alive! I thought for sure—" Lucy quieted when she saw Erilyn standing a few feet back, arms once again wrapped around her middle, Luna sitting warily by her feet with her ears pulled back. "Hello." Lucy brushed past Finn, but Finn stopped her with a hand on her arm.

"This is Erilyn," he said, keeping himself between the two. "She's—" panic flickered across her face. "She saved my life. She's my friend." Erilyn's eyes dropped from his and pain welled up in his own chest. He turned back to Lucy. "And that's Luna," he said, motioning toward the rigid cat. Luna wasn't growling, which seemed odd to Finn, but he was grateful.

Lucy looked between Finn and Erilyn before stepping around him and offering her hand to the small, blonde girl. "It's nice to meet you, Erilyn."

Erilyn hesitated a moment before taking the younger girl's hand in hers. The tension in her face eased and a small smile appeared.

"You too." Her voice was soft, but sounded calmer.

Lucy nodded and went to get candles to brighten the room. "We all thought you were dead, Finn." Her voice was accusatory as she lit a few candles in simple metal brackets. She motioned for Finn and Erilyn to join her on large cushions in one corner of the small apartment. "Cillian was starting to plan a grieving day and everything. I was going to have cook *so much food*." She smiled and hugged her knees, the candlelight making her light green eyes seem darker.

"Cillian's my brother," she said to Erilyn, holding her hand out for Luna to sniff as if having a large predator in her home was normal. "He's the mayor." She rolled her eyes and smiled. "He'll want to know you're back," Lucy said, turning back to Finn as Luna sniffed her hand and Lucy casually scratched between the large white cat's ears. "Where are you back from?" She asked, turning back to Erilyn. "Another city?"

There was a brief silence as Erilyn opened her mouth and no words came out. She looked to Finn and he shrugged.

"No." Erilyn's voice was as soft as the candlelight. "I lived alone."

"In the woods?" Lucy asked, seeming impressed.

"Erilyn found me after some Wylden tried to kill me." Finn pulled the neck of his shirt down to show the straight, pink scar. "She saved my life. Kept me alive since." He looked at her, remembering the feel of her fingers on his skin as she checked his wound each day, and the buzzing grew louder, more painful.

"I want to hear the whole story. *Everything*," she said. "But first, I need to get you both food and fresh clothes." She stood and dusted off her legs. "Erilyn, you go clean up first. We have a tap with warm water—not hot, but warm enough. I'll run down to the commissary." Erilyn's eyes grew worried. "I'll just tell them I forgot to bring anything back for myself—" Lucy looked around suddenly and laughed. "Which I did! Hold on." She went to a beautiful wooden chest. "Here." She handed Erilyn some folded clothes—warm, thick pants, a thick knitted sweater, and equally thick socks. "Go clean up and put these on. I'll put your clothes with mine for the next wash. Finn, I think some of Cill's clothes are in that bag over there—he asked me to mend them, and I hadn't given them back yet."

She put the clothes in Erilyn's hands and gently pushed her toward the small washroom. Inside was a round, metal tub with a window just over it. Lucy turned the water on, waited for it to warm, and then plugged the bottom of the tub with the stopper. "I'll be back soon."

Finn was still sitting on the floor, almost as out of sorts by Lucy's quick speech and movement as Erilyn seemed to be. Luna had curled in the middle of the floor, her head on the pillow where Lucy had been. Finn stood as Lucy came out of the bathroom.

"You're going to tell me everything, Finley. Ev-er-y-thing. Got it?" she asked, a finger in his chest. He nodded and she smiled, before kissing his cheek. "I'm really, really glad you're not dead," she said. "Be back soon."

In a flurry she left the apartment and he heard her quick steps down the stairs.

Finn found the clothes she'd mentioned and returned to his cushion. He heard the tap go off and the gentle sounds of moving water from the tub. He imagined the way the warm water would make her skin grow pink, the way her hair would float around her like seaweed.

Pain stabbed through his temple and he rubbed at his arms. The buzzing was like static all over. He shook his head and lay back, using the cushion seat as a pillow, and closed his eyes.

With the gentle sounds of Erilyn bathing in the next room, the soft candlelight, and Luna's gentle purr just beside him, he fell asleep.

Chapter Seventeen
Introductions

Erilyn

Without meaning to, I felt when Finn fell asleep in the next room, like a spider web had been gently laid over me like a blanket. With his sleep, my tension ratcheted higher, but I felt relatively safe in Lucy's home. Besides, I couldn't remember the last bath I'd had that wasn't in my small pond. The thought of my clearing sent a stab of pain through my chest and I pushed it aside.

Lucy had been a surprise. She was tall and thin with vibrant coppery hair and more energy than Luna on a perfect spring day. She'd accepted me without hesitation, and when I touched her, I was able to read every feeling as clearly as if she were telling me instead. But her face said it all, too. She was an open book. I'd saved Finn and she trusted me because of that. I wanted to trust her, too.

With a deep breath, I ducked my head under the water, bent knees rising above the surface into the cold air, and tried to run my fingers through the tangles.

I resurfaced and used a cloth draped over the side to scrub myself. It felt good. When the water had cooled and was an unpleasant shade of grayish brown, I pulled the plug in the bottom and stood into the cold. I was startled when I saw my reflection in a very old, very spotted mirror hanging above a water basin. I looked young—younger than I felt—and scared. Lifting my chin and squaring my shoulders, I stepped out of the tub onto a soft, woven rug. There was a towel hanging from a hook and I used it to dry off. I had carefully folded my thin, dirty clothes—I hadn't realized they were thin and dirty until I laid them next to the rich, warm clothes Lucy had given me—and put them in a neat stack next to Lucy's clothes. Carefully, I pulled on the socks—they enveloped my feet like warm water. The pants fit—the waist was a little big, but there was a drawstring—and the sweater was a pleasant weight against my skin.

I looked in the mirror again, wiping it off with my hand. It had been so long since I'd seen myself in anything except the reflection of rippling water. My skin was dark—I'd known that, but seeing my face was different than seeing my hand—and my hair was light, even as it hung in wet clumps down my back. The sweater she'd given me was the color of summer wheat and so soft. The pants were dark green. I wondered what they used to make these, what dyes, what materials, and why I had never learned to weave or knit. I could barely sew a patch.

As I pulled my hair away from my face, I was surprised at how gaunt I looked. I'd grown thinner than I'd realized. It hadn't mattered before now because I'd been alive, I hadn't been starving, but after seeing Lucy with her soft skin and curves, I felt like jagged old rock.

I turned away from the mirror, upset that I was even thinking this way. None of that mattered. Leaning over the tub, I wrung my hair out before hanging my towel and picking up the scraps that were my clothes. I was almost embarrassed to give them to Lucy, but these were my things, and I wouldn't give them up, not when so much had already been lost.

The front door opened as I left the bathroom. Lucy bounced in with a big burlap sack. She saw me and smiled before closing the door with her hip.

"Finn," she said, nudging him with her foot. He jerked awake. I felt lightheaded with his sudden confusion as he remembered where he was.

"Ouch," he said, rubbing his ribs where her toe had been. He looked over to me, his expression softening and causing my heart to beat painfully. It was the look he always had just before he kissed me. "My turn?" he asked. He winced and rubbed his jaw, then his arm. There was something off about his aura. It was usually a steady, deep green, but now it was wispy, somehow. I thought I saw little bits of black, there, but it could also just be gaps. I'd never seen that before.

Giving him a nod, I let my wet hair fall so that it covered my face more, wanting suddenly to hide from him. He picked up some clothes and went in the bathroom. I heard the water turn on and tried not to think of him sitting there as I had.

Lucy had been watching us, her eyes narrowed. Her curiosity was as bright and obvious as Luna's. Lucy's aura was orange—like sunrise—and strong.

"Hungry?" she asked. She took my hand and dragged me over to the chest she'd pulled our clothes from. We sat and from the bag she pulled a loaf of bread, a block of cheese, fruits, vegetables, and a covered bowl with some kind of meat inside. My stomach growled and I blushed.

She ignored my embarrassment and went to cutting the bread and cheese. She offered me a slice of bread—still warm—with cheese on it. I bit into it slowly and tears pricked the corners of my eyes. I hadn't had food like this in over three years.

I ate quickly, trying to enjoy the sweet fruit and crunchy vegetables, but I was so hungry it was hard. Lucy said nothing when I avoided the bowl of meat, and instead offered Luna bits of it between her own bites. When my belly felt pleasantly tight and I felt sleepy, there was still enough food left for three more people.

"Thank you," I said, embarrassed. I'd eaten like a starving animal.

"Not everyone likes my cheese," she said with a satisfied smile. "The fact that you did is thanks enough." She winked and ate a corner of the cheese that had broken off. Luna had fallen asleep with her head by Lucy's leg and I smiled.

"It was—" I'd forgotten how to talk with someone. "Good." I swallowed. Talking with Finn had been different—he'd been hurt, needed me, and by the time he didn't anymore we'd had an understanding. This was new.

"Good." She smiled and brushed her hands off. "Can I braid your hair?" Her eyes were suddenly big and her aura was glowing with excitement.

"Um." Lucy was all over the place. She was like a child and an adult in one. She was probably 16, a couple of years younger than me, and was looking at me excitedly. I nodded and she stood, disrupting Luna, who chirped in disapproval. She grabbed my hand and pulled me back to the hard cushions we'd sat on before. With a wooden comb she started gently working through the remaining tangles in my hair.

Her hands in my hair let me feel her out. She was excited to meet me, happy to be doing something for me, and so curious she could barely contain it. I sighed and sat up straighter.

"Thanks for all of this," I said, knowing she was dying to talk to me and wanting to control the conversation if I could.

"It's not a problem," she said, barely containing her questions. "But—" her hands in my hair hesitated, and then she went back to work, working through the snarls that had crept into the bottom layer. "I just really want to know what happened with Finn since he's been gone." She said it in a single breath and laughed, embarrassed. I smiled. I could tell her that.

I told her about Finn stumbling into the clearing where I lived, bleeding from the shoulder, being chased by

Wylden. That he'd climbed a tree, which was true, and that the Wylden had kept looking for him, which was partially true. I left out why the dogs had left—because of me. I told her that I'd nursed him back to health, taught him how to survive in the woods, and that we'd come back after the Wylden destroyed my home. Although I didn't tell her about us—whatever we were to each other—it seemed like enough.

By the time I'd finished my story, Lucy had worked all the tangles out and had almost finished a long, elaborate feeling braid that started at the top of my head and worked its way down until my hair hung just above my waistline. She tied it with a bit of string and then absently ran her hand over it in a way that reminded me of when Rosemarie used to fix my hair.

"That's—" she said, moving so that she was sitting beside me. "Just, wow." She shook her head and looked at me, and I smiled. "You're a hero," she said, and I shook my head.

"No, just a friend." She looked at me skeptically. Her emotions were as clear as her expression—she suspected something more had happened between us, but she wasn't going to ask about that. I instantly liked her more.

As I heard the water draining in the bathroom, that image of Finn—imagined and naked—flashed in my mind again causing my cheeks to redden.

Luna's ears perked and she crouched moments before a loud knock sounded on the door. I jerked toward the sound, heart pounding. I hadn't felt anyone coming, and I'd let my awareness expand quite a bit, since being around Lucy was so pleasant.

"It's just Cillian," Lucy said, seeing my alarm. "My brother. He wanted to meet you and see Finn." She went to the door as Finn was coming out. He looked alarmed, too, as his gaze met mine. For an instant it was like we were back in the woods, but it was gone as soon as the door opened.

A man walked in—tall, blonde, and handsome. He looked nothing like Lucy, and when he saw me his eyes widened in pleasant surprise.

A half a moment later, in a flurry of movement, a second person burst through the door. I hadn't felt this person either. She pushed past Cillian and Lucy and launched herself at Finn, wrapping her tan arms around him, her dark hair a silky sheet down her back. He hugged her back, his face blank with alarm as his eyes met mine. For a brief moment, I felt like the room was charged with static, but then it was gone.

I felt sick as I stood there in the sudden, thick silence.

Morrigan had come, too.

Chapter Eighteen
Morrigan

Finn

Finley had dreamed about this. Dreamed that he would go home and Morrigan would want him back, that they could go back to the way they were and be better than before. But that was before Erilyn. Before he knew what it was like to feel like he belonged, to be accepted for exactly who he was.

Over Morrigan's shoulder, Erilyn's face crumpled, but she turned and quickly schooled her features. Morrigan squeezed him tighter and he found himself holding her back. He didn't remember doing that. The buzzing he heard and felt was worse and he knew it had to be nerves.

"Oh, Finley!" she cried, pulling back to look at him, tears in her dark hazel eyes. "You're *alive*." She pulled him back to her, crying into his shoulder. He patted her back, feeling awkward.

"I'm fine, Morrigan," he said, his voice gruff. She pulled back and smiled at him, a single tear dripping down her cheek, her hair falling over her eye. He should push it behind her ear, wipe the tear away—he knew that's what she expected—but he didn't. "Fine."

She smiled, looking annoyed for a brief moment, before tucking herself under his arm and putting her head on his shoulder and her hand on his chest. "You must be Erilyn," she said brightly, never letting go of Finn.

Finn watched Erilyn, his heart breaking as she met Morrigan's gaze, her face a stone mask. She nodded, never looking at Finn.

"I must hear all about your grand adventures together."

Cillian was standing quietly in the doorway, letting the cool air in. Lucy was standing just beside him, her face tight. Erilyn stood in the middle of the room, Luna by her side, alone. She nodded once, her jaw tense.

"Oh," Morrigan said, moving away from Finn just enough to see his face. "Does she talk?"

"Yes," Erilyn and Finn said at the same time.

"Oh. Good." Morrigan smiled and put her head back on Finley's shoulder.

"Yes, well then." Cillian cleared his throat and stepped further into the room. Lucy closed the door behind him and Erilyn flinched. "Erilyn," he said, extending his hand. She looked at it for only a moment before taking it, her spine straight, her jaw tight. "I'm Cillian, mayor of Sunnybrook, and Lucy's big brother. It's a pleasure to have you here."

"Thank you." Erilyn's voice was quiet and her eyes wide, which told Finn she was afraid. He disentangled himself from Morrigan and moved next to Erilyn, feeling her tension melt slightly with his nearness.

"We were hoping Erilyn could stay for the winter," he said, facing Cillian. Morrigan's glare at his back made him tense and the buzzing was worse. He clenched and unclenched his hands. "Her home was attacked by Wylden and won't be able to be rebuilt until the thaw."

Cillian looked to Erilyn, pity in his brown eyes. "Wylden? How awful. Of course. Of course. We have more than enough for one more person." Luna growled by Erilyn's feet and Cillian smiled. "Even *two* more." Cillian smiled at Erilyn and jealousy flared in Finn. "Actually," Cillian said, moving so that he was closer to Erilyn without directly pushing Finn out of the way, "we do have a job for you, if you'd like it. So far, no one's been willing to fill it, and everyone in Sunnybrook has to work."

Finn stiffened. What sort of job would Cillian have, ready to offer? But Erilyn was independent and strong. He wouldn't intervene with a decision that was hers to make.

"We have a small library, a collection of very old books and copies of books, but it's a real mess." Cillian clasped his hands behind his back, his shoulders broad and straight. "Lucy tried her hand at organizing it once, but she couldn't sit still long enough." He smiled at Lucy who was bouncing on her toes slightly. "If you're interested, it would probably take most of the winter. I'm afraid of the knowledge we'll lose if it sits in disrepair much longer."

Erilyn nodded, but before she could answer Morrigan stepped into the conversation. Finn noted for the first time what she was wearing—a skin tight, black top and pants with tall, leather boots—her patrol gear.

"And if you need help learning to read, that can be arranged," she said, taking a stance next to Cillian, looking official now rather than like a lovesick girl.

"I can read," Erilyn said, no anger in her voice, but Finn felt it simmering just below the surface. "I appreciate the job, sir." Erilyn nodded to Cillian, never meeting Morrigan's eyes.

"Please, call me Cillian," he said with a smile and that jealous ping flared in Finn's gut again.

"Cillian," Erilyn said, the quiet word loud in the thick silence.

"Would you like to start now?" Cillian asked, holding his hand out.

"Actually," Finn cut in, stepping between them for a moment, "I wanted to show Erilyn the town first. Let her get acclimated. Lucy's already fed us—" he nodded to Lucy, "and given us clean clothes."

"Ah, I thought I recognized that sweater," Cillian said, eyeing the blue sweater Finn wore with a green patch over one elbow.

"Like you'd ever actually wear a sweater with a patch," Lucy said, finally breaking her silence and standing with Finn. Together, they were like a shield between Erilyn and the others, and Finn was grateful for the younger girl's presence. "Erilyn can work tomorrow, after Finn shows her the Sunnybrook ropes. Besides, I need to talk to you both about something. Someone's been raiding the gardens again."

"Of course," Cillian said with a pleasant smile, his hands once more behind his back. "Tomorrow then, miss Erilyn. Finley can show you where the library is in the morning, after breakfast and we'll get started."

"Perhaps I should go with them," Morrigan said, her chin high and a slight color to her cheeks.

"No, you have duties to attend to." Cillian's voice suggested there was no arguing, and she nodded. Cillian nodded to Finn and Erilyn, his eyes lingering on Erilyn a moment longer than Finn thought was appropriate. "Tomorrow," he said, before walking out the door.

Morrigan followed, not a word to either of them, and it left Finn reeling. Part of him wanted to turn to Erilyn and scoop her up, tell her they would take food and leave this moment, but another part of him was desperate to go after Morrigan. The buzzing made his skin itch.

Lucy looked back at them. "Stay as long as you want. Lock up when you're done," she said, winking at Erilyn before closing the door behind her.

"Eri," he said in the silence, turning to face her.

"You can go with them if you want," she said, her voice tight.

"I want to stay here," he said, believing it in that moment, even though his skin crawled with the desire to go. "I haven't eaten yet," he said, moving to the food, "and I don't want to leave you alone." He cut a slice of bread and put cheese on it. "I want to be here with you."

When she didn't say anything, he looked up at her, his heart feeling broken. Her expression spoke volumes—she knew he wanted to go after them. He had a feeling that she could do more than stop fires and scare away giant cats, that maybe she could know what he was feeling, what he was thinking, too. Shame welled inside him.

"Come on," he said, his appetite suddenly gone. "Let me show you Sunnybrook." He offered her his hand, but she didn't take it. "Erilyn," he said, his voice pleading.

"You don't have to keep pretending, Finn." Her voice was hard, but it cracked at the end. "You were alone. Scared. Hurt." She wouldn't look at him, her cheeks growing pink. "You needed comfort and I was happy to give it to you." Finally, she met his eyes, and he was shocked to see tears there, not falling, just pooling above her bottom lashes. "We all need comfort sometimes. You've comforted me and I've comforted you. You don't owe me anything."

Finn felt like he'd been punched in the gut. What he'd experienced with her, what he still felt for her, was so much more than that, but his mouth felt glued shut as his heart thudded dully.

"Show me your town," she said into the silence when he didn't speak. Her shoulders were slumped, her iron façade gone.

He nodded, feeling lost. He gathered up the food Lucy had left and took the bag with him. He didn't want to go to the commissary yet.

He held the door open for Erilyn, and she walked through it, her hair catching the sunlight as she stepped outside. Luna was right beside her, as nervous as she was, pressed against her leg.

Suddenly Finn hated Sunnybrook, hated being here. He knew it was their best shot to survive the winter, knew she wouldn't have made it on her own, but look at what it was doing to them now.

The lock turned over and clicked, and Finn re-hid the key behind the doorframe's molding. He went to offer her his hand, but pulled it back before he could extend it all the way.

"Follow me," he said, his voice empty. She did, without a word, and they headed down to the street.

She was wrong. He knew what they'd shared was more than just comfort. But he also knew he wasn't sure what he wanted anymore. Out in the woods, he'd wanted her and only her. She had quickly become his home. But now, everything seemed different. Morrigan wanted him back. He could go back to his old life, his old love. And part of him begged for that. When he started to acquiesce to that begging voice, the pain between his eyes lessened, the buzzing grew quieter. Yet, it still didn't feel right.

Beside him, Erilyn stood with her chin high, her cheeks red, and her hands in subtle fists. People walked in groups around them and Erilyn and Luna seemed to shrink in on themselves. No, they wouldn't be going to the commissary tonight.

They walked around Sunnybrook, Finn showing her the essentials—the commissary, the soldier statue in the square, the clock tower building which housed the library, where she would be working, as well as Cillian's office, and the main gates to the city, flanked by two white sycamores. The sycamores were the only place that caused Erilyn to come out of her shell a little. She gazed at them thoughtfully, touching one in reverence.

Finally, he showed her where he lived—his tiny apartment in one of the older buildings called The Finch. All the apartments were named after birds. Lucy lived in The Hummingbird and Cillian and Morrigan both lived in the executive apartments, aptly named The Hawk.

He led her to his door on the first floor, missing the sound of her voice. She'd always had quiet conversations with him as they walked through the woods. He walked right into his apartment having forgotten to lock the door when he left.

He walked in and immediately opened a window to let air and light in. Erilyn came in hesitantly, drawn to the open window. Luna curled in the long patch of sunlight on the floor.

"We can stay here tonight," he said, and Erilyn spun to him as if he'd slapped her. He sighed. "Please, stay," he said, not caring that his voice broke.

"All right," she said, nodding, her hands on her stomach.

"Erilyn, I—" he took a step toward her and she held up her hand to stop him, her fingers on his chest firm.

"I'm glad to be your friend, Finn," she said, a sad smile on her face. "I'm grateful for this," she gestured to his apartment.

He stood, staring dumbly, and then nodded. He longed to reach out and hold her. Her hand on his chest made the choice seem easier—he wanted to be with her—but when that hand fell away, his confusion returned.

"Not much to see," he said, gesturing to the space. Erilyn walked to a cup with a wilted, red lily in it and Finn flushed with embarrassment. "But make yourself at home."

Erilyn made pitiful small talk after that, walking around the small space, touching the carvings he'd kept for himself or hadn't quite finished. All Finn could do was watch her move through his apartment and feel like neither of them belonged here. The longer he sat, the more he fought the urge to get up and run out of the room—to either leave with Erilyn or find Morrigan.

"Finn?" Erilyn asked, her hand on his shoulder. With her touch, a gentle calm spread over his body like cool water on a hot day. "Are you ok?" Her touch soothed the buzzing on his skin.

"I'm fine," he said, giving her a small smile. "Let me tell you about my favorite carving," he said, standing and collecting a small tree pendant he'd been working on.

She took it in her hands and traced the branches with her finger, her eyes softening as she looked at it. He liked watching her like this—unguarded and quiet—but as soon as he thought this her mask went back on.

Until night fell, they talked awkwardly. Softly. Quietly. When Finn's urge to get up and run became almost unbearable, Erilyn was there to calm him with a soft touch. When Erilyn's face would dissolve into a sadness deeper than Finn could stand, he would talk to her about things he'd made or wanted to make until the sadness lessened.

It wasn't like it had been in the clearing, but it was better than it could have been. She was still here, with him, and he was content for the moment to just be near her while he figured the rest out.

Chapter Nineteen
The Library

Erilyn

I woke to find a wet pillow beneath my cheek. My eyes were bleary. I'd been crying. I'd had the dream, again—the dream where I was running through the woods, away from the Wylden, and running through the caves, away from the children of Citadel. I hadn't had it since I met Finn.

I rolled to my back, surprised to be alone and warm. Luna was stretched alongside me. I sat up and massaged my scalp, sore from the braid Lucy had put it in. Finn was asleep on the floor, wrapped in a blanket, turned away from me.

The sun had just started to rise and I felt stiff from sleeping on something soft. I pulled my braid over my shoulder and untied the bit of string Lucy had used to hold it together. It was stiff twine, and I left it on the bedpost. With warm fingers I pulled the braid apart, sighing as my fingers brushed through my hair—surprisingly soft—by my scalp. My hair hung in waves and I pushed it back over my shoulder, glad for the tension of the braid to be gone.

Beside me, Luna stretched, yawning and showing off the pink inside of her massive mouth and her many sharp teeth. I smiled and then winced as I felt Finn start to wake.

It was disconcerting to feel so comfortable with someone else's aura. I'd felt that way with Rosemarie, but it had taken months for me to allow myself to be this open to her presence, and when she died, a part of myself died. As I experienced Finn waking, I knew that when he went back to Morrigan completely—as I knew he was preparing himself to do—it would be like another part of me had died.

"Morning," he said, looking at me from the floor, his expression bland.

"Good morning." I stroked Luna, who stretched, her weight shifting the cloth and straw mattress around. My heart thudded dully. "I think I can find my way around today." I was ready—at least, I told myself I was ready—to allow him to do what I knew he needed to. It didn't feel right, but I couldn't stop him. I wouldn't stop him. I couldn't read Morrigan, couldn't feel out her intent, but she gave me a bad feeling nonetheless.

"Can we go to breakfast together?" His voice was tired and sad, so I nodded.

I washed my face in the basin in his bathroom—smaller and dirtier than Lucy's—and put on my old, worn boots over the soft green pants Lucy had let me wear.

I waited for Finn, Luna pacing uneasily by the door. We'd slept with the window cracked, but Finn had closed it when he woke up and both Luna and I itched to be out beneath the open sky.

The fresh air was stimulating as we walked toward the commissary and I felt the pain of losing Finn ease a little as we walked. I'd been alone for most of my life, even when I was around other people. I could do this.

The town was set up in rings of buildings, the old roads having been built over and replaced with smaller paths and alleys. In the middle of town was a statue of a soldier, green and brown with age and leaning a little to one side. There had been roads here once, now broken apart by vegetation and age. The commissary was one of the newer buildings, a single story, in the first ring around the statue. As the sun rose, people of all sizes and hair colors streamed into the two double doors that had been propped open with wooden blocks. I followed Finn in, drawn by the smell of baking bread, but was repelled by the close press of bodies already lined up to get food.

"Finley, Erilyn!" Cillian's voice rose above the quiet din in the hall like a bell. "Please, join us!" I turned, surprised to find him at a table all his own, food already on it. Morrigan was at his side, still in her black clothes that fit like a second skin. She eyed me angrily, and in anger I reached out with my mind to try and read her. It was like trying to see through granite.

I stumbled and Finn grabbed my elbow, concern on his face. I gave him a thankful smile and pulled away. I looked back at Morrigan, her anger replaced by amusement, which surprised me. Did she know I'd tried to read her? It should have been easy to feel her out—I could feel echoes of every person in the room—but she was a blank slate. I could see her aura, though—a deep, dark red that reminded me of old blood. It pulsed steadily and made me uncomfortable to look at.

Just before we reached the small table where Cillian sat, I felt Finn's hand touch my lower back and I couldn't suppress the shiver that radiated out from his fingers. "Are you OK?" he said into my ear, my braid-wavy hair falling between his face and mine. I nodded and I felt his breath as he sighed before stepping away. I hated being around all these people, but when he'd touched me it hadn't been so bad. I looked up at Morrigan who glowered at me.

"Erilyn!" Lucy said as she bounced out from behind the food line wearing an apron covered in flour. "I have some food in back for Luna. Think she'll go with me?" Her hair was pulled up in a messy ponytail and I noticed a bit of flour there, too.

"Luna." The big white cat, who was slinking against me and gaining more than a few startled stares from the people already seated, looked up at me, her eyes wide. "Go with Lucy?" I nodded toward Lucy with my chin. She chirped at me and followed Lucy around the back of the food line and into a back room. I sighed. Luna would be happier away from the noise and I wished I could go with them.

I continued through the crowd, people looking at me strangely, and closed down my awareness as trickles of fear and intrigue started to make my skin tingle. There were so many. *Too many*. It was like being back in Citadel.

Cillian stood and pulled out the chair next to him where Morrigan had been. "Please, Erilyn." He smiled at me, and I realized when I tried to feel out his emotion, his intent, I hit the same wall I had with Morrigan. With a smile in return, I took the seat, disoriented by his blankness. I looked out toward the people already seated and saw they were staring at us. The room held rows of long tables. Ours was the only small one and the only one with food ready to be served in the middle.

Morrigan had moved beside Cillian, her face a cool mask. I couldn't help but admire her. She was a beautiful, powerful-looking woman. Her nose was long and thin, her jawline delicate yet strong. Her lips were full and stained a startling shade of red. Her hair—silky and black like a raven's wing—was pulled up into a high ponytail. No wonder Finn was so drawn to her.

Finn sat in the seat across from Cillian's as Cillian held up his hands as if asking for silence. There wasn't much noise to begin with, but it stopped almost immediately.

"Yesterday, Sunnybrook gained a new citizen." He put his hand on my shoulder and I appreciated how light his touch was. I didn't *see* anything. "She's come here to be our new librarian. As the protector of our main source of knowledge, I expect her to be given the respect of any official. Please, let us welcome Erilyn to Sunnybrook, and welcome Finley home from his travels." He released my shoulder and took a step back. The crowd broke into a soft applause, and I held my hands in fists under the table, managing what I hoped was a convincing smile. I could feel their acceptance of what Cillian had said and their hesitance at accepting a new person into town.

Cillian sat and the applause stopped, replaced by the quiet murmur of conversations. Cillian and Morrigan sat and both began filling their plates.

"Please, eat," Cillian said, smiling at me. His eyes were brown and warm, and I thought it odd that he and Lucy could be siblings and look nothing alike.

Disoriented from the lack of information, I filled my plate with fruit, cheese, and bread. I ignored the meat and eggs, but both Cillian and Morrigan took a fair share. A boy—maybe 14—came around and filled our cups with steaming, dark brown liquid that smelled earthy and strong.

Cillian and Morrigan filled the silence at the table with talk about the crops that had been stolen, about what the crews manning the wall would be doing that day, about when they thought it might snow. Finn and I sat silently and ate, each focused on our food and not looking at each other.

I wasn't hungry yet. The food Lucy had given me the day before had been so much, but I didn't want to be rude. Finn ate little, too, though both Cillian and Morrigan had seconds. I sipped the strong, brown liquid—bitter with a spicy aftertaste.

"Does that sound all right, Erilyn?" Cillian asked. They were all looking at me—Finn looking concerned, Morrigan looking amused.

"I'm sorry," I said, putting my fork down and facing Cillian, back straight and cheeks red. "I was thinking about something else."

He smiled at me and my stomach fluttered. It caught me off guard. It wasn't like when Finn looked at me. This felt foreign, but pleasant.

"Lucy's meals do that to all of us," he said, leaning forward as if we were conspiring. "I was just asking if you wanted to walk with me to the library after we finish here. My office is in the same building." His smile was disarming and I nodded as my nerves ratcheted higher.

"Lucy has offered to watch your cat." My eyes darted to Lucy who was busy refilling peoples' plates. She waved when she saw me. I trusted Lucy, but I didn't like leaving Luna.

"OK," I said, and from the corner of my eye I saw Finn's eyes open wide, his shock a bare echo compared to how I was used to *feeling* him.

"Cillian," Morrigan said, her voice commanding and rich. "I've decided I'm taking today off." She looked at Finn, her hand going to his where it rested beside his plate. "We need a day," she said, her voice softer.

"Of course," Cillian said. Finn's eyes were on his plate. He didn't take her hand, but he didn't pull his away. After a moment, he looked up at her, his cheeks red and his jaw clenched. I could feel his confusion—his desire to say yes and his reluctance at the same time, but he nodded and I looked away from him, pulling my awareness away from him with fervor.

Cillian stood after a while, motioning for me to follow. I hadn't been able to look at Finn since Morrigan had taken his hand, and I didn't look at him now. Instead, with a quick look to Lucy who pointed back to where Luna was and then gave me a thumbs up, I followed Cillian, head ducked to avoid curious eyes, out into the brisk fall morning.

We walked in relative quiet, Cillian pointing out facts about the town he found interesting as we walked—the section of the wall that surrounded the town that was built first to keep the Wylden out, his first apartment where he lived before he became mayor and moved into the bigger rooms closer to the center of town.

We'd taken the long way around. The library was in the clock tower building, which was just across the square from the commissary. It rose above the town like a beacon and I knew I'd always be able to at least find my way there.

Cillian held open the large wooden door and motioned for me to enter. Two large windows lit the front lobby, but the library was deeper in, through a set of heavy wooden doors. The room was dark, though my eyes adjusted quickly.

"Oh," Cillian said, touching my arm in apology. "Let me get the drapes." He left me in the near dark, bumping into a table as he went. "There we are," he said as he pulled thick drapes away from a window.

The room was smaller than the commissary had been. Bookshelves filled the room with aisles in between. There were at least twenty shelves, each a head taller than me and as wide as my arms could reach, filled with books.

"It's not organized," he said as he rejoined me, brushing dust from his hands. "At all." He looked at me with an apologetic smile and that same, foreign excitement blossomed in my stomach. I found myself admiring the set of his jaw and the whiteness of his teeth. He looked to be in his late 20s, at least a decade older than me, but had managed to hold onto his youthful smile.

"The hardest jobs are the most rewarding ones," I said with a small smile. It was something Rosemarie had told me before we did our more strenuous chores. I thought I saw his expression shift for a fraction of a moment, but I couldn't read him, and it was gone so quickly I wasn't sure I hadn't imagined it.

It was odd. Lucy and the other townspeople I'd been near were open books to me, but both Cillian and Morrigan were closed off. He smiled at me, and I chalked it up to chance.

"I'm glad you feel that way," he said, smiling. "This one should be very rewarding indeed." I let myself see his aura, surprised to see that it was very similar to my own—a deep golden brown.

"I suppose I'll get started." I started to walk to the first shelf, but he took my elbow, gently. It startled me enough to jump and he let go, his face apologetic.

"Come to my office first. I can give you paper and a quill so you can make any lists you need to." I nodded and he offered me his crooked elbow. I took it, awkwardly. "I'll be in there most of the time. If you ever need anything at all, you'll know where to find me."

He led me through a door to the left of the room. His office was large with high open windows. The light pouring in made it feel calm, and there was an ornate couch across the room from his large, dark wooden desk, separated by two high backed, blue, fabric-covered chairs.

"Also, if you ever need a break, feel free to come in here. It gets lonely," he said, smiling a crooked smile and shrugging. "People tend to avoid me. It would be nice to have—" he looked at me and shrugged, "a coworker?" He laughed lightly and I felt that soft excitement that wasn't quite my own again.

"Thank you," I said, suddenly nervous. He smiled then, releasing my arm as he moved to his desk. From one of the large drawers he pulled bound sheets of thick, uneven paper, a long black quill, and a small glass bottle filled with black ink. "Thank you," I said again as he offered them to me.

"I'll be in here if you need me." He smiled and I nodded before quickly leaving the room. Why had I felt so nervous all of a sudden? Like the girls from my childhood when they liked a boy.

Back in the library, I felt like I could breathe again. The feelings that had overwhelmed me were gone—a memory.

The library smelled old, but good. I wished Luna were here, but was thankful for some time alone.

I set the paper, ink, and quill on a table with four wooden chairs around it and went to the first shelf. The books were old, some of the covers so coated with dust that I couldn't read them. With careful fingers, I pulled the first five books from the top shelf and took them to the table.

There were four tables and I made a list with four columns. In school in Citadel we'd had to make store lists as one of our classes. It was important to always know how much food we had, so this was old hat. I would use the tables to organize the books, and I would use the paper to keep track of all I did. At least the job I'd been offered here was quiet and I could be alone.

With a deep breath and my thoughts far from Finn, I opened the first book, being careful of the old, delicate pages, uncapped the ink, and began.

Chapter Twenty
Sweet Bread

Finn

Finn watched Erilyn leave with Cillian, something twisting in his gut as the buzzing against his eardrums grew worse.

"Finley, are you listening?" Morrigan leaned in front of him, blocking his view of the doors, and he shook his head.

"Sorry." He said, sipping the now lukewarm chicory, grimacing at the bitter aftertaste. He longed for pine tea. "What were you saying?"

"Nothing." She turned, her cheeks red in anger, and he felt a welling panic.

"No, please," he said, touching her arm. "I just didn't sleep well."

She spun to him, her hazel eyes flashing darkly. "I'm sure you and Erilyn had a busy night." Her voice was sharp and it felt like he'd been slapped.

"I slept on the floor," he said, taking her long fingers in his. He'd always loved her slender fingers, but holding them now felt strange. "That's why I'm tired," he lied. The floor had been fine. He hadn't slept well because he'd felt like he was being torn in two. He'd wanted nothing more than to crawl in bed beside Erilyn and take her in his arms while also wanting to run from the room with equal fervor in order to find Morrigan and make things right.

"Oh," Morrigan said, softening, squeezing his hand. "I'm sorry. I just assumed—" Tears welled up in her eyes. "Oh, Finley." She threw her arms around his neck and breathed against his neck, causing tingles to walk down his arms. He held her tighter, less conflicted. Her breath on his neck didn't let him think of anything except her. Within a few moments Erilyn was gone from his mind as if she'd never existed.

"Morrigan." His voice was a sigh and she tightened her hold on him.

"Come with me," she said, standing suddenly and offering him her hand. He took it and she led him out of the commissary, the last of their breakfast left untouched. Finn looked back once and saw Lucy watching them, a frown on her pale face.

Morrigan quickly led Finn through the streets. People ducked their heads and moved out of the way as they passed. Morrigan walked assuredly through the people, a few of them nodding nervously when they saw the red captain logo sewn just above her breast.

She led him straight to her apartment in the Hawk building. The last time he'd been here, she'd broken his heart. "Wait outside," she said. She turned to go in, then stopped, turned back around, and kissed him. Her lips connected to his and fire spread through his body from where they had touched. He'd never had such trouble fighting the urge to grab her and kiss her harder like he did in that moment, but she pulled away and was inside before he had to fight it long.

He stood there, reeling, thankful for the cool air that blew through and helped dampen his sudden, intense desire.

Morrigan came back out a few minutes later. She was wearing a deep red summer dress, despite the cold, and her hair was down and fell fetchingly over one eye. He felt like he needed to push it back behind her hear, to feel her face in his hand. She took his hand before he could, her skin warm, and pulled him after her, smiling over her shoulder as they descended the stairs.

"I have a sweet tooth," she said, slipping her arm around his waist as they walked. His arm went around her shoulder and for a moment he was disoriented by her height. Erilyn was so much smaller and part of his brain told him it should be Erilyn there, not Morrigan, but she leaned over and kissed his jaw and he forgot Erilyn again. "Want something sweet?" she whispered and he shivered.

"Sure," he said, feeling dizzy like when he'd had a fever in the woods. At least the buzzing was gone. He'd felt it all night long and its absence was a sweet relief.

They walked to a little shop just down the street. Usually this shop made breads and pastries for special occasions, but they always kept sweets on hand in case someone wanted to trade. Morrigan pushed open the door and a bell tinkled. A woman—thin as paper—came from the back dusting floured hands on her apron.

"Captain," she said, straightening.

"Sweet bread," Morrigan said, her chin lifted, her smile gone. "Two."

The woman nodded and hurried to the back. Finn bristled at her tone. No hello. No acknowledgement. He realized he didn't know this woman's name, but he still would have said hello.

The woman was back in a moment with two pastries wrapped in cloth. She handed them to Morrigan and ducked her gaze.

"We'll be in next week for inspection," Morrigan said, handing the bread to Finn. She took his hand and guided him from the shop. He looked back and saw the relief on the woman's face.

"You didn't trade anything," he said once they were outside, shifting so that he had to use both hands to hold the bread and Morrigan let go of his hand.

"I don't have to," she said, flashing him a dazzling smile. "I'm captain of the patrol now."

Finn bristled at this and told himself he'd take something in to the woman later to repay her.

Morrigan, the woman forgotten, tossed her head so that her hair flew over her shoulder. "Oh, I wanted us to have a picnic, but it's so chilly." She wrapped her arms around herself and pretended to shiver. "Come back to my apartment," she said, her voice growing a bit huskier.

Finn suddenly flushed as he followed Morrigan up the steps and into her home. The candles were already burning and the drapes over the two windows were closed. He wondered, absently, why the candles were lit if she'd planned a picnic, but his heart was racing too fast to think about it too much. He didn't know why. He'd spent many hours in Morrigan's apartment—both this one and the smaller one she lived in before she made captain.

This apartment was larger than most. There was a separate living area, bathing area, and sleeping area. All the apartments in the Hawk were huge—big enough for a family.

Morrigan took the pastries, still warm, and unwrapped them on the table beside the ornate cushions in the living room. She held her hand out to him, her hair falling over her eye. She led him to one of the cushions, sitting so close he could feel her warmth through their clothes, and the woman at the bakery was forgotten.

"Here," she said, tearing of a piece of the sweet, honeyed bread and holding it up his lips. He took the bite and watched her as she licked the sticky sweetness off of her fingertips. "I missed you so much, Finley."

"I missed you, too," he said. It wasn't a lie. He had missed her, had thought of her often. But then Erilyn popped in his head—the way she looked at him when he would hold her, her eyes open and honest—and the buzzing came back. He *had* missed Morrigan, and then he hadn't.

Finn suddenly wanted to get up and leave, to get out in the cold hair to clear his head, but before he could Morrigan's lips were on his and all he could think of was her touch.

One moment, Finn was sitting up, kissing Morrigan, and the next she had him on his back on the floor. She was pressing her body to his, her summer dress riding up, and he found his hands wandering to her back, her legs, anywhere he could feel her skin.

They'd been here before, and she'd always slowed them to a stop after a time. He slowed his frantic hands, ready to stop. He never wanted her to feel pressured.

She leaned up then, her hair falling over her shoulder and the candlelight making her skin look rosy. "Don't stop," she said, her voice deep and he heard himself groan. "Not this time." She dipped her head back toward his and captured his mouth, and he was lost in the wave that followed.

Finn lay on the floor, Morrigan's head on his chest, her hair splayed across his bare skin. He absently rubbed the back of her arm as he stared up at the flickering candlelight on the ceiling. This, he thought, was the way it should be. How could he have ever doubted?

She moved against him, asleep, and contentment rose in him like the sunrise. She was wearing a necklace—a thin cord with a large, flat, irregularly shaped, dark green-blue stone that shone almost iridescently. It dug into his side, but he didn't dare move. It was the only thing she'd kept on and he wondered why he hadn't noticed it before. He sighed and pulled her closer. He expected her to fit against him more securely, but ignored the thought. He had a vague memory of someone—it had to be Morrigan—lying beside him, fitting like they belonged.

Her long body stretched against him beneath the quilt draped over them. It was one he'd had made for her their first winter together with their initials embroidered into the corner. She lifted her head and looked at him, her hair tangled and beautiful, her gaze sleepy.

"Tell me about what happened while you were away." Her voice was soft and seemed to fill him up.

"I tried to attack some Wylden," he said, suddenly confused about why he would. He couldn't clearly remember anymore. "They chased me and I was hurt. A knife, I think." He kissed the top of her head and a stray memory tried to push its way forward. Her hair felt strange against his lips, smelled wrong. "Erilyn found me." Guilt swamped him, rose up like thick, angry fog and made him cold. He remembered in snips and flashes holding Erilyn in the cold and he couldn't remember why he had. He just knew it had been wrong. He kissed Morrigan's hair, his nose wrinkling as that same stray memory tried to surface.

"And?" Morrigan asked, pressing her chest against his side—her skin soft and warm.

"And she kept me alive," he said quietly. He hugged Morrigan tighter and breathed her in. She liked to bathe in dried flowers and the perfume coated her skin and hair.

"Why did it take you so long to come home?" She had scooted up and was nuzzling his ear and neck. He groaned.

"My shoulder." Guilt rose up so hard and fast he winced. Why was he lying? He should tell Morrigan everything. He loved her. He had to tell her what she wanted to know. He should tell her that he'd betrayed her with Erilyn, though he couldn't remember why.

But something was stopping him. He thought of Erilyn, of how this information would hurt her. He couldn't remember why he'd treated her like more than a friend, but he wouldn't make things worse for her than he already had.

"I have a scar," he said, pulling away enough to angle his shoulder toward her. She traced the fine, pink line with her finger and then kissed it. "It took a while to heal." Another lie. More cold, foggy guilt. His head buzzed painfully.

"I'll have to thank her for saving you," she said, kissing the scar again.

The buzzing grew loud and sharp on his skin. He had betrayed Morrigan with a girl he barely knew. Everything in him was screaming to be honest, to tell Morrigan everything. He would do *anything* for her, but something held his tongue. He couldn't remember much about Erilyn anymore, but he knew he couldn't betray her.

Finn pulled Morrigan close again, his hand moving down her arms and resting on her thin, tight waist. As he breathed her in Erilyn faded from his mind and the buzzing receded until he could barely hear it in the background.

He pulled the blanket up around them and held Morrigan tight. He was finally where he needed to be. Regardless of what had happened, he was back home.

Home. The word caused a flash of pain in his gut, but Morrigan's breath across his skin banished it instantly. He fell asleep holding her, feeling content.

Chapter Twenty-One
Lucy

Erilyn

I sat back in a hard backed chair with a sigh. The library was stuffy, and the dust I'd kicked up while moving books made the air hazy. I looked at the four tables, now piled with books, all from the first shelf alone. I was arranging them by topic and groaned as I realized I would need more tables if that strategy were going to work. I hadn't had to do work like this—work that didn't contribute to my personal survival—in years.

My stomach growled and I looked out at the sky, unable to see the clock tower as it was above me. It was just past noon. I'd missed lunch and felt good about that. These people ate feasts for every meal and I didn't want to get used to that for when I left again. I stood and dusted off my hands, ready to tackle the next shelf, when the door opened and a white blur bounded toward me.

"Luna!" I said, falling to my knees and catching her as she threw her large, white body at me. I rocked back and caught myself with my hand. She bumped her head against my face and rubbed against my chin and shoulder, purring so loudly my hands vibrated where they touched her. She was as tall as me, and almost as heavy. "Oh, I'm so glad you're here," I whispered. I couldn't remember a time I'd been without Luna. The last few hours had been the loneliest of my life.

"She made it clear she wanted to come to you," Lucy said, closing the door behind her with one hand, a plate in the other. My stomach growled and I grew red. She smiled and offered me the plate before sitting on the floor across from me. "You missed lunch." She shrugged and scratched Luna's back. Luna was draped across me and shifted so that she was lying beside me on the old, soft carpet. She purred loudly as Lucy scratched just above her tail.

"Thank you." She'd brought me a vegetable sandwich with more of that thick, soft cheese. "For this and for watching Luna," I said around a mouthful of food.

"She's great," Lucy said, scratching her under her chin like she liked. "Feisty as hell, but great." Luna batted playfully at her hand, claws retracted, and Lucy laughed.

The door to Cillian's office opened. He strode in confidently. "Erilyn, I—" he stopped short when he saw me on the floor with Lucy. "Oh, I didn't know you were here, Luce." He looked at me once as I swallowed a bite. "I didn't know you'd eaten. I was going to ask—" he looked at Lucy and cleared his throat. "Never mind. Maybe tomorrow." He met my eyes and something in my low belly flashed hot. It was hard to describe—almost desire, as if I were feeling his feelings, except they were mine too. My cheeks grew red. It was like he wanted me to feel what he felt, which was a foolish thought to have. Besides, I couldn't read him.

"I can come back later," Lucy said, grinning almost wickedly at her brother, but he shook his head.

"No, no. Please. Don't let me interrupt." He turned as if to go, but then turned back, his tan face open and hopeful. His blonde hair, which was long enough to touch the tops of his ears, had fallen so that it brushed the top of his right eye in a very disarming way. "Can I walk you to dinner tonight?" He was looking right at me, and that same feeling—warm and intense—flared to life.

Caught off guard, I nodded. He smiled before leaving just as swiftly as he'd arrived.

"He's incorrigible," Lucy said, laughing as she rubbed Luna's belly. "He likes you," she said, winking at me.

I went cold and my face went blank as I thought of Finn. Lucy's smile fell and she put her hand on my knee. "Erilyn?" Her caring filled me like water in a glass.

"That's nice of him," I said awkwardly. She squeezed my shoulder and let her hand fall back to Luna.

"It's Finn, isn't it?" she asked, raking her fingers through Luna's fur.

"What?" I hadn't meant to sound so harsh.

"You like him." I shook my head, but she kept on. "I know you do. I've seen it." Her voice wasn't accusatory or angry, just matter of fact.

"We're friends," I said, finishing the last bite of sandwich she'd brought. "Thanks for the food."

She sighed and stood. "Don't mention it." She looked down at me for a moment, her wild red curls partially obscuring her face. She pushed them back, annoyed. "You're staying with me, ok?" she asked, her head cocked to one side like Luna did sometimes. I nodded and she smiled.

"Good. I'll see you at dinner then." She leaned over and hugged me with one arm, catching me off guard, before standing and bouncing from the room.

I turned back to my stacks of books. Having Luna here made the space feel less empty, though my emotions were still roiling as I thought of Cillian, of Finn, of Lucy. I scratched under Luna's chin and she chirped at me before stretching out in the rectangle of sunlight from the window.

With a sigh, I got back to work.

I stood and stretched, my back cracking. I'd almost gotten through an entire shelf. The books still needed to be re-shelved, but they were sorted. Mostly. I'd had a similar job in Citadel with scrolls and parchments that catalogued food stores. I crouched to grab the last book on the shelf—an old Encyclopedia—when I noticed another book, smaller, wedged between the back of the bookcase and the second to bottom shelf. I pried it loose and dusted off the cover. It was a little larger than my hand and very thin. There was nothing on the dark green cover or the spine.

I retreated to the single candle I'd kept burning as the sunlight started to fail and flipped through the book once. The back pages were empty, but the front was full of someone's handwriting. It looked vaguely familiar. Perhaps it was from one of the scribes who'd copied one of the many books I'd already shelved. They all signed their books in the front cover and I opened this one there to see.

My heart jumped to my throat and my hands started to shake. I brought the book closer to my face, to make sure the low light wasn't playing tricks. In the upper corner, in a flowing, small script that I now realized I would know anywhere, was Rosemarie's name. I'd seen her write it in her own books of garden and plant records she'd kept.

My hands were shaking harder than they'd ever shaken. I turned to the first page with fingers that didn't seem to want to work and found her words, carefully scrawled. It was a research notebook, notes about vitium, about where it was in the earth, about how to mine it. Why were Rosemarie's words here? Why was she writing about vitium?

I'd only read a few lines when Cillian walked in. I dropped the book quickly onto the pile I was nearest and looked at him, hoping he wouldn't ask about the book.

"Am I interrupting?" he asked, his expression confused. I made myself smile.

"No." I cleared my throat. "No. My eyes are just starting to get tired." I maintained my smile, my heart pounding.

"Good." He smiled and offered me his arm. "Ready for dinner?"

I took his arm, hoping he couldn't feel my hands shaking. My mind was reeling. Why were Rosemarie's words, a book with her handwriting, her name, in Sunnybrook?

I whistled softly and Luna's ears perked. "Come," I said, and she followed languidly, only stepping close when we stepped out into the cold autumn air. I sniffed the air and shivered, even in my thick, warm sweater. It would snow soon.

"We'll get you a coat," Cillian said, patting my hand on his arm. It was still strange to pick up so little from him, even with skin on skin contact. I only felt a bit of nervousness, colored red with desire. I blushed as my mind still raced.

"Thank you." Luna pressed against my leg as we walked. I wondered if I could trust Cillian. I felt like I could trust Lucy, and she was his sister, and I had to know something. I took a deep breath. "Cillian?" It felt odd saying his name, holding his arm, walking so close. "Who took care of the library before me?" My voice shook and he looked down at me with a furrowed brow. "You said it had been a while. I was just curious." I looked away, pretending to watch my step. I wasn't good at playing the conversation game.

"Oh, well, I can't remember her name." He cleared his throat and his expression grew sad. "I think she died during the malady—a plague that came through about ten years ago and killed over thirty of us." He sighed and patted my hand on his. "I'm sorry I can't remember. I was 19 and trying to help with all the new orphans the malady caused. Lucy and Finn were in that group, I remember."

"Thank you," I said, resolving to try and let go of the mystery until I could get back to the library the next day.

"You need to stop thanking me so much," he said, gently pulling me a little closer to avoid running into people as we entered a more congested area, filled with people finishing their evening chores before heading to the commissary. "We're friends." He cleared his throat. "Or, well, I mean, I'd like to be. Friends, that is." He laughed and brushed his free hand through his hair. "God, I'm usually better than this. At speaking, I mean. Talking, you know." He laughed again and I felt myself relax.

He was taller than anyone I'd ever known and I had to look up to see his face. His skin was tan and his hair was light blonde and thick. He was very handsome, his eyes a dark, rich brown. He smiled at me with one side of his mouth and I smiled back, feeling a blush creep into my cheeks. He looked at me in a way I'd only ever been looked at by Finn and it felt kind of nice, if not quite right.

I felt awkward thinking of him that way, even if felt nice, so I focused on making a mental map of the city instead. The town was laid out like a checkerboard or a square bullseye. The library was near the square. The apartments were in a ring around that, and the businesses, including the commissary, were in a ring around those. The wall surrounded three sides of the city, and a dense copse of woods surrounded the back, backed up by the quarry cliffs.

"See that building over there?" he asked, pointing to one of the apartment buildings. I nodded. "It's called the

Grackle—all the apartments have bird names, you know." I hadn't noticed, but now that he mentioned it, I saw a small sign, near the roof, with the name and a rough outline of a bird with a long, pointed beak. "Anyway, that's where I lived. Before I became mayor and moved to the Hawk."

"It's nice," I said, though it looked more beaten than the other buildings we'd seen.

"It needs some repair," he said, blushing. "Only a few live there now, and we've offered them other apartments, they just won't move. We want to use the older buildings for public works." He looked at it and shook his head. "Most of the people who died from the malady lived there, and it's hard to get people to move in." He shrugged.

We walked slowly, though the crowd around us moved quickly. I felt Luna's growl through her side as the people pressed around us.

"Isn't the commissary that way?" I asked pointing to the moving people. The commissary was just off the other side of the square, which was quite large, but we were walking the other way.

"I just thought we could walk a bit first," he said, stumbling a bit in his step. "I should have asked. I just thought we could talk. We can go there now." He went to turn us, his grip on my arm and hand firm but not uncomfortable.

"Oh, no, let's walk." The words felt odd in my mouth. I hadn't even meant to say them. But he seemed so embarrassed, and he was being so kind.

He smiled ruefully and we kept going. Luna settled some as we left the throng of people, but still didn't leave her spot pressed against my leg.

He pointed out more facts about the town as we walked. We circled the statue in the center of town, and he told me about the riot—right after the malady struck and killed a few dozen people—that caused it to stand at such an odd angle.

"Couldn't you fix it?" I asked, thinking the man in the statue looked sad, leaning like that.

He nodded. "We could, but people need to remember." He patted my hand again and this time left his fingers there, resting atop mine. His skin was warm and my belly flipped.

We circled back around toward the commissary and suddenly I was overwhelmed with the smell of dead flesh. It made me sick to my stomach. Cillian grimaced.

"That's the butcher," he said, pointing to a door, propped open. I covered my mouth with my hand to try and keep the smell out. "You get used to it after a while, and it's not so bad when it gets colder." He shrugged and squeezed my fingers. He'd somehow curled his fingers under mine, and it was almost like we were holding hands. His skin was warm, but it felt off. "I worked there when I was younger, from fourteen to eighteen. The butcher's a good man," he affirmed, wrinkling his nose at the smell, too. We passed it shortly and a breeze blew the foul air the other way.

"What did you do after that?" I asked, able to breathe fully again.

He squeezed my fingers and smiled. "I became mayor."

Finally, as I shivered, he led me past the crowd lined up outside the commissary and into the open double door. People were milling about, settling their plates at long wooden tables and calling out to friends. The whole atmosphere was much more relaxed than it had been this morning. Luna was pressing into my leg as if she was glued there and I ducked enough to touch her head.

"Sir!" someone called, and Cillian gently pulled me to a stop. "May I have a moment?"

While Cillian talked, never letting go of my arm, I looked around the room. I caught Lucy's eye from her spot behind the line. She smiled at me, but her face was pinched, maybe a little angry.

The crowd shifted and my eyes went toward the table where we'd sat that morning. Morrigan and Finn were already there. Sadness settled in me as I saw them. Finn seemed like he was so far away. Morrigan, as if she knew I was there, looked over her shoulder and met my gaze. She smiled, but it didn't reach her eyes. She leaned toward Finn, her hand against his neck, and said something into his ear. He laughed, a big full laugh that I heard over the crowd, then leaned in and kissed her.

The room spun and I felt Cillian's grip on my arm tighten.

"Erilyn?" he asked, suddenly in front of me, between the table and me, blocking me from seeing. "Are you OK? You're pale."

"I think—" I had to swallow as tears threatened. "I think it's all the people," I barely whispered, my voice coming out almost a hiccup. "I think I'll just go to Lucy's."

"I'll take you," he said, taking a step closer. People were stopping to watch, and I had to get out. Their stares pressed against me and I felt suffocated.

"No," I said taking a deep breath and smiling up at him. He looked concerned. "I'll be fine."

I pulled away, but his hand lingered on mine. I felt a tingle of desire from him, but it just amplified the pain I was feeling. Finn had kissed Morrigan. I knew it would happen, but it had happened so quickly. Less than a day. I'd expected more time to adjust, to distance myself. I wanted to vomit.

"I'll have breakfast for us in my office tomorrow," he said, his face shadowed with concern. "Just for us. No crowd." I was backing away and nodded.

"Thank you," I said. He opened his mouth to say something, but I was gone, out the double doors, trying not to run past the people still in line in the cold.

The cold air seemed colder than it had just moments before, but I was flushed now, my heart racing. I walked blindly toward the row of apartments, not paying attention to where I was going.

Luna chirped a few moments later and I looked around. I didn't know where I was. I didn't know what building was Lucy's. I looked at the building names. The Cardinal. The Stork. The Swan. I kept walking until I thought I recognized it. Night had fallen and I was shivering in my sweater, but it didn't matter. I walked up the steps, recognizing Lucy's curtains through the window in the moonlight. She lived in the Hummingbird.

I reached the landing and her door flew open. She immediately pulled me into a hug and I gasped. She should still be in the commissary. "You're freezing," she said, pulling me inside and closing the door behind the tip of Luna's long white tail.

Two lanterns were burning and the room was lit in a comfortable, soft yellow glow. She pulled me toward a bowl of soup she had waiting.

After she'd settled my cold hands around the warm bowl, she sat in front of me and sighed. I brought the soup to me mechanically, still feeling shocky. "I'm so sorry, Erilyn." I looked up at her from my first bite of food. "I'm just so sorry. I didn't know until they came in, and I couldn't leave to warn you."

"What do you mean?" I asked, my tone not at all convincing.

"Finn and Morrigan." She shook her head and pounded the small table with her fist, causing Luna to jump. "Sorry, girl." She stroked Luna's back.

"I don't know what you mean," I said, taking a bite and not tasting it.

"Anyone with eyes can see that you love Finn." Her voice was firm, but full of empathy.

My eyes closed as tears sprung up. Love. I hadn't really thought about what I felt for Finn, but love seemed like an appropriate term. I sat the bowl down as my stomach clenched in pain.

She sighed and placed a slice of warm bread in my hand. "I thought—" her voice trailed off as she met my eyes bleary eyes. "I've known Finn for as long as I can remember. We were in the same group home until Cill adopted me. I *know* him. And I was sure, *sure*, that you and he. Well, he just had that look." She sighed again and angrily shoved a piece of bread in her mouth.

"We're friends," I said, my voice quavering and my hands shaking. Lucy took my hands in hers. Her hands were larger than mine, thinner, and covered in a smattering of freckles.

"He shouldn't be with her," she said, squeezing my fingers hard. "Something isn't right there. They were over. I saw it." She shook her head. "He cares about you. Deeply. It's as plain as the freckles on my nose." My heart jumped. I'd thought the same.

"And Finn would *never* be this callous on his own. He's always put everyone else's feelings before his own. He knew you'd be there, he wouldn't have—just, something isn't right. But I'll figure out what's going on." She squeezed my hands again and handed me more bread, I hadn't realized I'd eaten the first piece. This one had soft cheese spread across it.

Lucy didn't say anything as tears trickled down my face. Instead, she dipped more soup from the small pot she'd brought into my bowl and then made a bowl for herself. We ate in silence as I calmed myself down. Lucy's presence was a balm.

"So," I said, my stomach distended and full, "Cillian adopted you?"

Lucy smiled and we settled into more comfortable positions, Luna laying across my lap like a very heavy, very long, child. Lucy told me about how the malady had claimed her parents' lives and Cillian had taken her in. Lucy loved Cillian and in that moment, some part of me grew angry. Cillian was a good man. Why was I so resistant to the idea of his friendship, or whatever it was he seemed to be interested in? Finn was with Morrigan. I had nothing stopping me from forming new relationships.

We talked until we both grew sleepy. I'd heard people come to their apartments and go home, heard murmured conversations, but it was quiet now. We'd talked for hours.

Lucy made up a bed for me on the floor with her cushions and blankets—she had so many—and promised to have a real cot for me, like hers, by the next day.

I still hurt, but I felt better. I wasn't used to having a friend like Lucy, and I knew that being here would be OK with her to talk to like this.

As I drifted off, still hurting, the last image I saw in my troubled mind was Morrigan's look toward me, full of something dark, as Finn kissed her.

Chapter Twenty-Two
The Workshop

Finn

The day after he came back to Sunnybrook, Morrigan presented Finn with a workshop. He'd always worked from his apartment, or outside for larger pieces. The old carpenter had had a workshop, but after he died the city had reclaimed it.

This new space was perfect. It had been an old patrol shed that had been gutted and refilled with new benches, saws, and chisels ready and waiting for him. It was deep in the woods, unlike any of the other shops in town, because Morrigan said she wanted him to have the freedom to work without prying eyes, and she visited at least once a day.

When she visited, he tried showing her some of his new work. The other local shops had been flooding him with orders, which surprised him, because before he had to go around and almost beg for work. But Morrigan rarely had time to do more than look behind the curtain beneath the counter check to make sure he had enough firewood and check inside the single cabinet to make sure he had enough materials to work with. She always ended her short visit with a kiss, though, and it held his loneliness at bay and left him thinking of her for the rest of the day.

As the weeks passed, the air grew colder and the walk to and from town after breakfast and before dinner became more and more uncomfortable. He started to crave those moments she was there with him, dream about her kisses, since she always seemed to work late now and he never saw her after dinner for more than a few minutes.

One day she was particularly attentive during her midday visit. She'd pinned him to the closed door and his hands roved over her back and sides, trying to find her skin somewhere around the skintight black leather.

"Now, Finley." She playfully smacked his chest before biting his earlobe. "You know I'm working right now." She kissed him hard once more before pulling the door open to leave.

He followed her out, letting the air cool his overheated skin. "What about after dinner?" he asked.

She shrugged as she walked away. "I have to work late." She blew him a kiss over her shoulder and disappeared into the shadowed forest.

He stood in the cold for a long moment before he realized it was snowing. He held his hand up and caught a few of the tiny white flakes. The ground was coated with a thin powdering of white.

As he watched the snowfall, a thought tugged at him, though he couldn't quite place it. He looked up into the snow, falling in dizzying spirals, and then out into the shadowed woods. He imagined Luna there and scratched his arm as his skin buzzed. Luna would be hard to see in the snow, hiding in shadow and light alike.

He hadn't seen Luna, except for from a distance, since their first morning here. He imagined her, pressed against Erilyn's legs, chirping. He imagined her playing in the snow. He couldn't picture Erilyn's face, and when he tried, the buzzing grew quickly so that it was nearly unbearable.

He quickly thought of Luna again instead. He would like to see her playing in the snow, to see her running through snowdrifts. There beside her was Erilyn. He closed his eyes, and despite the buzzing, he pictured her—cheeks rosy, hair hanging in a long, dark golden sheet down her back, watching the snow fall with him. He grabbed his head, a sudden pain behind his eyes, and the image vanished.

With a sigh, he went back into his shop and resumed his work on a chair Cillian had requested for his office. He hadn't told Morrigan about it. She hadn't seemed interested in his work, but the reason he hadn't mentioned it was he was afraid she wouldn't let him deliver it, since Erilyn might be there. He could barely remember his time with Erilyn, but he knew she was his friend, and he wanted to see her, to make sure she was OK. He thought maybe he should be worried about her, but he couldn't remember why.

The chair Cillian had ordered was large and ornate, but he was working quickly, hoping to get it done today. With frozen hands he went back into his workshop, stoked the fire, and worked as fast as he could on the chair, suddenly eager to get it into town.

He borrowed a hand wagon from Arlie, the boy he got his firewood from. Arlie had been the carpenter's son and always gave Finn a fair price for the wood. Finn often borrowed Arlie's cart to deliver larger pieces and in exchange, Finn repaired the cart, and anything else Arlie needed fixing, for free.

He almost ran the wagon back to his shop once he had it. Carefully he loaded the heavy chair, careful not to dent or scratch the intricately carved roses in the arms and back, before covering it with an old quilt. It was more intricate than the other chairs in Cillian's office, but Finn didn't ask questions. The general rule in Sunnybrook was the mayor was to be given whatever he asked for and in exchange he wouldn't ask for much. That had always been true, but this time Cillian had made promises to Finn. He would have free choice of all the wood that had been salvaged from the forests outside the wall for his shop for this particular chair.

It took him over an hour to pull the heavy cart over tree roots and through trees, and by the time he reached town, he'd missed the noon meal. It didn't matter, though, because he never came back into town for it anyway. It was too far to walk and he was rarely hungry until dinner. His time in the woods had changed his eating habits.

The wagon moved more easily on the stone streets, though he was careful not to jostle it against the sides too much. He had to move even more slowly because the streets were slick from the slight snowfall. But when he saw the clock tower his pace increased.

The wagon wouldn't fit through the doors that led into the library, so Finn made sure the quilt was covering it adequately before pushing it up to the building with a deep breath.

He made his way back to the library first—the only way to get to Cillian's office. It smelled less musty than he remembered. He hadn't been in here since he was a child, and he hadn't been back since his mother died. His heart was pounding as he walked deeper into the dark room.

His eyes adjusted to the low light slowly. Books were stacked on the floor and on tables. One table was clear except for pages of notes. Finn leaned closed to see what they were—book titles and authors' names in loopy, lovely handwriting. His stomach flipped as he realized it had to be Erilyn's handwriting he was seeing. His skin buzzed and his head started to ache.

He looked around, ignoring the headache. She was in here, wasn't she? Just the thought of it set the buzzing to an extreme, but still he looked and hoped.

There was no one, but faintly he heard a sound—voices coming from Cillian's office. The last time he'd been in there was when he was ten and Arlie's dad had asked if he could adopt Finn as an apprentice.

He walked to that door now, his headache growing worse with each step, the buzz growing louder. He could just bring the chair in and leave it here, but he wanted to give it to Cillian in person. He could hear their voices more clearly now. He thought he heard laughter—Erilyn's laughter. He didn't think he'd ever heard her laugh before. Then again, his memory of their time together was a fog, so he couldn't be sure.

Despite his headache growing worse and moving between his eyes, he knocked on the door. The door opened and Finn looked up at the slightly taller, more muscular Cillian. The mayor's hair wasn't slicked back, as it normally was, and he was smiling in a way Finn had never seen. He always had seemed so stoic before.

"Finley!" he said jovially, clapping him on the shoulder. "Finished my chair already?" he asked, looking behind him for it.

"Yes sir," Finn said, fighting the urge to look past him to see if it was Erilyn in the room. "It's outside. Covered. I didn't have a key for the big double doors on the side to bring it in."

"I'll get it," Cillian said, smiling at Finn as if he were a child. "I'll be right back," he said, turning back to whoever was in the room.

Cillian brushed past Finn. If it had been any other client, he would have offered to help, gone with him, but he felt glued to the spot as his eyes landed on her.

Erilyn sat on the couch, staring down into a mug in her hands. Luna, who had been stretched in the sunlight from one of the room's large windows, saw Finn and sprang toward him. She rubbed around his legs, almost knocking him over, and he smiled. She stood on her hind legs—her front paws resting on his chest, and head butted him with a loud purr.

"Luna," he said, his headache easing slightly. He rubbed under her chin and between her ears. He took a deep breath and looked up to see Erilyn—her gray eyes wide, her cheeks pink. Seeing her now made the fog in his brain begin to lift. He could remember, suddenly, the way it had felt to hold her, to talk quietly with her, the way it felt to hold her small body against his. His headache was gone. The buzzing was gone. He remembered she could do things and he knew as her eyes widened and her cheeks flushed that she was feeling what he was. He remembered her, remembered them.

And then just as suddenly, the headache came roaring back. He winced and pushed the heel of his hand against his temple. "It's snowing," he said, his voice breaking. He winced again as the buzzing spread across his skin. Erilyn stood, still silent, as if she were going to come to him, when Cillian's voice rang out into the library. Luna chirped, dropped from standing against Finn, and returned to her space in the sunlight.

"Finley!" Cillian said, smiling as he carried the chair easily, even though Finn knew how heavy it was. "It's beautiful. Erilyn, come see." He sat the chair in the library in the shaft of sunlight.

Erilyn looked at Finn for a long moment and then glanced at the window where snow was starting to gather. She walked past him, brushing against him even as she turned to avoid it. That slight touched cleared the fog again and Finn almost gasped with the pain he felt at losing her, at having forgotten her.

"It's beautiful," Erilyn said, letting her fingers trail lightly across the roses.

"Very well done," Cillian said, moving to stand near Erilyn.

Jealousy sprang to life in Finn only to vanish a moment later. He'd been the one to walk away and he was with Morrigan, though in his moment he couldn't figure out why. It was as if the last few weeks had been a dream, and not one he'd wanted to have.

"I thought you could use your own chair," Cillian said to Erilyn, collecting a cushion Finn hadn't seen leaning against the way and placing it in the seat. "You're always sitting on the floor," he said with a shrug.

Erilyn gave him a small smile and placed her hand on his for a moment, causing Finn to bristle. "Thank you." She glanced at Finn, saw his face, and her hand fell from Cillian's.

Finn cleared his throat, confused, sad, and angry. The buzzing was making it hard to think. "I should get the cart back," he said. He wished Cillian would leave so he could talk to Erilyn, though he didn't know what he would say.

He stared at Erilyn for a long moment and she stared back, her expression unreadable. Cillian moved so that he was standing just behind her.

"Thanks again, Finley." He smiled, hands behind his back. "I've just asked Erilyn to the gala. First snow and all, it'll be in a few days. Will you and Morrigan be attending?"

"The gala," Finn said, nodding. "Yeah. Yes. We'll be there." The buzzing was so bad it was all he could do to stay upright. It hurt. He met Erilyn's gaze again and promised himself he would talk to her at the gala.

"Good," Cillian said, putting his hand on the small of Erilyn's back. She looked up at him, a little startled. "Should we finish our tea before getting back to work?"

She nodded and let him guide her toward his office. She looked over her shoulder once toward Finn, who still stood dumbly in the middle of the room, his hands clenched. The door closed behind her and Finn was left alone.

He returned Arlie's cart and walked slowly back to his workshop. Some days, Morrigan would come to walk him back into town for dinner, but he didn't feel like it today. He stopped at one of the patrol stands and left a message for her—he was sick and would see her for breakfast. He needed time to think, alone. He would stay in his shop.

As he walked, the snow picked up. The grass and leaves were almost covered. Back in his small building, he stoked his fire and slowly added scrap wood until it filled the room with warmth and light. He barred the door and sat at his worktable. He had a dozen projects—small gifts, a few tables, even a pipe—waiting to be started, but had no motivation to start any.

He pulled a small bag to him. It had been a gift from the local stonemason—small bits of stone that were beautiful, but oddly shaped. Finn dumped them into his hand and sifted through them until he found the one he wanted—a piece of turquoise shaped like a tiny raindrop.

He replaced the rest in the bag. His head still buzzed, but he ignored it along with the pain between his eyes. The look Erilyn had given him as she walked into the office was stuck in his head. It was a look of hopefulness.

He decided he would carve a ring with this teardrop stone inset. Something beautiful. As he worked, he thought of Erilyn, of that look. The buzzing stuck with him, but he ignored it as best he could.

He spent the rest of the night working on the ring. He fell asleep with his head on his arms, lulled by the fading light from the fireplace.

Chapter Twenty-Three
Metamorphosis

Erilyn

I hunched over the table in the chair Cillian had given me—the one Finn had made—and I tried not to think of either of them. Cillian, the man who would escort me to my first gala, who had brought me gifts each day and eaten with me in private so I didn't have to eat with a crowd. Finn, the man who had broken through the walls I'd carefully constructed around my heart, who'd shown me that I was capable of loving and trusting someone, and then walked away. Thinking of either of them was too painful, too confusing, and I needed a clear head for what I was doing.

For days now I'd been carefully copying Rosemarie's notes onto my own paper so that, even if one copy were lost, one would survive. I planned to hide my copy and keep Rosemarie's with me. I needed to have that piece of her, even if I wasn't sure what it meant yet. It was cryptic, but slowly I was finding new bits to piece together.

I'd asked Lucy about Rosemarie, but she didn't remember her. She'd been so young when Rosemarie left, but I knew she'd been here, in this room, touching this table and these books, and it made this place feel more like home.

In her notes, Rosemarie had written references to other books. This alone made me keep organizing the books, to find the books she mentioned. Most of them were science texts that were filled with words I didn't understand and concepts that sounded like gibberish, but she'd left bookmarks, underlined things, and I carefully copied those pieces into her notebook and then onto my own pages. It was a long, drawn out process, and it was exhausting.

I paused to check the time. From the way the light slanted into the room, it was almost noon. Cillian would be in soon with lunch. I carefully tucked her notebook into my bag, the one I'd saved after the Wylden burned my tree, then tucked my copied pages into the book I was currently working from. I stacked other books on top of it. Right on time, Cillian came in carrying a covered tray with a cloth flower lying on top.

"Here or my office?" he asked, closing the library door with his foot.

"Your office is warmer," I said with a smile, surprised that it felt genuine. I'd grown accustomed to our meals in his office over the last couple of weeks. I couldn't read him except when he was feeling something very strongly, so being with him was soothing, whereas being in town around other people grated on my nerves. Being with him was like being alone without the loneliness.

I opened the door for him and Luna darted in, stretching luxuriously in front of the fireplace. The library was much cooler, but there were vents from the fireplace's chimney that piped the warmer air in, so it wasn't cold.

Cillian sat the tray on the small coffee table and I sat on the couch, closest to the fire, where he always invited me to sit. He smiled as he uncovered the tray with a flourish.

Most days, lunch was made up of leftovers from breakfast or dinner the night before, but this was a feast in and of itself. Boiled eggs, beautiful salads — where they got the fresh produce in such cold weather, I didn't know — with nuts and a creamy dressing, Lucy's goat cheese and fresh, steaming bread, and some kind of pudding on the side. There was even a bowl of raw scraps of meat that Cillian sat in front of Luna.

Cillian sat beside me and held out a flower made of stiff, red cloth, shaped like a rose. "For you," he said with a smile, and I took it, feeling silly. "There aren't any real ones in bloom." He shrugged. I liked these moments alone with Cillian. He often walked me home at night, but if we saw other people he grew stiff, like he was better than the people he passed, and it made me uncomfortable. But when it was just the two of us, he was softer, more carefree.

"It's beautiful," I said, laying it carefully in my lap.

"I was hoping you'd wear it tonight. To the gala. If you're still planning on coming with me. I mean, letting me escort you there." I'd never seen him this flustered before. It was disarming and I smiled. His eyes were deep brown and looked warm in the firelight.

"Of course I haven't changed my mind," I said, feeling that strange tightening of my gut that I only felt around

Cillian. It wasn't nervousness, and it wasn't that deep, pure desire I'd felt with Finn, but it was something that made me stop and take a breath. The hints of shared desire, perhaps.

His posture relaxed and we ate in companionable silence. As we ate, I wondered what was expected of me at a gala. I didn't have any clothes except the ones Lucy had given me and it suddenly occurred to me I might need something else.

With the food gone—Cillian had eaten most of it—he made tea from rosehips and raspberry leaves. While it steeped, I moved to the floor, flower still in one hand, to pet Luna. Cillian watched me from the couch and the weight of his gaze caused that feeling in my lower belly to increase. I'd never felt his desire this strong and it piqued something in me.

I ducked my head, suddenly nervous and a little shy. He poured two mugs of tea and offered me one, joining me on the floor.

I sipped it, the hot liquid burning the tip of my tongue. "Thank you," I whispered.

When he didn't answer, I looked up. He was sitting so close my breath felt caught. Cillian was a handsome man. His hair, though thick, always looked wispy and soft. I'd never noticed the flecks of gold in his eyes until this moment. I felt my cheeks warming, and it wasn't from the fire.

"Erilyn," he said, setting his mug down and taking mine and to put beside his. "I'm really glad you came here." He took my hands in his, warm from the tea.

Normally I'd pull away. He touched me often, but I rarely let it go on for more than a moment or two. I didn't pull away this time. I'd felt strange ever since Finn's visit a few days earlier. Reckless.

I nodded at Cillian. "Me too," I said, which was more true than I'd realized. He smiled then and slowly leaned toward me. My heart didn't race as it had always done with Finn. My hands didn't shake. I felt frozen. And when his lips touched mine, warm and soft, I felt that tingling desire in my low belly grow the slightest bit.

He pulled away after a moment, a smile on his tan face.

Lucy burst in the room before I could even figure out what it was I was feeling. Cillian had kissed me and I'd felt...something.

"Are you ready?" she asked me, then immediately turned to her brother. "Is she ready?" She was smiling, her nose red from the cold.

"Ready?" I asked, mind still reeling.

"Oh, I forgot." Cillian blushed and stood, brushing off his pants as if the immaculately kept floor had been dirty. "Lucy has offered to help you get ready for tonight." He offered me his hand, our tea forgotten, and I let him help me up.

"Come on!" she said, grabbing my arm. "It's already past noon."

She pulled me away from Cillian, whose hand was still lightly in mine. As she tugged me out, I grabbed my bag from where I'd left it by the door.

The office door closed and I looked toward my books where my notes were hidden. They'd have to wait until tomorrow.

Lucy shook the snow from her hair once we were back in her apartment. Each of our two cots had a dress lying atop it. Sometimes I still felt overwhelmed by how generous Lucy was with me—inviting me into her home and making it mine as well as hers. Luna sniffed the table where Lucy usually had food waiting when we came back in the evenings. She dropped a handful of crumbled cheese there before scratching the cat between her ears.

"What's this?" I picked up the dress on my cot and looked at it in the light from the window. It was long, silky soft, and a dark, burnt gold.

"Cillian picked it out," Lucy said with a wink and a smile. "Go put it on and then we'll work on your hair." She shoved me into the bathroom with a smile.

The dress slipped on as if it were made for me. The neckline rested in a scoop against my collarbone, covering my shoulders but leaving my arms bare. Fabric gathered at my waist and then flowed in gentle folds down to the tops of my feet. The only embellishment was some finely done embroidery in a lighter gold across my torso.

I stepped out of the bathroom and Lucy smiled. She was wearing the other dress, green like summer grass, and fitted to her waist where it grew loose and swishy.

"Perfect." She clapped her hands. "Now, let's get to work!" Her long legs took her to a bag sitting by the door in only a couple of strides, her dress swishing around her pale legs. She pushed the curtains open wide and motioned for me to sit on the wooden chest.

From the bag she pulled combs, clips, rags, and many jars of varying sizes and shapes filled with different colors and textures. I opened one and sniffed it—crushed up rose petals and something else sweet and pungent. I opened another and quickly closed the lid as my eyes started to water.

"I need all this?" I swept my arm across the things she'd laid out.

She nodded, her green eyes sparkling like dew-drenched grass. "Ready to get started?" I could feel the excitement vibrating from her, and found myself smiling.

"Do I have a choice?" She laughed and shook her head, wild curls flying.

For the rest of the day, Lucy remade me. She'd braided my hair the night before—something she'd taken to doing before we went to bed at night when we weren't too tired—and now she took the braid out of my hair and brushed out the main tangles with a comb and her fingers. As she worked, she talked. I was able to sit quietly and listen to stories about Cillian as a younger man. Before he'd been made mayor, he used to sneak out of the wall at night and sleep under the stars just to prove he was brave enough. He'd stopped when Lucy had tried to sneak out with him. It made me smile to think of him, wild and free, tamed only by his desire to keep his adopted little sister safe. And then the memory of his kiss resurfaced and I felt confused again.

It had been nice, kissing him, but something about it hadn't felt quite right.

I had to sit stock still with my eyes closed as Lucy put things on my face. Some things were cool and soft and others made me sneeze as powder tickled my nose. I smiled when she dabbed whatever had been in the rosy smelling jar on my cheeks and lips. It was cool and I could smell it even after she'd moved on to other things.

When I was finally allowed to open my eyes, my face felt funny, like I was wearing a second skin. She turned me so that I was facing away from the window and I watched her shadow as she began gathering my hair in her hands, pulling it into sections and braiding little bits back, tying them all together in some intricate knot on top of my head. She worked quickly, talking the whole time, and I relaxed with the sun on my back and her voice lulling me as she told me about her first kiss to a boy named Arlie. She stumbled over her words and I felt her mood shift from relaxed and happy to anxious in a moment. She was back to happy shortly after, though, and I quickly forgot her anxiety.

"Almost done," she said, her words soft as she pulled a wooden box from the bag. From the box, she pulled a thin wreath of green leaves with tiny red berries. She sat the wreath on my head and with two final pins secured it. "There." She stood back and smiled. "Perfect. You can go look in the mirror in the bathroom while I get ready!" Her good mood was back and I made my way back into the bathroom through the darkening room.

I used the a bit of flint to light the candle that sat on the basin and held it up to see myself in the old glass. My eyes opened wide as I took in the face that looked back at me. My eyes were lined with black, making them look bigger and bluer than they were. My lips and cheeks were rosy and my skin looked impossibly smooth. My hair was woven into countless braids of different sizes, which all were tied together in a beautiful array at the crown of my head. But what I loved most was the way the leaves and berries, sitting like a crown woven into my hair, made me feel like I was back in the forest. I missed my pine, my pond, my quiet, simple life, and this little bit made me feel less like I'd left it all behind.

"Do you like it?" Lucy was just outside the bathroom door, her hands in her own hair, taming her curls into a sleek knot on top of her head.

I turned and wrapped my arms around her thin frame and she laughed, hugging me back with one arm while the other held her hair. "Yes." I pulled away from her, tears in my eyes. "I've never—" I turned back to the mirror and shrugged as I looked at Lucy's reflection behind me. "I never thought about the way I look. At least, I didn't think about what it might be like to feel—" I looked at the wreath in my hair again, at the way the gold fabric on my shoulders made my skin look warm, "beautiful."

She smiled with one side of her mouth and shrugged. "Happy to help." She finished tucking a metal pin in her bun, her hair tame for the first time since I'd known her. "Oh! I almost forgot." She pulled a thick, knitted dark green shawl and matching, soft looking dark green shoes from the foot of my bed. I hadn't seen them before as they'd been in a shadow. I slipped the shawl over my shoulders and then the shoes on my feet and felt the slight chill dissipate.

Lucy was dabbing some of the rose-tinted liquid on her lips when there was a knock on the door.

"Can you get that?" she asked with a wink. I smoothed the soft fabric over my belly nervously. I opened the door and looked up at Cillian, who smiled at me with one side of his mouth, his dark eyes bright. He wore warm looking wool pants with a matching jacket that were a few shades darker than my dress and fit him like a second skin. His hair, which he'd been leaving loose and free lately, was brushed back again. His smile grew as he looked at my face and I felt myself blush as he glanced toward my overly red lips. I fought the urge to feel them as I remembered his mouth on mine.

"Erilyn." He closed the distance between us and took my hands before bringing them to his lips to kiss my knuckles. "You're breathtaking." He breathed the words and my skin tingled. I met his dark brown eyes and felt that odd tingle in my gut. It was stronger, like when he'd kissed me, and it made me nervous.

"Thank you." I said softly. "You look very handsome." I took a steadying breath.

"No one will notice me if I'm next to you," he said, smiling and showing his straight, white teeth. He turned to Lucy. "Are you ready?"

She laughed. "I am, but I'm going to go by the commissary to make sure nothing was left behind." She winked at Cillian. "Someone has to make things run smoothly."

My smile fell. "You're not coming with us?"

"I'm sure I'll see you," she said, giving me a full, noonday smile. "The party has probably already started," she said, looking out at the setting sunlight. "And I have to go do damage control with the food." She gave me a one-armed hug as she slipped a white knitted shawl over her own shoulders and zipped out of the room.

Cillian offered me his arm and I took it. He patted my hand where it rested in the crook of his arm. "Some of the children are anxious to give Luna some toys they've made—little mice made out of bits of cloth and straw. They've worked on them in their free time since you first brought her in the commissary." He laughed. "She's become a celebrity—the great white cat from outside the wall."

Luna chirped at me and cleaned her paws as if that were the only suitable title for her and I laughed. "Good. I mean, that's nice."

"Shall we?" He motioned toward the door and I nodded. Luna followed us out. Snow was falling lightly and I tucked myself closer to him without thinking about it. He smiled and leaned down to place a chaste kiss against my temple. My face warmed as an image of not Cillian, but Finn, rose up in my mind. I remembered Finn holding me, kissing my hair, telling me it would be OK. I squashed those thoughts and tried to focus on the here and now—on Cillian's arm beneath my hands, on the way his lips had felt against my skin instead of Finn's. I stood up taller. More than ever, with Cillian on my arm and Finn still buried in my heart, I felt more out of control than I ever had before.

Chapter Twenty-Four
The Gala

Finn

The sun was starting to set. Finley had hastily changed into the clothes Morrigan had brought for him—pants and a shirt that were such a dark shade of blue they may as well be black—and a single red lily made of cloth that he pinned to his shirt. He had just finished shaving in his small sink when she'd burst into his apartment, a dress draped over her arm. Her hair was pulled back into a high ponytail and slicked back to show off her striking cheekbones, and her lips were a deep, dark red. She looked fiercely beautiful.

She kissed him, her lips warm. He held her close, but he didn't feel as strongly about her as he had before. Before he saw Erilyn in the library and started to remember. She smiled into his mouth then gently pushed him away. "I just need to change and then we can go." He nodded and started to leave the room when she grabbed his arm and smiled. "No need to leave." Her voice was husky and low.

Before he could respond, she slipped the long jacket she wore off her shoulders, revealing that she only wore her underclothes beneath it. Finley's mouth went dry. "Help me slip it on?" She turned, exposing her back to him. He wanted to run his hand between her shoulder blades, to rest it in the small of her back. He carefully removed her dress from the hanger—the same red as her lips—and stepped around her so she could step into it. He slid it up her body. She wriggled a little as he did so until he pulled it up to her shoulders. Two straps draped over her shoulders and it buttoned just behind her neck. The back was left open. He buttoned the single button slowly and allowed his hand to trace the line of her spine. She leaned into him and almost purred.

"Thank you." She leaned up and kissed him once more—her lips against his opened the tiniest bit and she gripped his shirt in both hands before stepping away.

As night fell, Morrigan and Finley walked into the town square, her hand hot in his. It was brightly lit with torches and colorful glass lanterns. In the center of town, near the statue, was a larger fire that smelled of pine and herbs. Finley breathed it all in. As a child, he and his mother had come to this celebration every year and watched from the outskirts, enjoying the sights and sounds before trying to trade some of his mother's knitted wares at one of the tables just outside the heat of the main fire. He'd never wanted anything more than to smell the smells and watch all the interesting people, but here he was, dressed richly with the captain of the patrol on his arm. He'd never wanted this, but it felt good.

Morrigan smiled, the red stain she'd put on her lips drawing his eyes down to her mouth, and leaned close. "We may be the most attractive couple here." Her breath tickled his ear and he shivered.

He was about to lean down and kiss her bare shoulder—she'd refused a shawl, saying she wasn't cold—when soft applause across the square drew his gaze. The crowd shifted and Cillian stepped through, Erilyn at his side. Finn felt his mouth go dry, felt his heart stutter. Morrigan's hand in his was suddenly too hot and he wanted to let it go.

Even from a distance, all Finn could see was her, and the way the firelight made her look like a sunbeam on the surface of a lake. He was aware of every heartbeat. Time seemed to slow.

After an eternal moment of watching her unnoticed, her eyes met his. They looked bluer than he'd ever seen them, even from such a distance. Cillian saw them and waved, a smile stretched across his face. He whispered something in Erilyn's ear and she looked up at him and nodded. Finley's hands began to sweat as he watched them circle the statue toward them. The crowd resumed its meandering around the tables of food that were already set out, as did the vendors who'd set up shop to try and trade wares while people were merry and a little drunk.

"Morrigan, you look ravishing," Cillian said, bowing slightly as he reached them. Morrigan smiled and gripped Finley's fingers painfully. He'd forgotten she was there, holding onto him. Guilt ripped through him, but his eyes kept going to Erilyn. His head had started to throb as soon as he'd seen her.

"You both look very fine as well," Morrigan said, smiling and showing all of her teeth. "Don't they Finley?" she asked, squeezing his hand again.

"Oh." Erilyn was focusing on Luna at her feet, and Finn wished she'd look up at him. Luna chirped at Finn, as if chastising him for something. "Oh, yes. Very fine." He cleared his throat and turned to Cillian.

Cillian patted Erilyn's hand on his arm and winked at Finn as if they were old pals. "One of the perks of being in charge is that we get the best seats in the house." He nodded toward the empty table just the right distance from the fragrant fire and leaned toward Erilyn. "And I'm sure Luce will make sure we get the best food, too." Cillian stroked the back of her hand with this thumb.

Anger shot through Finn like a bolt of lightning. Then Erilyn smiled up at Cillian and the lightning sizzled to be replaced with ice.

"How wonderful," Morrigan said, but from her tone Finley knew she wasn't happy. "Don't you think it's wonderful, Finley?" Her nails dug into the back of his hand.

"Yes. Great." He looked over at Morrigan. Compared to Erilyn, she looked harsh in the firelight, her ponytail making her skin look too tight, the red of her lips looking garish. The buzzing was back and his skin itched with it.

"But first things first," Cillian said, straightening and gently pulling Erilyn an inch closer. "First we need to show Luna where her anxious fans are." Cillian nodded toward a group of children on the outskirts. It was where Finn had stood as a child. All the children were holding something in their hands, bouncing on the balls of their feet. Erilyn looked at them and laughed so softly Finn was surprised he heard it.

Morrigan pulled Finn to the table, but he kept watching from the corner of his eye as Erilyn and Cillian walked to the children. Erilyn released Cillian's arm to crouch in front of the children and talk to them. He wished he could hear what she was saying. They all looked at her with big, awe-filled eyes and nodded. He imagined her voice, soft and kind, and longed to hear her speak to him that way, like she'd done before they'd come to Sunnybrook. Erilyn then rubbed Luna's ears and stood. Luna circled her legs once before walking into the throng of children who all squealed with delight as they sat around the cat, showing her toys made of strings and feathers.

Finn made himself look away as they walked back. He only looked up when Cillian pulled out the seat in front of him for Erilyn to take.

With trepidation, Finn looked up, their eyes locking for a breath, and his heart seemed to break. He was jerked back when Morrigan grabbed his arm and started talking about something—the decorations or the food. He felt distracted, and though he nodded and looked right into Morrigan's hazel eyes, he wasn't listening.

The night grew louder as more and more people arrived to eat and dance and drink. More than once, Morrigan had to slap his arm as his attention drifted to

Erilyn when Cillian would lean down and whisper something in her ear and make her smile or blush. Finn tried to focus on Morrigan, on what she was saying about the patrol, about other partygoers, but his eyes kept betraying him and traveling back to the soft curve where Erilyn's neck met her shoulder—her green shawl having been discarded when the fire in the center of town made her skin grow rosy. He finished the honey wine that had been in his glass and poured another.

It wasn't that Finn hadn't always known Erilyn was beautiful, because he had, it was just that he'd never seen her let that beauty shine so brilliantly. Her cheeks and lips were pink, as if she was slightly flushed, and her eyes were lined delicately. She looked like a ray of sunshine in her golden gown that reflected the fire and looked like a sunset. As he watched her as discreetly as he could, he felt something in him shift. The buzzing was roaring now. His head was pounding.

"Finley, did you hear me?" Morrigan's voice was hard and brought him back to her like an icy blast of wind. Her cheeks were red and angry. "I asked if you were ready to dance?" Her grip on his arm was like iron. He focused on the music. He knew some of those instruments were ones he'd made. Her fingers gripped his arm with bruising strength.

"Oh, yes. Of course." He stood and offered her his hand, making sure not to look at Erilyn as he did so. He was with Morrigan. He'd made a choice. He loved Morrigan. Didn't he?

Finn led Morrigan to the dance floor, his hand going around her waist, and pulled her to him. Her eyes were almost level with his. "What's wrong with you tonight?" she asked, her body unyielding against his. The image of her back to him earlier, almost naked, flooded his mind, but it didn't have the same effect as before. It was like that memory had happened to someone else. Even as he felt her press against him, felt the heat of her body, he didn't feel the need he usually did.

"I think I'm just tired," he lied, keeping his gaze from the table where Erilyn still sat. "I didn't sleep well again last night. You know I haven't been sleeping well for a few days." He hadn't slept well since he'd delivered the chair. "You look beautiful tonight," he said as he squeezed her waist, trying to be reassuring despite the pain and confusion in his head.

Her fierce expression softened a little. "Well, I can't imagine being here with anyone but you." Her unyielding form quickly pressed into him, like a log that caught fire and burst into flame. Her dress was slick, the fabric thin, and left nothing under his hands to the imagination. His hands on her waist slid around her back as if she'd pulled them there.

"Me too," he said. A flash of gold over Morrigan's shoulder caught his eye. Cillian and Erilyn were dancing, her dress moving like the morning sunlight on gentle waves. Morrigan nearly forgotten beneath his hands, he couldn't tear his eyes away. His heart was racing and he hoped Morrigan would think it was because of her and not because of how beautiful Erilyn looked. The buzzing increased to a painful pitch. He could feel it, could hear it.

After a few songs, Finn grew restless, the buzzing in his skull combining with the struggle of keeping his eyes off Erilyn starting to wear at him.

"I need a break," Finn said to Morrigan, pulling away slightly. He smiled. "I still don't feel great. I need to cool off." Before he could walk away, she pulled him to her and kissed him hard, her body a wall of heat against his. He expected to be swept away in emotion and desire, but he wasn't, and he pulled away quickly, eager for the cold air of his childhood, away from the center of all this.

He walked away quickly, moving between people, his head spinning. Once he broke from the central ring and moved past the merchant tables, he closed his eyes and took a deep breath, letting the cold air fill him up. He kept walking for a bit, still able to see the light from the party, but not as overwhelmed by it. His skin still itched with that damned buzzing, but it was easier to ignore out here.

He was about to turn around and head back when he saw her a few yards away, standing in the bright light of the full moon, her back to him. *Erilyn.*

He wanted to call out to her, tell her he was here, but he didn't. Instead he just looked at the way the silver moonlight painted her hair and dress, at the way she looked so at home surrounded by snow and her little puffs of exhaled air. She'd forgotten her shawl and her fingers gripped her arms as if trying to hold in warmth that wasn't there. He suddenly wanted to cover her hands with his and wrap her up in his arms as he'd done so many times when it was just the two of them.

She turned then, her eyes as big and round as the moon itself. The buzzing in his head grew to a fever pitch, but as he looked into her eyes it lessened, his headache backed off. "Are you cold?" he asked, his breath a light fog between them.

"I'm fine." Her shiver as she spoke gave her away.

He'd worn a sweater—a light gray one with a hole near the hem—even though Morrigan had insisted that he not because it made him look plain. He crossed the space between them and draped it over her shoulders. He'd meant to do that and step away, to give her space, but he found his hands resting on her upper arms, rubbing warmth into them with the pads of his thumbs. His heart was pounding now, but each beat of his heart seemed to push the buzzing away.

"Thank you." Her voice, though a whisper, seemed to wrap around him and hold him there. Just as he had in the woods, he wanted more than anything to pull her against him, to hold her. But he didn't. He had no right. He'd gone back to Morrigan, had forsaken what they had without a thought. He let his hands fall from her arms.

"Eri," he said, swallowing hard. "You look—" He didn't know what to say. The word *beautiful* didn't seem like enough. "Like sunlight." He immediately felt stupid. Morrigan would have been angry if he'd ever said that to her, but Erilyn smiled and looked up at him, her expression soft and open in a way he hadn't seen since they left her home.

Standing here now, looking down on her in the snow and moonlight, he felt more confused than ever. Why had he left her? He couldn't remember ever choosing to, only that one day they were together and the next they weren't. And Morrigan. He was with Morrigan.

Erilyn's smile fell suddenly and she took a step back. "Morrigan looks beautiful."

"*You* look beautiful," he whispered, staring into her eyes and hoping she could see his soul. "You look—" he sighed. "You're perfect."

"Finn—" the word was pained.

"I'm sorry." He wrapped his hands around her arms as he choked the words out and felt hot tears well up in his eyes. "I don't know what—" he shook his head, the buzzing back with a vengeance. She looked up at him, her own eyes sad. "I don't know. I'm just so, so sorry." A single tear fell from his eye. He was shaking, trying to ignore the painful buzzing against his skin, to get out the words he hadn't known he needed to say.

"I've missed you," she whispered, so much emotion in her voice he felt it like a palpable thing. She looked up at him, her gray eyes silver in the moonlight, and he took a step closer.

As if riding in on the snowflakes, which were growing fatter as they fell, Finn heard the light sound of strings drifting over from the gala. His hands slid down her arms and found her waist. As if thinking the same thought, she put her hands on his shoulders, then up around his neck. As her fingers touched his skin, the buzzing stopped and he sagged with relief. He held her loosely and together they swayed, their feet barely moving. With each breath, they moved closer together until finally her head rested on his chest. She fit there, perfectly. As they moved, his sweater slipped from her shoulders, unnoticed.

Her hands moved down his chest and slipped around his waist as his hands moved and slipped around her shoulders, hugging her to him. He sighed and realized the last of his headache was gone. He felt like he'd had it since they came here. With her against him, he could remember. He remembered the moment he'd realized he wanted to be with Erilyn more than anything in the world. He remembered that she was special. He remembered that he'd chosen Morrigan when they'd come back, though even now, he couldn't say *why* he had.

The song that had drifted in with the snow changed to a livelier tune. Their swaying stopped, but neither of them let go. After a moment, Erilyn pulled away enough to look up at him, a snowflake caught in her eyelashes. He looked at her lips and she lifted her head as if giving him permission. With a tentativeness they'd never experienced with each other, Finn pressed his lips to hers.

For a moment, everything fell into place. This was where he should be. This felt *right*. And then a sharp pain sliced through his skull and the buzzing was back with force.

Erilyn pulled back, hands still on his sides, a concerned, confused look on her face. "Finn?" she asked, her breath fogging between them.

"I'm fine." But when she went to touch his face the pain flared and he jerked. Her face grew determined and angry.

She picked up his sweater handed it to him. "Thank you for the dance. And the sweater," she said, her tone unreadable. Her face was stern. Angry. He couldn't figure out why and the pain between his eyes was so intense he couldn't think straight.

"Eri." His voice broke as he reached for her, but she was gone, moving swiftly back toward the square, leaving small footprints in the newly fallen snow. He stood still, as if in shock for a moment, before following her. He'd nearly made it to her; he could almost *feel* her just ahead, when a hand closed on his arm. He stumbled as the pain in his head intensified brilliantly for a moment before fading to almost nothing.

"There you are." Morrigan smiled brightly and put her body in front of his. He could see Erilyn with Cillian, saying something to him across the square. Erilyn looked back at him, her eyes wide with worry, but then the people shifted and she was lost to his line of sight. He had to get to her, to explain. Morrigan grabbed his face and kissed him passionately, her warm body pressing into him in all the right places. But his eyes were on Erilyn still, even as she turned away, Cillian's hand on her low back as they left through the crowd.

He gently pulled away from Morrigan, her hazel eyes flashing dark with anger.

"I'm sorry," he said, trying to keep his voice steady. His skin almost itched with buzzing. "I think something I ate disagreed with me." He needed to get away, to talk to Erilyn, to figure out what was wrong with him. Even if she'd chosen Cillian over him, he needed to explain why he'd left. "I got sick in the alley," he said, knowing Morrigan hated anything to do with bodily functions. She pulled away, a disgusted look on her face.

"Maybe you should just go home then," she said, looking at his mouth with a sour face.

"I think you're right." He kissed her cheek and felt nothing. "Stay and have fun, ok?" He didn't wait to see if she answered.

Finn pulled his sweater back on and tried to go in the direction Cillian and Erilyn had gone, but once he broke through the crowd, they were gone. He didn't seen Luna anymore, either. He needed to find Erilyn, to talk to her, to explain his confusion, the pain he'd felt, everything, even if it didn't make any sense. He just needed to talk to her.

He headed toward the Hummingbird and spotted them as they moved up the snow-dusted stairs, Luna leading the way.

He would wait until Cillian said goodnight and then he would go up and talk to her. It was getting late, the gala winding down, but he would wait as long as he needed. He leaned against a building, thinking his sweater had been warmer when he put it on than it should have been having lain in the snow.

Through the single window in Lucy's apartment, Finn saw a candle spring to life and the curtain close. When Cillian didn't come out right away, jealousy grew in Finn like a monster. He could still feel her hands on his waist, her lips against his. His hands were in fists as he waited. He just needed to see Cillian leave so he could talk to her. He knew if he could talk to her, even if nothing changed, everything would be better.

He waited until his hands and toes were so cold he could barely feel them. The gala ended and people had passed him, heading to their homes. There was only one door to the apartment. Lucy hadn't come home and Cillian hadn't left. Finn's stomach dropped as he realized what that meant.

Moving stiffly from the cold, he walked through the snow, through the stragglers just leaving the gala, back to his apartment, regret heavy on him like a dead weight.

Chapter Twenty-Five
The Buzzing

Erilyn

I woke with a groan and turned away as the bright light from the window assaulted me. Lucy was already up and getting dressed. I never slept this late and my head hurt. I turned and glanced toward the corner where Cillian had sat the night before. He'd stayed late to help Lucy replace a hinge on the bathroom door. She could have done it herself, but he'd insisted, and he'd stayed late into the night talking.

As he was leaving, I could sense that he'd wanted to kiss me. He asked me to walk him outside, well after midnight, but I'd kept a careful distance, the memory of Finn's lips on mine still fresh in my mind and my heart still aching from the loss.

Lucy had fallen asleep waiting for Cillian to leave, so I'd come back in and carefully placed the dress across the chest by the window and fallen into bed after changing into clothes to sleep in. I wasn't used to having so many clothes, so many options, but Lucy kept bringing me things, and I felt rude saying no, even if it was excessive and unnecessary.

She looked at me now with a quizzical expression. Her hair was wild and curly again. I'd only caught her eye a handful of times the night before and we hadn't had a chance to talk yet.

"Lazy bones," she said with a laugh, sitting on the foot of my bed with a crinkled nose. Luna, who'd been stretched beside me, chirped and batted at her hand. Lucy batted back before she rubbed her belly. "So, what happened last night?" She lifted an eyebrow and I swung my legs off the cot and stretched my toes.

"Cillian left after midnight, but nothing happened," I said, shrugging. Lucy laughed.

"I know. I wasn't really asleep." I pinched the bridge of my nose. I should have been able to *feel* that. I'd been so distracted. She laughed and said, "I meant, what happened at the gala?"

Finn's lips, soft and warm on mine. His hands around me, holding me close. Feeling his thoughts again had felt like coming home after a long time away. I took a deep breath. "You were there," I said and she rolled her eyes.

"I saw you slip off and I saw Finn follow you. *What happened?*" She was smiling in a way that reminded me of a fox.

"Lucy—" I'd wanted to tell her that nothing happened, but my voice cracked when unexpected emotion rose in me like a tide.

She scooted closer, her smile replaced by a look of concern, and put her hand on my shoulder. Suddenly tears leaked from my eyes. I wondered if the black stuff she'd used to line them would streak my face.

I shrugged and sniffed, letting my shoulders drop. "I think Cillian is a good man," I said, sniffing again.

She nodded. "I know you do." She squeezed my shoulder and then abruptly pulled me into a one-armed side hug. "But I also know you're in love with Finn."

I jerked away from her and she shrugged, a scowl on her face. "I know you are. I've seen it since the moment I saw you together. And clearly *something* happened last night. Tell me!"

She sat there, red curls wild, green eyes kind, and an expression so open and earnest that the words came tumbling forth.

"I left, because it was too much. The noise. The crowd." They had all been in my head, the wine that had been passed around making everyone's thoughts looser and louder. "And then Finn was there. He let me borrow his sweater. And—" I took a deep breath, another tear dripping heavily onto my legs. "And then we danced in the snow. And he kissed me." I looked at her, blurry through the welling of water in my eyes. "It was like I was home."

I sniffed, wiping my nose on the back of my hand like a kid. "And then something happened with him. He got distant, like he was in pain, so I left. Found your brother. And I saw—" I closed my eyes as the pain of seeing Morrigan and Finn together was like a knife stabbing through me again. "He was with Morrigan again." I shrugged again, feeling my shoulders sag further forward.

His pain had been real when we were alone, but I couldn't pinpoint it. I was worried about him, but seeing him with Morrigan had made the worry take second place to jealousy.

Next to me, Lucy's aura shifted from the sweet, subtle green of curiosity and care to the dark, deep green that meant she was angry. Everyone's aura was different—different colors meant different things—but with Lucy, dark, vibrant, green, like pines in deep summer, meant she was agitated.

"Something's wrong with him," she said, a quiet fury in her voice.

"He loves her," I said, shrugging, though I'd felt the same way. His aura, which was normally green like Lucy's, except brighter, had been crackly—like it was shot through with tiny black cracks.

"He *used* to love her. This is different," she said, standing up and pacing. "I saw him when he loved her. And I saw him with you. With her now, it's like—" she gestured around with her hands. "It's like he's a different person. A shadow of who he was. Don't get me wrong, he's always doted on her. But now, it's like he can't help it. Something is missing in his eyes."

She turned to face me, her hair swinging around in a wild arc. "We're going to go see him," she said matter-of-factly.

"What?" I asked, standing in shock. "No. We're not." I shook my head and held my hands out even though part of me was desperate to go.

Lucy put her hands on her hips and cocked them to one side. "Yes, we are." She walked over and took my hands in hers. "Don't you want to know why he's been so weird? Why he's basically disappeared?" She sighed and shook my hand gently. "Don't you want to just *ask*?"

Her skin on mine, the purity of her intent, convinced me. And I could leave whenever I needed or wanted to. "I'll have to tell Cillian I won't be in today. He brings lunch for both of us."

"We'll stop there first. Go get changed. It snowed more last night, so wear the new boots." She smiled then and hugged me, a hug that was so firm and warm that it sank into my bones and I hugged her back.

I changed into the warm pants and yellow sweater she'd given me my first day here, then laced up the boots she'd given me more recently—they fit my feet like they were made for me, which they probably had been. I tucked my pants into them, above my socks, to keep the snow out.

I'd taken my hair down the night before and in the mirror I saw that it was a wild halo of kinks and curls and reminded me of a less lovely version of Lucy's. My berry crown hung from the side of the mirror and I looked at it longingly. Black roughly ringed my eyes and I splashed cold water on my face and then scrubbed it away with a cloth. I wet my hair and dragged my fingers through it to pull the kinks and curls straight, then closed my eyes and sought out the fire below the building to dry my hair quickly. When I opened my eyes, I looked like myself again. It had been fun to look so elegant, but it felt good to be me again.

"Luna, come," I said as I joined Lucy, who'd been lacing up her own boots. I slipped my bag over one shoulder and tightened the strap so that it rested snugly against my side. I still carried my ratty blankets, though Lucy had washed them and gotten most of Finn's blood out, and the old, burned cup I hated so much, but now Rosemarie's book filled a good portion of the satchel. I wouldn't leave any of it behind.

The snow covered the tops of our shoes as we crunched down the stairs and headed toward the library. Lucy told Cillian that she was abducting me for the day, since I'd worked in the library every day since I'd arrived. Cillian, who looked at me longingly, making me uncomfortable, agreed. I felt that feeling—pressure that was almost desire, in my low belly—graze my awareness just before we left. It had felt good at first, but now it felt like an invasion. I didn't think they were my feelings at all.

Morrigan was on patrol and Finn spent all his free time in his workshop. I let Lucy lead the way, having never been there, or outside the city center, before.

We trudged through the snowy woods and I wondered why I hadn't been out here yet. Why had I allowed myself to stay cooped up in the library? Rosemarie's notes had held me—I touched the bag and felt the reassuring pressure of the journal inside—but I'd missed the outdoors, too. It felt good to be back beneath trees and sky.

My fingers grazed tree trunks as we passed them and I relished in the feel of the cold bark, the smell of snow and clean air, not filled with the smells of people and food and fires.

The further we went from the center of the city, the calmer I felt. Until we saw the workshop. It was a small wooden building with a stream of lazy smoke curling from the chimney, curtains open to let in light. There were no trees around it, and behind it a ways back I could see the edge of the quarry cliff.

My heart started to pound a little more rapidly as we approached. I could feel Finn inside—not as clearly as I'd been able to feel him when we'd been alone out in my woods, but I knew it was him. Now it was as if he had something shielding him from me. But whatever it was had cracked and was letting bits and pieces through. He was tense. Worried. Scared. Angry.

Lucy knocked on the door.

He opened the door with a scowl, but it vanished as soon as he saw us. "Erilyn," he breathed before his forehead scrunched. I immediately let myself see his aura. It was stricken with black lines like lightning flashing all over.

"Can we come in?" Lucy asked, anger in her voice. She couldn't see what I could—that he was in pain. I wanted to reach for him, but I was afraid it would make whatever was happening to him worse.

He held the door open wider and she strode into the small room. I followed, and he closed the door after Luna, who ran to the small fireplace and curled up before it to lick the snow drenched fur between her toes.

"Erilyn," he breathed, his shoulders hunched. He met my gaze and his face contorted with pain again, his body shaking slightly.

"Finn?" Lucy asked, realizing he wasn't OK.

He reached for me and his knees buckled. He held his head between his hands, shaking it back and forth, his face screwed up with pain. The black cracks in his aura were growing in number and size.

I was in front of him in an instant. As soon as my fingers touched his, his posture softened. He looked at me as his hands fell, holding mine tightly. "What's wrong?" I asked him, and he squeezed my fingers so tight they hurt.

"I don't know." Tears leaked from his eyes, but his voice was too tired sounding to waiver. "I hear this—this *buzzing.*" He grimaced and gritted his teeth. "I *feel* it. All the time. Except when you're here, when you're touching me." He held our hands between us and I rubbed the backs of his hands with my thumbs. "When I make myself not think about you, or forget about you, it's better, but it's still there like it's waiting to spring back up. It makes my skin itch. Ache." He shook his head. "I sound crazy." He looked up at me with wild eyes. "It didn't start until we came back." He was breathing erratically.

For a moment I forgot about Lucy standing there, quietly, behind me. I looked into Finn's bright blue, scared eyes.

"I'm not crazy," he said as another tear fell. I nodded and released one of his hands to wipe the tear away as he'd once done for me.

"I know you're not." I rubbed his cheek, feeling the coarse stubble there. "I know." I let my hand fall to his neck and he gripped my other hand with both of his.

This close, if I looked at his aura, I could see that the black spider-web cracks that forked around like lightning weren't true black at all, but a deep, dark, blood-like red. I'd seen that color before—it was the color of Morrigan's aura.

"Finn," I said and his gaze focused on mine. "Do you trust me?" I whispered.

"Yes," he said, squeezing my fingers tightly in his.

"Lucy," I said, not turning to look at her. "Will you go outside and make sure no one comes in?" It was an odd request, but she was out the door in an instant. Her presence had filled up the room and her willingness to do what I asked, even though she was scared and confused, emboldened me.

"Do you trust me, Finn? I mean really, *really* trust me?" I whispered and leaned toward him. He gazed at me with almost clear eyes and the emotion that swelled from him almost made me weep.

"With anything," he said. "With everything."

"OK. Close your eyes." I didn't know what I was doing. I just knew I had to see more, see what was *inside* of him.

He did and I gently pulled my hand from his to place both hands on his face. His breaths were short and ragged.

With a deep exhale I let my awareness expand, moving forward like it had over the tall grass in the field so many times and through the woods, only now I let it see inside of him. I let it follow the lines of light that made up his aura. They were tethered somewhere inside him. I wasn't seeing blood and bone. I was seeing energy, hundreds and hundreds of strands of energy all leading toward something in middle. His heart. Maybe his soul.

I followed it, but kept my awareness split so that I could still feel the stubble on his cheeks beneath my hands, feel the steady breaths in my lungs. I followed the light until my vision slowed and I saw it—a glowing ball of dark green light, pulsing in time with his heartbeat.

Except, there was something wrong with it. It was choked with the black spider web cracks, except this close I could see they weren't cracks. They were thick and ropey, like vines, and they pulsed reddish black, dimming the beautiful green light beneath. With every pulse of the green orb the ropey vines tightened and pulsed brighter. And there *was* a buzzing—I could hear it now, loud and incessant, though it wasn't really an audible sound, but more like a grating vibration on my aura. It felt angry. It didn't belong here.

I didn't have hands or feet here, but I wanted to rip the vines away. Chop them to pieces.

Finn? I whispered in my mind, not sure what would happen.

Erilyn? He was confused. His mind sounded tired. *What's happening? It hurts.*

I'm here. I needed to remove those vines. Destroy them.

With a thought I watched one of them disentangle and move toward me like a snake. I didn't have hands, but I imagined lashing out at it, like I had a knife, and it recoiled. A righteous anger grew in me as it slipped back around the ball of light that I knew was Finn. Now that I knew how, I attacked them, using only my thoughts to rip them away from him.

They squeezed tighter. I felt Finn beneath my hands start to shake, though he stayed quiet, trusting me even as I felt his pain grow. His pain fueled my anger and I hacked and slashed at them, screaming in my mind, wanting to throw them on a fire to burn.

I hacked and slashed, pulling myself closer and closer to him, to his aura, until the vines were mostly gone. There were small pieces here and there, but their dark light had diminished and I realized, with a shock, that I had no energy left to pull those last bits away. Finn would have to do it. I turned my attention back toward the glowing ball of light and saw that though it was brighter now, it still fluttered, weak.

Do you really, truly trust me? I asked, sounding tired. I felt him nod against my hands and I scooted my body a little closer to his to hold him up if I needed to.

My aura—a bright, sunshine gold—glowed brighter as I moved toward his light and started to merge with it. It felt right, like a hug or a bandage. As our auras blended I felt the last bit, the buzzing faded to nothing.

I saw the last of the reddish black tendrils slowly fade until they were gone. Together, our aura was a swirling mass of green and gold, and though I knew I should leave, knew I needed to let him have his aura back to grow strong on his own, I stayed just a moment longer, basking in what felt like bright sunshine after a long, hard winter.

Chapter Twenty-Six
Tucked Away

Finn

Erilyn's hands on his face were hot. Finn's head ached, his stomach ached, and the longer Erilyn held his face in her too hot hands, the worse it got. The buzzing had never been this bad, this painful. It grated at every nerve and he didn't know how much he could take. But he trusted Erilyn. She was special, and she would help him.

He gritted his teeth as the buzzing turned especially painful, and then it was gone. It was like he'd been doused in ice water after being on fire. For a moment he couldn't breathe, and then he could, and it was gone.

He sagged in relief, lifting his hands to hers where they were still pressed against his face. His own hands shook as he curled his fingers around hers, his eyes closed still. And then the memories started. They played behind his eyelids as if they were happening again.

He thought he'd remembered everything, but he hadn't. He'd only remembered a little and now he was overwhelmed by the sheer volume of detail, of emotion, all of which he'd somehow lost. He remembered how she'd been so cautious of him at first, at how quickly and naturally that had changed into something so beautiful. And then, Morrigan. His fingers on Erilyn's tightened as she entered his memories, except it all looked different now. He could see her coming to him, see the way he started moving around her like a moth around a flame. He remembered how it had happened and realized that something had been guiding him, controlling.

The memory of having sex with her in her apartment flared and he stiffened, hoping Erilyn couldn't see it, too. He still wasn't sure what she could do. He remembered moving against Morrigan mechanically, could remember the desperate desire for her, though now it made him ill.

He opened his eyes to escape memories of Morrigan that didn't feel like his own. Erilyn was staring back at him, her eyes like the water of a stream just before a storm.

"Are you OK?" she whispered.

He realized he'd been holding her hands to his face. He pulled them down and kissed them—her palms, her knuckles—then reluctantly, as he remembered Cillian, he let them go.

The absence of her touch didn't result in an onslaught of buzzing, of pain behind his eyes, and he gave her a small smile. "I'm OK." He scrubbed his face with his hands. "I don't know what you did," he said, looking at her again. He took on his, needing—no, *wanting*—to touch her. "But thank you." He kissed her hand again and didn't let it go. He would never force anything on her, and if she were with Cillian she would pull away, but now that he was himself again, he couldn't sit here like they were strangers. He'd woken from a waking nightmare and wanted to once again live.

"I—" her face contorted, conflicted. "It's so hard to explain," she said, her eyes sad.

Finn sat up on his knees and gathered her to him, her head tucking just under his chin as he wrapped his arms around her and kissed her hair in the way that felt right, in the way that had always felt off with Morrigan. "You don't have to." If she was here and he was himself again, he didn't need her to explain anything. He just needed her to stay, at least for a little while.

She nodded against him before gently pulling away and Finn let her go. Cillian—he'd never left Lucy's that night. Finn knew they'd worked closely together for weeks. He was handsome, powerful. Why wouldn't Erilyn be with him? And Finn had given her no reason to think he wanted to be with her.

"Lucy," Erilyn said, standing and going to the door. Lucy was pacing around outside, picking up autumn leaves that still peeked through the snow. She turned when the door opened and darted back inside, rubbing warmth into her hands.

"Is he OK?" she asked as Erilyn took her hands and rubbed them for her. It was strange to Finn to see Erilyn so familiar with Lucy, but he was glad for it. He'd been away for a few weeks, but a lot could change in that amount of time.

"He's OK. You were right, though. He wasn't—" Erilyn looked back at him, her eyes locking on his in a way that made his knees weak. "He wasn't himself. But he is now." Erilyn turned back to Lucy and dragged her to sit beside the small fireplace. Even though Luna was as long as Erilyn was tall, she dragged the sleeping cat and laid her across Lucy's lap to warm her faster.

"Well Finn, you have some talking to do," Lucy said, facing him square on. The snowflakes in her hair and on her clothes were melting, but her eyes were hard and angry again now that he was OK.

"Lucy," Erilyn started, but Finn stood and shook his head.

"No, I do." He offered his one, ragged, padded chair to Erilyn and started to pace. He locked the door and closed the curtains, then lit a candle from the fire. He wrung his hands.

"I don't know how," he said, sighing as he sank onto the stool where he sat most of the time to work, "but it was like I wasn't in control of myself. Like I was stuck in a fog. Or a tunnel, maybe? Like all I could see was *her*, and if I thought of anything else—" he met Erilyn's eyes and felt sadness swell in his chest. "If I thought of you," he said and she blinked slowly like Luna sometimes did, "it hurt. That buzzing felt like it would crack open my skull. I felt it on my skin. It was awful." He rubbed his arms with the memory. "And if I thought of her," he shook his head, "the buzzing went away almost completely. I felt like I *had* to think of her. It was just easier, I guess. And I could ignore the buzzing when I was with her, so I did."

He shrugged. "So I ignored it. All of it. Until the gala." He couldn't look away from Erilyn's stormy gray eyes. "Until I saw you. The buzzing got so much worse until we were dancing. Once I held you in my arms—" he shrugged, "it was gone. Until the end."

He dropped his head into his hands as a headache, a normal headache, started to pound there. "Since last night it's been unbearable," he said into his fingers. He looked up at them, up at Erilyn. "But it's gone now. I don't feel like I have to go to her. I don't *want* to," he said, standing. "If anything, I want the opposite. I don't know what was wrong with me, but I know she did it somehow. It's the only explanation, even if I don't understand it."

Erilyn nodded slowly, but Lucy looked confused. "Finn, I love you," she said as she stroked the light gray stripe that ran between Luna's ears, "but none of that makes any sense."

"I know it doesn't," he said, sitting down again with a thump, head in his hands.

"It does," Erilyn said softly and both sets of eyes turned to her. "It does if you have all the information." It was her turn to stand and she fidgeted nervously with the hem of her yellow sweater. "It does if someone *was* controlling you." She glanced up at him then looked away.

"How?" he asked. He'd seen what she could do. It only made sense others might be able to do things like that, too.

"Vitium." Her answer elicited a light laugh from Lucy.

"That stuff's long gone," she said, shrugging. "Since the nightcrawlers went into the caves and died off trying to find it after the war."

"It's not gone." Erilyn took a deep breath. "Please, don't ask me how I know, but it's not." She met Finn's gaze, begging him to be quiet with his eyes, and he nodded. "If someone were to be exposed to vitium—by accident or on purpose—it might give them the ability to do this. To do things with their mind." Her eyes were wild as she turned to Finn. "I found some notes in the library. Notes from *Rosemarie*. All about vitium, about the mayor—not Cillian, the one before—who was trying to find more about vitium, how to use it, trying to find the cave cities. I think—" she took a deep breath and squared her shoulders. "I think someone in Sunnybrook is trying to do that again. Maybe they already have."

"Cillian?" Lucy asked, and Erilyn shook her head.

"I don't think so. But maybe." Erilyn was pacing now, absently touching little half finished projects in the workshop in a way that made Finn's heart swell. "If he's part of this, he's hidden it well," she said finally with a shrug. "But I think, maybe—" she trailed off and looked at Finn. "Morrigan."

Memories that he'd not been aware of surfaced and he pinched the bridge of his nose. She'd said things to her patrol in passing about taking a boost, about practicing new skills. He'd seen maps in her apartment of the woods around Sunnybrook, but in his previous state, he hadn't cared about those things. Now he did.

"Maybe." He nodded with a grimace. "She had maps. Maybe of caves outside the city wall. I'd forgotten 'til now." Had Morrigan found a way to harvest and use vitium? The war had been fought over vitium as an energy source, but there were stories still told about how vitium could change a man into something more. Had Morrigan done that? Had Erilyn?

Erilyn stood, suddenly energized.

"I have to go," she said quickly and chirped for Luna, who was up and beside her in a heartbeat. "You both need to stay here. Keep the door locked. I'll be back. I have to get the notes from where I hid them, to give them to you to keep safe." She looked up at Finn, her expression fierce, but sad. "Then I have to see exactly what Morrigan's been up to."

"I'll go with you," Lucy said, standing and dusting off her pants.

"No." Erilyn shook her head and gave her friend a small smile. "No, stay here. You're safer together. If this is what it seems to be, Finn's not safe alone. Not if Morrigan can come in and do whatever she did to him again." Lucy nodded before hugging Erilyn, who was substantially shorter.

When Lucy let her go, Erilyn looked up at Finn. He wanted to hold her, too, to keep her here with him instead of letting her head out into the snow into what now felt like a dangerous world, but he didn't know if she wanted him to. As if reading his mind, she closed the distance between them and hugged him. He kissed her crown, not caring about whether he should or not, and she hugged him tighter.

"I'll be back as soon as I can. Stay here," she said again. And then she was gone, the door closing softly behind her. He looked out the window and watched as she and Luna disappeared into the trees, silent as ghosts.

Chapter Twenty-Seven
Silent Shadows

Erilyn

I flew through the woods, silent as Luna, quietly reveling in the feeling of freedom the trees and snow-covered earth gave me.

I thought as I ran. The vines I'd seen around Finn's aura, they were Morrigan's. I knew it as surely as I as I knew that she'd been exposed to vitium. It was why I couldn't read her. It had to be. But then why couldn't I read Cillian? I had to assume he had been affected, too. I couldn't trust him, and that realization stung.

I reached town quickly and slowed to a walk so I wouldn't draw any attention. Maybe Cillian wouldn't be there and I could go in and just grab the notes I'd left behind.

I reached the clock tower and ducked inside the warm building. The library was silent as I carefully gathered my copied notes and folded them away inside my bag next to Rosemarie's notebook. I was going to be in and out in less than a minute. I'd made it almost to the door when I heard heated voices in Cillian's office. I should go, but something held me rooted. I stepped closer.

"It has to happen. *Now.*" Morrigan's voice was as clear as if she'd been standing in the room with me and my hands curled into fists. Her voice dropped low again and I took another step to try and hear her.

It was quiet for a moment and then the door swung wide, catching me off guard. I stumbled back and Morrigan glared at me.

"What are you doing?" she asked, hands on her black leather clad hips, hair pulled into a high, tight ponytail that pulled the skin on her face tight.

"Finn's sick." The lie rose up in a rush and I forced myself to believe it in case she could see into my thoughts like I could see into everyone else's. I let the image of him crumpled, holding his head be at the forefront of my mind. "In his workshop." I pushed past her, wanting to run away but knowing I had a chance here to give us some space, some time. I turned to Cillian who was stacking papers on his desk. I saw the corner of a topographical map for a fraction of a second. "Lucy and I were out in the woods. He's feverish. Can't keep any food down." I hitched my bag a little closer while Luna hugged my legs, facing Morrigan with a deep growl in her throat. "Cillian, I thought you should know so you could keep people away."

I turned to Morrigan then and her aura flared a deep dark red, just like the tendrils I'd hacked away from Finn. "I'm going back, since I've already been exposed." The last bit had been petty—letting her know I could go, but she couldn't. Her aura flared dark and angry, almost black, and for a brief moment I caught a glimpse of her feelings—she hated me. Good.

Cillian was approaching me, but stopped when he realized I could be sick. I didn't feel that thing in my stomach anymore—that thing that felt like his desire pushing my own.

"You should stay here." He took a step toward me to show that he wasn't afraid, and I held up my hand. "If you're sick, I'll take care of you."

"Thank you," I said, and that feeling in my belly surprised me with fresh tingles. I looked into his deep brown eyes and something stirred deep inside me. I could feel what he wanted and it made me nervous that part of me wanted it too. "But I should go."

He took my hand, surprising me, and kissed my knuckles. The tingles grew and I sucked in a breath as my cheeks burned red.

"If you need anything," he said, looking at me over my fingers, "come find me."

I nodded and left without looking at Morrigan. It was hard to catch my breath as I hurried from the library with one last look at the stacks of books I'd yet to search.

I dashed outside. The snow had stopped but the sudden cold shocked me and what was left of those strange tingles dissipated into nothing.

I raced through the woods back to Finn's workshop. Luna darted ahead. I breathed the icy air and for the first time that I could remember, I was grateful for it. I'd always hated the winter, but right now it felt like freedom.

The door to Finn's cabin opened as we approached. He must have been watching from the window. It was stifling hot in the small building.

"You're OK?" Finn asked, worry lines etched across his face.

I nodded. "I told them you were sick. Throwing up. They should stay away for a while."

"They?" Lucy asked, arms crossed as she leaned against Finn's worktable.

"Cillian and Morrigan." I avoided Finn's gaze as I felt a sudden sadness pour off of him like steam. "They were in his office, arguing about something." I sighed, thinking of Cillian and his kindness to me over the last few weeks. "I saw maps on his desk that look like they may lead to the caves."

"How do you know where the caves are?" Lucy asked, eyes narrowed. I read her quickly. She was either genuinely curious or the world's greatest liar.

"Because I'm from there," I said, matter-of-factly. Her eyes opened wide for a moment, then returned to normal.

"Weird," she said with a nod, and I nodded back. It was for reasons like this that I loved her.

"I went to get these," I said, taking my copied notes from my bag. "They're copies from the notes I found of Rosemarie's," I said, handing them to Lucy while looking at Finn.

"Are you sure it was *your* Rosemarie who wrote them?" Finn asked, forehead crinkled.

"I have no doubt." I straightened my spine. They were both so much taller than me. "I would know her handwriting anywhere. She lived somewhere before she lived in her cabin alone," I said with a sigh. "It's like I was supposed to find them."

Lucy was flipping through my notes, her brow furrowed.

"Patrols have been leaving more often lately," she said, looking up at me. "They come for extra rations from the commissary. Cillian told me, a few months ago, to give them whatever they needed whenever they asked." She looked toward Finn, her expression pained. "They started going out more when Morrigan made captain."

"But she hasn't been leaving much," he said absently, some part of him still holding onto the hope that she was innocent, though I knew she was anything but.

"She's not always with them, but the change started when she was promoted." Lucy's voice was stern. It was easy for me to forget that Lucy was only 16. She'd had to grow up so fast, but it suited her.

"I'm going to follow them the next time they leave," I said and both Lucy and Finn turned to me, ready to protest. "I am." I cut them off. Lucy looked almost proud. Finn looked furious.

"And what will you do if they catch you?" he asked, stepping toward me until he was right in front of me, blue eyes shining bright, cheeks through his stubble pink from the fire. "You're not a Sunnybrook citizen. They know you, but we aren't allowed to leave the city walls without express permission and papers, and—" his hands were balled into fists as he met my eyes. "If they were to hurt you out there, they could cover it up and no one would know except us. It would be their word against our guesses." He unclenched his fists and put his hands on my shoulders, gripping tightly, but not hurting me. "Please. Don't."

His worry overtook me as his hands leaned heavily on me, and I almost agreed, but I knew I had to figure out what they were doing. I shook my head and he closed his eyes.

"They're going today," Lucy said quietly and Finn grimaced. "They came yesterday to let me know they'd need food for ten for one night and one day. They may not have left yet."

"They haven't," I said, thinking of Morrigan in her black leathers and the maps, of her insistence that something had to happen today. "I have to go," I said, and Finn's grip on my shoulders tightened. "I'll be back. Tonight. I'll see where they are, what they're doing, and come straight back here. I won't stay long."

"Erilyn." His voice broke and something in me broke with it.

"Just wait here for me. You're sick, remember? I told Cillian so they'd stay away. Let you recover." I pulled his hands from my shoulders and held them in my hands. "Luce, I need you to go keep an eye on your brother. I don't know how much of this he's wrapped up in, but we should know if he tries to go anywhere, do anything."

She nodded, pushing away from the counter with a grim look. "I'll go now." She stepped toward the door, but stopped and looked back at me. "Be careful." The ever-bouncy Lucy stared at me for a long, soulful moment, and then was gone, out into the bright midday sun reflecting off the snow.

"Please," Finn said as I turned back to him. "It feels wrong for you to go alone. I could go, too."

I thought of Finn in the woods with me, searching for food. He'd tried so hard, but his feet were loud. He left tracks. He didn't know how to be silent and invisible like I did.

"I have to go alone." I squeezed his hands, suddenly reluctant to let them go.

He looked at me for a long moment before grabbing me and pulling me to him. His lips met mine and fire spread down through my fingers and toes. I clung to him as my suppressed pain from losing him roared forth and started to slowly heal in this new, desperate heat. He pulled away and pressed his forehead to mine while his arms held me securely.

"I'm so sorry." His whispered breath tickled my lips.

I nodded and stepped away. Luna jumped up with a chirp. "I'll be back soon."

He nodded, looking forlorn as he stood alone in his workshop, now dark from the fading fire and closed curtains.

I darted outside, the whole world looking too white until my eyes adjusted to the sunlight shining up from the crisp snow, marred only by mine and Lucy's footprints.

I had to find the patrol. I had to hope they hadn't left in the time I'd been with Finn. I closed my eyes and let my awareness loose. It zoomed through the trees, fueled by my desperation to find them. I'd never tried this, searching for people instead of a specific place, but I'd never looked for someone's soul before today either and that had worked. I let my thoughts go and let my instinct lead.

The world tilted as my vision sped along and then stopped suddenly near the wall where Finn and I had snuck into Sunnybrook. Morrigan was there directing a group of black-clad patrollers down into the quarry. The path we'd taken in hadn't been as secret as Finn thought.

I opened my eyes, the world shifting again, and took off.

I was already near the quarry's edge. I could follow it until it met the wall and then follow their tracks. A group that large would leave them, especially in freshly fallen snow. I used the cold, crisp air to push me with Luna as my ever-silent white shadow.

I reached the wall faster than I thought. I stopped for a moment to catch my breath. My two weeks in Sunnybrook had left me soft. Weak. The cold air hurt my lungs.

Dimly, I felt something at the edge of my awareness. I'd felt it the first time I'd come into town, too. It felt familiar. Warm. But it was too subtle for me to identify and I had to move quickly.

The rocks were slippery with snow, so I had to carefully pick my way down and back up the trail that would lead me outside. There, I saw their tracks clearly. They'd been careless.

Erilyn. I jumped as I heard my name whispered on the wind. I shook my head angrily. Now was not the time for imagined voices. I hadn't heard this since before Sunnybrook, before Finn, and I pushed it away. Nothing could distract me right now.

Luna chirped at me and looked back toward the quarry, but I followed the tracks, knowing she would follow. If this patrol could do what I could do, and do it better than me, I had to try and hide. I was sure I'd been able to lie to Morrigan in my thoughts, so now I imagined a wall around myself that hid me from everything. I held that image, that belief in my mind, as I ran. I was invisible. I didn't exist.

I ran for a few minutes before I heard voices through the trees. I slowed and hid so I could see without my eyes. With eyes closed, my vision sped forward and stopped abruptly, closer than I thought it would. I was seeing through someone else's eyes again. I could tell by how clear it was, and by the way my vision stayed still, focused on Morrigan, like a soldier should look at their commander.

"Have you all been wearing the stones I gave you?" she asked, holding up a stone on a cord. It was the same color as the walls in my nursery had been—dark teal that shone with a dull, green-blue light. *Vitium.* "Good. We'll need an extra boost for today's excursion." She grinned without mirth. "You know the drill."

The eyes I was seeing through looked toward my arm—a man's arm, the sleeve rolled up. My other hand pulled a short knife from a sheath and sliced my forearm. Phantom pain sliced through my actual arm, though the man I was looking through didn't even flinch.

The man's arm extended and Morrigan walked by with a drawstring bag. From it she sprinkled a finely ground powder into the cut. The bleeding instantly slowed and a breath later my shared vision blurred before becoming painfully sharp. The snow went from being bright to blinding. The man looked to Morrigan and her aura—a dark blood red—was glowing more brightly than I'd ever seen any aura glow. I could hear the breaths, the heartbeats, of all the patrollers present. I could hear their thoughts, all except Morrigan's.

"Today we find the caves. Tomorrow we *take* them." Morrigan's voice was a growl. The members of the patrol all grunted in unison. From her pocket she pulled a rolled up map. She looked at each of her patrol intently. Erilyn wanted to recoil when she looked into her eyes.

"Let me in," she said, eyes flashing dark. The man I was seeing through took a deep breath and I felt him open himself up. In my mind I was seeing a map that led to Citadel. For this brief moment I could hear Morrigan's harsh, static-filled thoughts, feel her anger. And just as I recognized her thoughts, she recognized mine.

My eyes flew open as my heart went into my throat. I started running, trusting instinct to guide me back, trusting Luna to follow. I let my awareness expand without loosing my vision with it. I wanted to feel them, but I needed to see where my feet needed to go. They were following me, though slowly, which confused me. I pushed myself faster. Finn had been right. If they caught me out here, they could do anything they wanted.

No matter how hard I ran, I knew they'd find me. They were tracking me like Wylden, tracking me like I could track someone if I tried. My only hope was to get to Finn and tell him what I knew. Then, at least, when they caught me, I'd have someone who would be able to try and stop them.

Chapter Twenty-Eight
Revelations

Finn

He worried the small, wooden band between his fingers. Erilyn had been gone for a few hours—long enough to finish the ring he'd started with the raindrop stone. Now he just sat, holding it, growing more nervous with each minute.

The days were rapidly growing shorter and the sun was already sinking toward the horizon. He'd opened the curtains again to let some light in and to maybe catch sight of Erilyn as soon as she returned, but the elongating evening light made him tense. His tension ratcheted higher and his heart beat erratically for a moment just before the door burst open.

"Erilyn," he said, putting the ring down and going to her. He took her shoulders in his hands and looked into her eyes, which were wide with panic.

"They're going to the caves." She looked up at him and clutched the fabric across on his chest. "To Citadel. They're going to—" she shook her head and gripped the fabric of his shirt in her fingers. "They're going to take the people.

Use them in the old vitium mines like slaves." She was shaking as she looked up at him, her look somehow now wilder. "They know I know. They're coming for me any minute."

An icy chill darted through him and he gripped her arms tighter. "What? What happened?" Luna was staring at the door and Erilyn was staring at Finn. "Did they see you?"

She shook her head and closed her eyes, her fingers losing some of their grip.

"I know because of what I can do." She opened her eyes and looked right into his, begging him to understand. "The same way I helped you heal from that knife wound, helped you earlier break away from Morrigan's control." She shook her head and looked toward the fire. "I know they're after me because I can do things like this." The fire behind Finn, which had burned down to coals, roared to life and he whipped around to see it just as it settled back into a small flame.

Though he'd known she could do things for some time, it was different seeing it so bluntly. She was inching away from him, and he was sure he could feel her worry, her fear, that he would pull away first, so he gently pulled her to him and held her under his chin. She relaxed, her shaking subsided.

"Tell me everything," he said into her hair and she nodded.

"I saw Morrigan and her patrol in the woods. They've all been exposed to vitium. They wear it—"

"On a necklace," he said, remembering Morrigan's naked body pressed against his in the floor of her apartment, remembering the strange necklace digging into his side, how it reflected the light. She wore it almost always, now that he thought about it. He squashed the memory of her naked body, hoping that Erilyn hadn't somehow seen.

"You've seen it?" she asked and he nodded.

"The stone was odd."

"Vitium." Erilyn shook her head and stepped away from him. "And they cut their arms, dusted the wounds with more to get it right in their blood." She shivered and her arms went around her body. "I saw into Morrigan's mind." Her voice was quiet as she stared at him with eyes as wide as Luna's. "For less than a moment, but I saw everything. They want to enslave the people in the caves, use the vitium mines, and make more people like them. Like me." She held her hands out as if in supplication. "They want an *army*."

Finn's mind was reeling. He went to her again and took her icy hands. Her eyes shot to his, suddenly wide and afraid.

"We have to stop them." Erilyn's head swung toward the door and Luna chirped. "Keep Luna safe," she said, pulling away from him. "Tell Lucy everything."

Finn opened his mouth to speak as the door burst open. Two patrollers walked right in and grabbed Erilyn's arms. She struggled, but not hard enough to matter. Her eyes were locked on Finn's.

"What are you doing?" Finn asked, stepping forward, only to be stopped by a third patroller who pushed him back as they dragged a now silent Erilyn out into the snow. "Where are you taking her?"

Morrigan walked in, blocking him from following, nothing but a silhouette in the fading daylight. Luna hissed at her and she ignored it, motioning to be left alone.

"Did she hurt you?" she asked as she reached for Finn. He stepped back, scowling.

"Hurt me?" He shook his head. The buzzing was back—faintly in the periphery of his senses. He thought of Erilyn, her stormy gray eyes and proud stance and it vanished. "She would never hurt me."

"She's dangerous, Finley. A cave witch." They'd all heard stories growing up about the albinos in the cave who practiced magic and stole children. It would be an easy lie to believe. "What did she say to you? She told us you were sick to keep us away." Morrigan's voice was soft, alluring, but Finn held firm, the memory of holding Erilyn keeping him grounded.

"That she was scared." He knew if he lied, Morrigan would know. So he repeated that in his mind. *She was scared. She was scared.* And he pictured Erilyn, looking up at him, frightened. If Morrigan could read his thoughts or see his mind, this would be all she saw.

"Scared of being caught," she said, putting her hand on his stubbled cheek. He stiffened and the buzzing grew louder, but it still didn't touch him, like a swarm of bees just outside the door.

"Where are they taking her?" He didn't move and she dropped her hand, anger replacing the faux concern on her face.

"She's to stand trial for endangering Sunnybrook," Morrigan said with a smile that never reached her eyes. He could see the bump beneath her shirt where the flat pendant rested.

Anger roared forth, but he tried to keep it in check. He didn't know what Morrigan could do. It would be better to give her as little as possible. He kept thinking of Erilyn's eyes in the firelight and nodded.

"She's poisoned you against me," she said, the sudden pain on her face an act that Finn could now see through. "Maybe, after she's executed, you'll come back to me." She touched his shoulder and he felt a static shock. The buzzing grew louder and he thought of Erilyn holding his face, thought of her holding him up when he was injured, and it backed off again.

Morrigan stared at him for a moment as if she'd been slapped, then she stormed out without a word, slamming the door behind her. Finn sagged, exhausted, and Luna pawed at the door.

Finn watched through the window as Morrigan and the last few patrollers disappeared into the woods before he moved. He grabbed the ring he'd made and shoved it in his pocket. He grabbed his sweater—the gray one with the hole near the hem. Just next to it was Erilyn's bag. She'd left it for him, he knew.

He knelt and opened it. Inside were Rosemarie's notes, their two ragged blankets, and that horrible metal cup. He repacked everything neatly and put the strap over his shoulder.

Luna was pawing at the door still, mewling, and he knelt next to her. She bumped his face with her large head and cried once. He rubbed down her back. She listened to Erilyn, but now he needed her to listen to him.

"Stay with me," he said, looking into her large, orb-like eyes. "OK, Luna? Erilyn wants you to stay with me."

She cried again, then blinked slowly and dipped her head. Did she understand?

With a sigh, he stood and opened the door. It was almost night and the air was still and cold. When Luna didn't dart off after Erilyn he took a relieved breath.

"Let's go find Lucy," he said, and she jumped into the snow and waited for him. The fire had dimmed after Erilyn had left, and it was now nothing but coals. He looked at the room and exhaled a long breath before shutting the door. He had a feeling he might not be back here for a very long time.

Chapter Twenty-Nine
Caged

Erilyn

The patrollers who'd grabbed me from Finn's shop took me to the basement below the library. They'd left me in there and locked the door behind me over an hour ago. The moon had risen, and I could barely see it through a small window near the ceiling—barely large enough to fit my head through—with bars across it.

My stomach growled and I silently cursed myself for having let myself eat so much since coming here. I'd gone much longer without food when I was in my woods. My stomach ached, but I knew I was fine. To distract myself, I closed my eyes and sent out my awareness. It wouldn't hurt to see who was close by, to see if I could find Finn, Lucy, or Luna.

I could feel two people outside the door—their auras faint behind my closed eyes, one a grayish-pink, the other a dull red. I couldn't feel anything past that. I needed to *see* past it. My vision sped through the door as if it weren't there and then stopped so hard my head jerked back and my eyes popped open. It was like I'd run face first into a brick wall. I shook my head and tried again, ready for the wall this time, so I didn't hit it so hard. I couldn't move past whatever it was. I could see through the eyes of one of my guards, but that was it. A single candle burned in a glass-covered lantern down the hall, but I was stuck seeing no further than that.

The woman whose eyes I was borrowing was sleepy and a little anxious. Her aura had been the red one and I was curious, because she felt so unsure about what she was doing. She looked up and I saw someone approaching in the dark hall.

Cillian stepped into the light of the lantern, his hair disheveled, his clothes wrinkled, with something draped over his arm. He stood straight as he approached the guards and they straightened as well. He opened the lantern and lit a free candle he had in his hand.

"I'm here to see the prisoner." His voice was strong and his free hand was clenched.

"Captain said no one in or out." It was the other guard who spoke, a young man whose voice broke with nervousness.

"Morrigan's your boss," he said with a nod as his gaze turned fierce. "I'm hers. You will let me in that room."

The two guards looked at each other before the girl took out her key. I heard the key turn and pulled my awareness back to myself, prepared for the room to tilt for a moment. It was easier in the dark to deal with the dizziness.

The dim light from the lantern poured in followed by Cillian's long, lean frame. The guard closed the door behind him and I heard it relock. He grimaced and placed the lit candle in a sconce by the door.

"Are you OK?" he asked, moving to sit beside me on the wooden bench I'd been on for the last hour.

"I'm fine." I grimaced when my stomach growled.

He had a blanket draped over his arm and laid it down, then pulled a bag with an apple and a sandwich from it. "From Lucy," he said as I took them.

"Thank you, both." I sat them aside and tried to smile. I felt odd sitting here with him. Not long ago he'd kissed me. The memory of his lips on mine was foreign, as if I'd seen it happen to someone else, but it was a sweet memory, too, which was confusing.

He took my hands and brought my knuckles to his lips where he kissed them three or four times. Then he pulled me to him, his lips near my ear. "You need to fight your way out," he said so quietly I barely heard. "Lucy told me what you can do." I felt my stomach drop as he leaned back so that I could see his eyes. I felt that ping in my belly again, weaker this time, and he pulled me back to him. "You have to use that. Use those abilities to get out." His lips brushed my cheek, warm and soft. "Morrigan *will* kill you if you don't." His grip on me tightened painfully and I felt that tingle in my belly again.

Lucy had told him. My head was spinning. How could she? And then the spinning stopped, replaced by a single, crystal clear thought. Only Finn knew what I could do. Lucy couldn't have told him.

I looked into his eyes, black in the near darkness. He was lying to me.

"I can't," I said, shaking my head. "I don't know what she told you, but I don't have *abilities*." I shook with sudden anger and hoped I sounded afraid instead. He looked at me as if he didn't believe me, but then pulled me to him again.

"OK," he said, holding me. "You're freezing." He picked up the blanket he'd brought and wrapped it around my shoulders. It was warm from being on his arm. He wrapped me up in it and then pulled me to him again. I felt constricted. Trapped.

He held me for a long time, his heart beat loud and steady. What was he doing? I started to fidget. He was lying to me. He'd kissed me, made me feel things for him, but he was lying. I felt my heart rate increase.

He leaned back with bright eyes. "Erilyn," he whispered with longing. Then, my arms still trapped inside the blanket, he pulled me to him and kissed me.

I was so shocked my lips popped open to try and grab a breath, and he took that as an invitation. His tongue in my mouth was forceful and invasive. His clean-shaven skin pressed against my face. And even though I didn't want this, didn't want to be kissing him at all, I felt that sensation in my belly—a stirring of desire that I could now recognize as definitely not my own. I'd felt desire with Finn and this was nothing like that.

I was trapped beneath the blanket, trapped against him. I started to pull the blanket off and pull away from him. I needed to free my hands.

I wiggled my arms loose and grabbed hold of the blanket to rip it away, his lips still pressed to mine and his arms still holding me, but as soon as I grabbed the blanket with my fingers, something icy hot shot through me. I gasped with the sudden pain. Cillian must have thought it was a gasp of pleasure because he crushed me against him, his kiss turning almost painful.

It was almost like I was following my vision again, but different. My body was flooded with a desire not my own and white hot. I saw a room. It was hazy, lit dimly. There was a fire burning and it was so warm. I was lying on top of someone, their body beneath mine lean, kissing them, moving against them.

And then I sat up, dark hair falling so that it landed on a man's naked chest. On Finn's chest.

"Morrigan," he breathed, and I dipped forward again.

With a gasp and a rush of air I pushed Cillian away, pushed the blanket away, and stumbled to my feet, my hands trembling.

"What's wrong?" he asked, taking a step toward me.

I held my hands up and shook my head. What was that? Was it happening now?

"Nothing," I said, hands to my stomach. The bag of food Cillian had brought was still there, but I felt too sick to eat it. Finn and Morrigan together. Had it been real? "I think I should sleep."

"I can stay." He took another step, his eyes hungry.

"No," I said quickly. "No, please. I need some time. Some rest."

He looked at me for a long time. His face was unreadable, and as always I couldn't hear his thoughts. His aura had never been reliable, always changing color and intensity, as if it were on purpose. Right now it glowed a bright orangey-red, and though I could never read him, right now I could feel that tingle in my belly that I recognized now as his desire, his lust, thick in the room.

"I'll be there tomorrow," he said, his shoulders slumping. "At the trial. I'll do what I can, but in matters like this, Morrigan has jurisdiction." He sighed, his wrinkled clothes making him look distraught and I wondered if he'd wrinkled them on purpose.

"Thank you," I said, keeping my arms around my middle as a sort of shield. He stood for a moment before turning and asking to be let out.

When he left, and the door was relocked and bolted behind him, I sank to the ground, my heart beating wildly.

I could still feel Finn's hands on my skin—on Morrigan's skin—feel his lips, the way his naked skin had pressed against mine hotly.

This couldn't be happening. When I'd left him just hours ago, he was with me. I knew he was. We were going to fight this together. He wouldn't be with her now. Even if she'd somehow managed to control him before, enthrall him, I knew he wouldn't be with her now.

Fighting the urge to panic, I closed my eyes and made myself revisit the memory. It was as vivid as any memory I had and it made me feel ill.

Firelight causing shadows to dance around the room. Finn's hands, rough from his woodworking. Heat. I made myself remember Finn's face. He had stubble, like when I saw him today, but there was something different.

Morrigan. He'd breathed her name and I'd felt tingles spread from his fingertips, tingles that didn't belong to me. I made myself focus on his hair. Not the way his warm skin had felt. Not the borrowed desire I had from her. In the memory his hair was longer, shaggier, like when we'd first come to Sunnybrook. Earlier today, his hair had been short, cut for the gala.

My eyes popped open and I breathed a little easier. I'd been seeing a memory. I'd seen them before. Rosemarie had called them memory imprints. The cabin where we lived was full of them—places where something emotionally intense had happened and left an energetic stain—and now that my heartbeat had slowed and I could think clearly, I recognized the telltale haze around the images. Some were clearer than others—the more recent the memory had been imprinted on something, the clearer it was. I looked down at the discarded blanket on the floor. With hesitant fingers I picked it up and studied it in the fading candlelight. It was a quilt of squares with embroidery in one corner. I lifted it to the light. F + M was stitched inside an embroidered heart. I dropped it as if burned.

Why had Cillian brought me a blanket that belonged to Morrigan or Finn? His kiss, the pressure of his desire, had brought forth that memory as if he'd done it on purpose.

He'd been lying to me, too. For some reason, he wanted me to fight, and somehow, he knew about my abilities.

I sat down, angry that I'd let myself trust him, and pushed the blanket away with the toe of my boot. I opened the bag of food—a sandwich and an apple. The sandwich had meat on it so I knew Lucy hadn't made it—another lie. I threw the dried meat into the corner of the room and ate the meager meal—bread with cheese and a mealy apple— then lay back on the wooden bench. I could just barely see the sky through the slit that was the small, barred window.

I stared there, into that tiny piece of sky, long into the night.

I woke with a start as the door to my prison cell slammed open. Eyes blurry, I looked to the window where the sky was just starting to brighten. Two patrollers— women who I hadn't seen yesterday—came in and pulled me up. I stumbled, waking more slowly than usual. I hadn't slept much and my bones were stiff with cold. One of them tied my hands in front of me with a coarse rope. The pain of the cord biting into my skin helped shock me awake.

One pulled the rope behind them like a leash while the other held a knife at my back, the point pressed into my shoulder. They were both shielding their thoughts, but not as well as Morrigan. I could *feel* that they were afraid of me.

"Where are you taking me?" I asked, looking back at the girl with the knife. She was younger than me, maybe fifteen, and her white blonde hair was gathered at the nape of her neck in a tight bun, pulling her features tight. She looked almost like a cave dweller, except for her brown eyes and peachy skin.

"Move," she said through gritted teeth. Her aura—a wild, vivid orange—pulsed erratically.

I stumbled forward as the girl in front of me pulled the rope. I could try to escape, but I knew I wouldn't make it. There were more guards waiting outside the room, and even more as we stepped out into the frigid morning air.

They led me through a crowd that had gathered around the leaning statue in the center of town. It wasn't breakfast time yet, but it seemed the whole town had come out.

A rough stage had been constructed beside the statue and Morrigan was standing behind a podium in her black leather patrol gear. Her hair was left long and free, a red lily tucked behind one ear and a dark blue-green pendant rested against her collarbone. I had never seen it before but immediately knew it was the vitium necklace Finn had mentioned. I opened up my senses to it and saw that it radiated a light that reminded me of my glowworms—green-blue and bright.

The guards led me to a spot separate from the crowd. The crowd murmured as they watched me and I tried to block out the waves of feeling they were putting off—fear, confusion, mistrust.

I took a deep breath, my hands going numb from the ropes, and tried to find Finn or Lucy in the crowd by seeking their auras. I found them both quickly near the middle of the crowd, Luna a nervous bundle between them.

I didn't look, but breathed a little easier knowing they were here.

Morrigan, standing tall and proud behind the podium, lifted her hands as the sunlight finally broke over the top of the buildings and lit her up. The crowd quieted and she smiled.

"We're here today," she said, her voice loud and commanding, "for the trial of this woman from the wilds, Erilyn. She is being charged as a cave witch."

The crowd exploded with sound, their fear rising in great waves. I felt like I might be suffocated by it all. Their voices in my head were too much, too great. I tried to look calm, but I couldn't breathe. Morrigan smiled at me and I felt anger flare, only it wasn't mine. Finn was standing closer now, having pushed his way nearer to the front. I held onto his anger and added to it with my own. I used it to burn away the confusion from the thousand voices until I felt only his feelings and my own. I could breathe again and Morrigan's smile turned sour. She knew what I was doing.

She held up her hands and the crowd quieted, still restless.

"I had planned a civil trial, officiated by our mayor, but he isn't here." She motioned around and the crowd's murmur rose again. "He refused to come, locked away in his office, because he says whenever he's around this woman," she motioned to me, but didn't meet my eyes, "she tries to seduce him. He feels like she's using her powers to control him. Bewitch him." She finally met my gaze and I saw her lip twitch, though I couldn't tell if it was in humor or anger. "Because of this," she said, her voice steady but causing the crowd to quiet, "I have made a decision." The crowd was silent. The only sound came from the winter wind blowing through, promising more snow. "Erilyn will be escorted, blindfolded, from the city, by a company of no less than *twenty* patrollers. She will then be released." Morrigan turned to me, the smirk on her face making her normally ravishing features ugly. "And if she ever returns, or makes contact with any citizen of Sunnybrook, she will be killed." Her quiet voice carried over the now silent crowd as if she'd yelled it.

The crowd exploded then, demanding justice, demanding that something be done to protect them from the witch, but I sagged in relief. I could still try and stop them from going into Citadel, could still try and warn my people that the upworlders were coming.

Morrigan was still talking, quieting the crowd, when suddenly my awareness was active, my vision moving without my direction. I gripped the wooden rail next to me as the world spun and I was suddenly seeing through someone else's eyes. A man was standing on top of a building. It was an old building overseeing the crowd. I could see me, holding onto the rail, could see Morrigan. The vision swung around until it stopped on a spot of white and a spot of vivid orange—Lucy, Luna, Finn.

The man felt calm as he lifted a bow and sighted down an arrow. He'd found Lucy's hair, but he was aiming for Finn—the largest of the three. Finn's eyes were toward the stage, toward me. I felt the man take a deep breath as he prepared to fire.

A moment before he did, I was able to jerk myself back—it felt like trying to move through mud, but I did it. I spun to where he was, standing in all black, aiming at my friends. I felt a familiar, dreaded heat well up in my belly.

"No!" I screamed as the arrow flew loose. I threw my bound hands up and I felt energy expand from them in an instant. The ropes around my wrist snapped apart. The people nearest me fell back. The arrow splintered in mid air.

And the man on the roof screamed as he fell forward and hit the earth.

"Grab her!" Morrigan's voice was lost in the din as the crowd scurried to get away from me. The people were so dense that the patrol couldn't reach me.

I wanted to go to my friends, to Luna, but I knew I had to leave. They'd all seen what I could do and any fear they had was now justified. The people before me made a path, terrified, and I ran through it, shaking feeling back into my tingling hands as I went. I ran as hard as I could toward the towering white sycamores that would lead me to my freedom.

The streets were nearly deserted. The few people milling about just stared as I ran in a frenzy. The patrol would be able to calm the crowd enough to follow me soon. I kept seeing the man who had fallen, in my head as if in slow motion.

I'd pushed. *Pushed.* Not pulled. He'd fallen forward. I hadn't done that, had I?

I ran until the sycamores rose like giant white beacons straight ahead, and then I ran faster.

Only one guard was posted in a stand at the edge of the wall, the rest having been stationed to guard me. He was young and panicked as I ran closer, his bow and arrow forgotten as he held onto the wooden banister around where he stood and yelled for me to stop.

I was through the sycamores before his voice had carried far. After a minute or two I slowed a little, looked back and saw the tracks I'd left—great depressions in the snow. I was shaking, already growing tired, but I dug down deep inside and found an energy reserve. I let it trail behind me like a wave and it covered my tracks with windblown snow as I kept moving forward.

I ran all day, growing more and more tired, more and more hungry, wishing I had more than just this one sweater and then chastising myself for having become so weak.

The hearing had been just after dawn. By midday, I didn't think I could keep going, but I did, stopping only to drink water from semi-frozen streams and eat the few berries I could find that were safe. I let my instinct guide me more than my eyes. The further I ran, the more I started to hear. *Erilyn.* My name on the wind. I didn't push it away now as I had the day before. It was almost comforting now, and when I started to lag, when I tripped, it was there to call me forward, to keep me moving. I didn't care if it was in my head or not.

When I passed the field and then the metal signpost, I knew I was almost home. My energy spiked one final time, the voice almost singing my name to keep me moving.

I stumbled into my clearing—almost unrecognizable from the flames that had burnt half my pine—and collapsed to my knees, my energy finally spent.

In front of me was my pine covered in snow, lopsided as the snow hung heavy on the branches that were still green. The burned side held snow on crisped limbs that looked like bone.

I crawled to the pond, no longer hiding my tracks. A layer of ash had settled over the top and I pushed it away like pond scum, thankful it wasn't cold enough for the whole thing to freeze. I scooped water into my mouth with hands that shook.

My lungs were heaving, my heart trying desperately to keep up with the breaths I needed. I needed a plan. I needed to do something. I'd come here because it was the only place I knew to go.

My heart was beating loudly in my ears, but I thought I heard footsteps and wanted to cry. They'd found me too soon. I turned, crouched, too tired to stand. A second before they burst through the clearing I was assaulted with a wash of rage and lust of the Wylden.

And then he was there, a Wylden man who looked barely older than me. His hair was long and dark, his eyes huge with anger, his chest heaving, a knife in his hand. On his side I saw old, dried blood, and I remembered the Wylden Finn had stabbed.

The man looked at me, his muscles tight and ropey, coiling as he readied himself to spring, and I felt more than heard his one muttered word. *Mine.*

I barely had a second to think before he dropped his knife—a long blade that was easily the length of my forearm—and lunged at me.

Chapter Thirty
Escape

Finn

Finn grabbed Lucy's hand as the crowd scattered, people screaming and rushing in different directions. He kept his eyes on Erilyn as best as he could through the throng. She looked around, eyes wild, before darting into an opening the people left. She was fast, and small, and he lost sight of her far too quickly.

"We have to go after her," he said in Lucy's ear, and her curly red hair bounced against his face. "Luna," he said, the white cat crouched, scared, pressed against him. She hissed and growled and Finn looked up to see Morrigan trying to get to him through the panicking people clogged around the hastily constructed stage. "This way," he said, and pulled Lucy after him, Luna on their heels.

They made it away from the crowd and ducked into an alley that the morning sunlight hadn't lit up yet. He knew that the only way they'd stay away from Morrigan was to leave the town. If she could do what Erilyn could do, if she could control his mind, she could find them.

He kept a tight grip on Lucy's hand as they ran down the alley, Luna darting out in front, muscles coiled. They ran from the alley and headed straight for the gates. Lucy didn't question where they were going. She was right beside him, running hand-in-hand to avoid getting separated if they came across a group of people again.

When the white sycamores were in sight, Lucy pulled Finn to a stop and dragged him into the shadow of a building. The gate was swarmed with patrollers. Morrigan was there as well, her cheeks red as she gave orders. How had she beaten them here? Finn looked at her and anger grew in his chest. He was angry because he'd loved her and she'd betrayed him. The girl he'd loved, who he'd laid on a blanket with and made shapes out of stars, had become something else.

"Finn!" Lucy yanked him back. He'd been walking toward them and hadn't even realized. "We need a plan. We can't leave her out there alone."

He shook his head, pushing his anger away to focus on Erilyn. "Right," he said, crouching so that he could comfort a very tense and very distraught Luna. She was shaking.

"We should go to Cillian," she said. Finn shook his head.

"No." He didn't trust Cillian, even if he was Lucy's brother, even if Cillian seemed to care for Erilyn.

"Why not?" She pulled her hand away, her whispered voice angry.

"You heard Morrigan," he said, still shaking his head. "He said Erilyn was bewitching him, and we both know that's not true. We can't trust him." He meant it, but part of him didn't want to involve Cillian, because he'd seen the way Cillian looked at Erilyn. There was a hungry light in his eyes when he watched her and he wanted to keep Cillian far from her, even if she cared for him.

"Or maybe he tried to stop Morrigan and she locked him up and made up that cock and bull story." Her face was screwed up as she tried to contain her anger with him. Her righteous rage made Finn sag as he realized she might be right. Maybe his feelings for Erilyn were clouding his judgment.

"OK." Finn sighed. It still felt wrong going to him, but they had to move quickly. He nodded as Lucy motioned for him to follow.

They made it to the library without incident. There were patrollers on the street, but they had ignored Finn and Lucy as they walked, hand in hand, as casually as they could. Finn stopped just inside, his eyes moving quickly over the stacks of books. He hadn't come to see her here except to deliver the chair, which now sat pulled up to a table with the smallest stacks of books, but he could imagine her here, flipping old pages in the quiet.

"Cillian?" Lucy banged on the office door. "Are you in there?"

"Lucy?" he said as he tried the knob. "I've been locked in. Is there a key?"

She pulled a large, old looking key from a hook and pulled the door open. Cillian burst from the room, looking frazzled. "Where's Erilyn? What happened?"

Finn watched him with narrowed eyes. Cillian's face was panicked, but something felt off, rang false.

"She ran," Lucy said. "Morrigan was going to exile her and then something happened. A man fell from the roof and panic broke out in the square." Lucy shook her head, confused. "We're pretty sure she's out of the city."

"Good." He sagged in relief. "Good. Morrigan said she was going to kill her. I tried to stop her, but she hit me." He showed them his cheek, which sported a darkening purple bruise right on his cheekbone. "I'm glad Erilyn got out."

Finn grew impatient with the chatter. "We're going after her." Finn scowled.

"You?" Cillian's look was pointed.

"Who else?" Finn shot back, fists at his sides, Luna pressed against his leg, growling softly. That, if nothing else, told Finn something wasn't right with Cillian. "We need your help getting out of the city," Finn said through clenched teeth.

Cillian glared at him. Lucy stood between them, calm and silent, which helped Finn calm down a little.

"Are you going to help us or not?" Finn tried to relax his clenched fingers. "We need to move quickly. Before the patrol finds her."

Cillian looked at Finn, long and hard, and then his shoulders sagged. "Head for the quarry—the west wall. I'll make sure there's no patrol."

Finn nodded, though still suspicious

Cillian turned to Lucy and pulled her into a tight hug. "You're all I have," he said so quietly Finn almost didn't hear. He pulled back and looked at her like a parent might look at a child. "Please, be careful."

She nodded and then turned to Finn. "Ready?"

He nodded once and they were off, Luna beating them to the door.

They walked slowly at first, Luna crying softly as if urging them to hurry.

"We have to watch the wall, wait until Cillian can pull them away." Finn looked toward the wall in the near distance and saw that patrollers once again occupied it. They only waited a few minutes before messengers came and the wall was abandoned. "Let's go," she said, darting off toward the back end of town.

The quarry was a long jog from where they'd been in town. Once they were out of the city, they ran instead of walked. Finn grew more and more anxious. When he saw the quarry cliff, he sped up, sprinting toward it, Luna just in front of him.

Finn had just reached the wall, Luna already headed down the zigzag path through the quarry, when behind him Lucy screamed.

Finn whipped around and saw her held by two patrollers, kicking and fighting. Two more were running for him.

"Go!" she screamed, kicking the man nearest her in the groin and twisting away from the girl holding her other arm. She dove after the two running for him.

He hesitated only a second before crashing headlong down the path, the sounds of Lucy's scuffle fading as he moved swiftly through the rock.

He scrambled up the other side toward Luna who was crying from the cliff's edge. They immediately took off, running into the snow-covered trees, their breath leaving a foggy wake.

Finn felt a surge of guilt at leaving Lucy, but the patrollers wouldn't hurt her. She was Cillian's only family. Anger welled up as Finn ran. He was sure Cillian had told the patrol where they would be. He told himself he'd come back for Lucy after he knew Erilyn was safe.

Luna was impatient as Finn ran behind her. She kept crying, kept darting ahead and then circling back like a shepherd, trying to push him faster. He pushed himself as hard as he could, but he tired quickly. Each time he felt like he couldn't take another step, he would think of Erilyn—hands outstretched toward the falling man, her anguished cry, her panic as she looked all around—and he would find more energy. She was scared. Alone. He had to find her.

They stopped only twice to get water. Luna paced and cried as Finn gulped from icy streams, but she never left him. His side ached as he ran, his legs burned fiercely and his lungs burned even more. The cold air in his throat and nose was like fire itself.

They reached the field much faster than he thought possible. They were close, but now even the thought of taking another step seemed impossible. He was stumbling, ashamed as Luna cried, urging him forward.

He fell to his knees, catching himself with his hands on the cold ground. He wanted to keep going, but felt as if he had nothing left. He hit the ground weakly. Luna head butted him, a low growl in her throat. She cried.

And then something strange happened. Like hearing a bell in a silent room, he felt her. He didn't know how, didn't know if it was real, but he used that feeling of knowing where she was to push him back to his feet. Before long he was running again, though he didn't know how. He ran as hard as he could, something pulling him forward as his anxiety ratcheted up.

He skidded into the clearly, stopping when he couldn't reconcile what he was seeing. The tree was half burned still, nothing looked the same, but what caught him off guard were the two bodies, rolling through the snow. A Wylden was attacking Erilyn.

Luna yowled and launched her long, muscular white body toward them. The Wylden threw her off as if she were a doll. She hit the nearest tree with a crack and sank to the ground, unmoving.

Beneath the beast, Erilyn fought, grunting, trying to push him off. She had to be tired from running here and he was easily twice her size.

Gasping for his breath, Finn scrambled. He needed a stick. A rock. Something heavy or sharp. Just like in the caravan, he saw nothing.

And then something in the snow caught his eye—a long blade a few feet away. Finn ran to it and lifted its awkward length and weight.

Erilyn gasped in pain as the Wylden man did something he couldn't see and fear shot through him like an icicle. With the knife in hand he ran across the clearing and brought the blade down on the man. The Wylden's arm was bleeding now as he looked up at Finn. Beneath the man, Erilyn lay, eyes wide with fear, her shirt pushed almost to her breasts.

Anger burned through Finn and with a scream he stabbed the Wylden and yanked the blade back. The Wylden roared in anger and stood, blood dripping from his side. He charged Finn, his face a mask of anger. Finn held the knife out with both hands and the Wylden impaled himself on the long, sharp metal.

The Wylden's eyes grew wide as he sank to his knees, hands around the blade in his gut, and Erilyn started to scream.

Finn ran to her, circumventing the Wylden completely. He pulled her shirt straight as he gathered her to his chest. She was screaming and clutching her gut as if she'd been the one stabbed. He gathered her hands and held them firmly to his chest, but she continued to cry out.

"Erilyn!" he called, trying to look into her eyes, but they were darting around, looking everywhere except at him. She screamed again and then went silent, her body shaking much harder. She was looking straight up, her eyes wide, and then she went limp, her eyes closing, her breaths turning shallow. "Oh god. What did he do?" He pulled her closer, cradling her against him, though her body was listless.

"Erilyn?" He kissed her forehead—it was hot, as if she had a fever.

Luna woke then and walked on unsteady feet toward them. Finn shifted Erilyn to feel her pulse at her throat— weak. Luna licked her cheek and nudged her head as if that would wake her.

She'd been lying in the snow and her clothes were wet with it. He stood and lifted her against him with a grunt. He stepped over the snow bank on the burnt side of the pine and moved them inside, as far from the opening as he could get. Luna followed, her eyes never leaving Erilyn.

"She's going to be OK," he said as he carefully sat, still cradling her against him. He still wore her pack and awkwardly pulled their thin, holey blankets from it. The bloodstain from their first encounter had almost been washed out.

He arranged her in his lap so that her head was against his chest and as much of her body was touching his as possible. He could feel her small, shallow breaths against his neck. She whimpered and grew tense, then went limp again.

"You're OK," he whispered, kissing her hair as he covered them with the thin material. "You're OK." Once she was covered, Luna darted over, mewling like a kitten.

"Help me," he said. It was cold beneath the pine, but her skin felt colder than it should, and she wasn't shivering anymore. Luna curled her long body around Erilyn's back and tucked her large, white head into Erilyn's lap. Finn wrapped his arms around her. He felt like each breath was shallower than the last.

"Erilyn," he said, his lips against her hair. "Please." He kissed her hair over and over, his grip around her body tightening as he started to shake with fear more than cold. "Please. I need you."

He still had the little ring in his pocket, the one with the turquoise stone shaped like a raindrop. Holding her more tightly with one arm he pulled the ring from his pocket with the other. With hands that shook he slipped it onto her cold, pale finger, and then gathered her close again, rocking slightly, shivering himself. He didn't have a reason for doing it, but it felt right.

"Come on," he said, pressing his lips to her chilled forehead. "You have to be OK." His voice was a bare whisper. He rubbed her arms to try and get her circulation moving. Luna lay silent, staring into Erilyn's face without blinking.

Finn closed his eyes as tears started to make his vision swim. *Erilyn,* he thought when his words failed him. *Please be OK.*

A heartbeat passed and she didn't breathe, and then Erilyn gasped. Finn's eyes popped open and Luna jerked up, but Erilyn had settled again. She started to shiver. She huddled closer to him. Her fingers found the fabric of his shirt and gripped it weakly, but she didn't wake.

Luna watched her for a long moment, and then settled back against them with her own eyes closed. A single tear fell from Finn's eye as he kissed her hair one more time.

"You're going to be OK," he said into the quiet, believing it this time, his breath fogging up around him as he held her against his chest.

Chapter Thirty-One
Phantasms

Erilyn

Curled in a dark space. I don't have arms, legs, a body. Darkness presses in like a living weight.

Like being torn to shreds, I felt the man die. Like I was dying, too. My aura, myself, shattered like glass. My body cooling snow stained with his blood. I screamed without sound.

The Wylden—a beast who was more man than I thought. Whose aura was like mine—golden—except broken somehow. Jagged. All sharp edges. As he'd tried to force his way inside me, his energy had merged with mine, painfully, sharply. He was binding me and I couldn't fight him away.

And then he was gone, ripped from me like a dagger torn from flesh. It felt like bleeding. Like having no air. Like water leaking from between clenched fingers I slipped away until—

Erilyn. A voice on the wind, but different, like it was inside my mind, inside me. *Please be OK.*

Like the dinging of a crystal clear bell I remembered. *Finn.* I shifted, shook, started to take shape again. I felt arms around me, felt breaths in me, felt a heart that beat out of rhythm.

"You're going to be OK." Lips pressed to my hair.

And then, after the numbness of oblivion, pain. I wanted to scream, but my lips wouldn't open. I was trapped in the dark. I could feel Finn's hands, feel the cold air, feel Luna's head on my belly, but I was trapped. So I did what I always did when I felt trapped.

I ran.

My legs didn't move, but I did. I moved through the dark until I saw light—like the rivers of energy that had led me to Finn's center, I saw my own. My aura was gold, like sunshine, but it was fading and flickering like a candle without much wick. I followed the flickers, moving faster and faster, my body clinging to Finn's, until I saw golden light.

If I'd had knees to fall to I would have as the light washed over me. It was sunset gold. It was me. But it was dissipating. It pulsed and faded with each staccato beat of my heart.

Finn! I called, wishing I could see with my eyes. Wishing my body would do more than shake and cling. *Help me!*

And then I saw a new color—deep, rich green like summer grass, like pine boughs. His light traveled along the rivers of gold and made them grow brighter. Green and gold twined about one another like lovers. I followed them without eyes to the center—a glowing, golden orb. When the green connected with it, it flared bright white and then returned, glowing soft gold, a bit of green pulsing steadily at its center. An egg in a nest.

I felt my body relax, felt my fingers relax, felt myself sigh, felt Finn's even breaths as he slept, still holding me against him like a child.

I traveled back along the rivers of light, wishing I had hands to dip in them like I would a stream of cool water. The further I got, the stronger the green rivers became. I continued on, following them even after the gold was nearly gone. They connected to rivers of green, interspersed with bits of gold. I followed this to Finn's center.

At first, I was relieved to see that the tendrils were gone. No sign of Morrigan's corruption at all. It was calm here now. Peaceful.

Then I noticed the gold. Finn's aura was bright, beating steadily with his heart, the green full and deep. But it wasn't just his light. I saw my own, woven through it like threads, like ribbons.

It didn't look like what Morrigan had done, didn't look like what he'd done—intentionally or not—to save me, but it felt wrong. I wanted to reach out, to leave him pure and untouched, but I was afraid.

Truthfully, it was beautiful, but it wasn't right and shame filled me up. My soul had a bit of him and his had a bit of me. And I didn't know how to fix it.

My body was finally calm and slipping toward sleep. I tried to hold on, to stay here and fix this, but I had no hands. I needed to untangle the web that we were in. I wanted to release Finn from whatever I had done to him. To us.

Like wind pulls smoke up and away from the fire, I easily returned fully to my body. Sleep pulled at me deeply. I felt hot tears leak from my eyes and sink into the soft fabric of his sweater as the world went dark.

Chapter Thirty-Two
Subterranean

Finn

Finn woke with a sore neck from sleeping upright, propped against the tree. It was cold, but they'd managed to stay relatively warm, all piled together beneath their blankets. He lifted his head and felt it crack and strain. His shoulders ached—his arms had been locked around Erilyn all night, keeping her tucked against him—but he didn't dare move more than that.

He craned his neck to see her in the gray morning light filtering in through the burned side of the tree. Her face was peaceful, her breaths even and deep. Whatever was wrong from the night before seemed to have passed.

He looked at her—her small nose, the way her lips turned down slightly at the corners as if she didn't expect to ever be happy, at how small she seemed, curled against him almost like a child.

He sighed again and she shifted against him, burying her face in his chest as she woke. He gingerly shifted his arms so that he wasn't holding her so tightly, so possessively, and watched her eyes open and clear.

For a long moment she looked up at him as if confused, then a small smile formed on her face. "Finn," she whispered. And then her smile vanished to be replaced with fear or disgust.

Gently she disentangled herself from him, the blankets falling away as Luna stood and stretched, yawning widely enough to show her many sharp teeth and bright pink tongue.

Erilyn moved to Luna and wrapped her arms around the large cat. Luna leaned into her, rubbing her head and cheeks all over Erilyn's face, purring louder than Finn had ever heard.

"Are you OK?" he finally asked, moving stiffly from where he'd sat all night. His backside was numb and his shoulders and back ached.

"Yes," Erilyn said quietly, finally looking at him over her shoulder, her hair falling to cover her face in way that reminded him of their first days together.

He wanted to ask her what had happened, but her fearful, tentative gaze made him hold his tongue. Instead he stood and stretched, his spine cracking in a dozen places. "Will you stay in here for a little while?" He wanted to go take the body somewhere she wouldn't have to see it. She looked toward the dead side of the pine then back to him, a haunted look in her stone gray eyes, and nodded.

He walked away, stepping over the bank of snow that had acted as a shield for the wind and shivered at the sudden cold. The inside of the tree had been warmer than he'd realized and he was thankful for it, though it made the sudden bite of icy air harder to stand.

The Wylden man still lay, face down, in the snow. His body had been dusted by it during the night, and some of his blood had been covered.

The knife Finn had used to kill him was in the man's hand, dark with dried blood. Finn shivered at the memory, of how it had felt to pierce his clothes and flesh. He'd never killed anything in his life and the urge to vomit rose. It hadn't been real until now, looking down at his lifeless, waxy-looking purple skin.

Finn looked back toward the pine. Erilyn was inside, alive, because he'd killed this creature. This man. He grabbed his feet and started to drag him, the knife still gripped in frozen fingers. He was heavy and left a deep trench in the snow. Finn pulled him back into the woods. He wanted to bury him, but he knew the ground was too hard and he had no tools, so the best he could do would be to take him somewhere Erilyn wouldn't see, maybe somewhere he could cover him with stones.

He dragged him until his arms and legs grew too tired. He was in the woods, far enough from the clearing that Erilyn wouldn't have to see him, though there were no stones or rocks here.

Finn flipped the man so that he was on his back. Knife still clenched in his white fingers, Finn crossed his stiff arms over his chest. In death, the Wylden looked more like a regular man, the anger and ferocity gone from his hairy face. Finn looked down at him and thought back to his mother's funeral. They hadn't let him see her—all those who had died of the malady had been burned—but they'd held a service.

The mayor at the time had led the attendees, primarily the children of those who'd died, in a simple wish for the deceased. Finn couldn't bring himself to say the first part, to thank this man for his contribution to the world. But he could say, "I hope your spirit is at peace." His breath reflected the morning light filtering through the bare-boned trees. "And I'm sorry."

He stood in silence for a moment before turning and following the trail he'd made, back to the clearing.

In the clearing he kicked the snow around to hide the blood, glad Erilyn hadn't come out yet. He had just finished when he heard a sound—soft lilting words from beneath the pine. He walked closer, listening, as Erilyn sang a sad tune without words. A song of mourning. He listened, captivated, as the melancholy slowly changed and was replaced by something a little brighter, if still sad. He thought of grass breaking through frozen ground during the first days of spring.

Her voice slowly faded away and she emerged from the tree, not surprised to see him there. She looked at him critically for a moment, that same sad, worried expression etched into her face as when she'd woken. He wondered how different her life would be, how much less painful the last month would have been for her, if he'd never come to her.

His face crumpled and she went to him, her arms slipping around his waist as he drew her close. They stood that way while the sun rose higher in the sky. The air wasn't quite so cold.

She finally stepped back, an unreadable mask on her face. "Why are you here?" she asked, her expression hopeful and doubtful at the same time. He put his hands on her shoulders.

"Because I want to be." He squeezed her shoulders gently. "And because I didn't want you to be out here alone."

She looked into his eyes until the doubt in her own vanished and she nodded. "We need to go to Citadel. To the caves."

"The city you're from?"

She nodded slowly. "We have to warn them."

In Sunnybrook, children were told that the caves were filled with white-skinned troglodytes who practiced magic and stole babies. But he looked at Erilyn now and knew those stories were false. He took Erilyn's hand and twined his fingers with hers. "Lead the way," he said.

Despite being hungry, tired, and sore, Finn trudged after Erilyn. Luna led the way, leaving perfect cat prints in the snow that were quickly covered by their footprints and kicked up snow.

Erilyn didn't say much as they walked. He knew she didn't want to go back, knew she'd never meant to go back. Some of the things he knew, he couldn't remember being told. It was more like he'd always known them. He wanted to ask her about it, to ask her about all this, but her body language was tense, so he kept quiet.

After a few hours they came to a rock outcropping in a hillside. Erilyn looked at it for long moments before turning to him. "You won't be able to see anything after a few minutes." She took his hand in hers and even though her skin was cold, it warmed him. "But I will. I'll get us there. You just have to trust me."

The darkness came upon him sooner than he thought it would. He thought he'd have more time to acclimate, but it was pitch black in minutes.

"Erilyn?" he whispered, and she stopped, still gripping his hand.

"Stay close. OK?" She squeezed his fingers and he squeezed back. She walked a little slower. Luna walked behind them, almost silent, as if she were protecting their backs like a rear guard.

It was hard to keep track of time in the dark, but Finn's calf muscles were aching from their slow descent. The pressure in his ears built and built until they popped. The deeper they went, the stranger the air felt. Finn tripped over and over despite Erilyn's whispered warnings to step here or not step there. It was warm down here, and muggy, and his winter clothes stuck to his skin. If he let himself think about where he was, what he was doing, he started to feel like he couldn't breathe. Only Erilyn's firm hand in his, and her repeated assurances that she had him, kept him from the brink.

Finally, after what seemed days, Erilyn stopped and turned to him. He only knew because she'd stepped close enough to put her hand on his chest and leaned in close enough for him to feel her breath on his ear.

"The city center is just up ahead," she breathed. He shivered and pulled her to him, needing to feel more than just her hand in his. She hugged him back, and like slipping into a warm bath after a long, hard day, he started to feel a little better. "There should be people there, but—" she took a long, slow breath, "but there aren't. Only a few."

He didn't know what that meant, but he didn't want to say much and risk being heard.

She kept his hand in hers but stepped back. "Just stay with me."

"Like I have any other option," he whispered and she let out a single, breathy laugh.

"Luna, come."

They walked in what felt like a zigzag for a few more minutes, and then Finn saw light up ahead. It was all he could do to keep from running toward it. It was dim, but after hours of pitch black it seemed bright.

He followed Erilyn, whose steps slowed as his begged to speed up. She stopped at the mouth to the cavern— barely large enough to walk through. Finn looked past her to see a cavern much larger than he would have expected. In the center was a statue of a man, roughly carved from the stone itself. From what he could see, the cavern was round and went up and up past his line of sight. Doorways and holes like windows dotted the walls, and a staircase, cut from the stone, spiraled up.

"Where is everyone?" she breathed as if to herself. "We have to go up," she said to him, knowing he was tired. "Chief Roark, or whoever's Chief now, lives on the top level. The stairs are the only way." She sighed. "People should be here."

With only a second for another breath, Erilyn darted through the doorway as Finn squeezed through behind her. Looking back, he realized it wasn't a door like the others, but a fissure in the rock.

He followed her to the stairs and swallowed hard as they started to walk up. He held onto the rail as Luna ran up ahead. The top stretched high above and he hoped he had the energy left in him to make it there.

Chapter Thirty-Three
Aiyanna

Erilyn

As we made our way up the stairs, I kept my awareness half focused on the city center to see if I could figure out where all the people were. I felt a few people in the lower rooms, frantic about something, but most of the homes were empty. It worried me, but I had to focus on getting to the Chief, on warning him about what was coming.

Behind me, Finn lagged. He was pressed against the wall, avoiding the rail. I could feel his anxiety increase the higher we got. My own did as well, but for different reasons.

I hadn't seen Chief Roark since I was a girl. I remembered him as a huge man, tall and powerfully built with a long, thick white beard and dark red eyes. Not everyone in Citadel had red eyes, but those who did were revered as special. It was only those with red eyes would could truly see without any light.

I was nervous about seeing Roark, but even more nervous that I might see—or not see—his daughter Aiyanna. Seeing her would be hard—she'd hated me, tormented me—but not seeing her might mean she was dead, that I'd killed her four years ago when I caused the earthquake.

"Erilyn." Finn's voice was a harsh whisper and I stopped, turning to see him holding the rail against the wall, clutching his side. I backtracked a few steps and put my hand on his back. He was shaking and exhausted.

"We'll rest a minute." I itched to keep going, but I was pushing him too hard. He'd volunteered to come along, but down here I was responsible for him. This was my world, not his.

He only took a few breaths before nodding and I was off again, Luna impatiently waiting a dozen steps above. I let my awareness seek out people inside the Chief's home. I only felt one person and my heart dropped. Maybe I had killed her. Maybe I'd killed all the children that day.

We reached the top landing and Finn clutched the rail at the top, chest heaving, shoulders hunched. I needed to give him time to compose himself before we entered, to present a unified front. I turned to see if he was OK when the door—made from wood scavenged from the upworld—swung open.

A girl stood with a bag over her shoulder. She looked shocked to see us—her straight, white hair in many braids, hanging over her shoulders, her mouth opened in surprise, though she didn't make a sound. Her eyes were a bright, icy blue.

"Aiyanna," I breathed, relief mixing with dread.

She closed her mouth and looked at me quizzically for a long moment before her hand flew to her mouth. "Erilyn?"

I braced to pull Finn with me if we needed to flee. If she raised an alarm before I could warn her of what was coming, we wouldn't make it out.

I loosed a tendril of my awareness and felt her surprise, her fear, and an unfocused desire.

We stood there for a long breath before she shook her head, grabbed my hand, and pulled me inside. Finn and Luna followed without being asked and Aiyanna shut the door behind us, the light in the room so dim I wondered if Finn could see at all.

"Erilyn. You're alive." She'd let go of my arm but hovered next to me, as if I might disappear at any moment. As children she'd been taller than me, but now she was smaller, much smaller, as if she hadn't grown at all in the last four years. She was slight, waif-like, with delicate, thin features and chalk white skin, though when I looked carefully, I could see maturity in her eyes and the set of her mouth.

I let that tendril of awareness expand and immediately wished I hadn't.

Erilyn! The voice—no, voices—were so loud I had to fight the urge to cover my ears. "I'm alive," I said, hoping she hadn't noticed me jump. "So are you."

She just nodded and we stood for a long moment, those same conflicting emotions wafting over me, but never becoming clear.

"I'm Finn." He was standing beside me, close but not touching, and I realized he had to duck.

"An upworlder." Aiyanna shied away as if she'd only just seen him. "Why are you here?" She turned back to me, her posture now closed off and tensed as if to run. "Are you part of the group coming to kill us?"

"No," I said, confused. "No, we came to *warn* you. There are upworlders coming to capture you, capture everyone. They want the old mines." Being with Finn had made me brave and I gripped her delicate arms with force.

"My father's already evacuated the city." She was shaking beneath my hands and I loosened my grip. Her strange desire, one I couldn't place, had strengthened as I touched her and I thought it might be the desire to run. "I stayed with the last group, to make sure they got out OK. They're all on the lower levels, lower class. Just a few are left."

"Evacuated?" I turned to Finn. He was squinting in the darkness. Luna was silent beside me. "How did he know to evacuate? Do you think there could be a spy in Sunnybrook?"

His expression was grim and he shrugged. I put my hand on his arm, took strength from the strong muscles there, from the way he leaned into my touch, and then turned back to Aiyanna who was watching us with a haunted expression.

"I'm supposed to leave soon. It's a good thing no one saw you. They would have thought you were scouts. You look so—" she reached as if to touch my hair, then dropped her hand. "Different than you used to."

"We have to warn your father that they're on their way. *Now.* And—" I took a deep breath. This was the part I dreaded. People in Citadel had always known what I could do and they hated me for it. "Aiyanna, do you remember when we were kids. That I could do things? Strange things? " My voice was soft. I expected her to be alarmed, to shy away, but she only nodded. "The people who are coming, they're all part of a patrol, they're soldiers, and they can do what I can do, except they're much stronger than I've ever been." I took her shoulders, feeling huge next to such a bird-like person. "We have to get the rest of the people away and *hidden.* Where are people being evacuated?"

Aiyanna visibly swallowed. "The grotto."

I closed my eyes and took a calming breath. The grotto was a huge cavern that opened up to the night sky. Only a few people were allowed there to work the fields at night where we grew our crops. If they were all gathered there, beneath the open sky, Morrigan and the others would find them quickly.

"Take me there," I said. "It's not safe. We have to—"

The door behind Aiyanna opened and in strode Chief Roark. He was still impressive with broad shoulders and a great, white beard, but he was smaller than I remembered. Finn was inches taller and his shoulders were just as wide and it made Roark less daunting.

"Release my daughter." His voice was gravelly and quiet. I did as he asked as two other men, shorter than him, shorter than me, stepped in around him. My back pressed into Finn's chest and he found my hand with his. "Take them."

"Father!" Aiyanna stepped between the men and us, hand outstretched. "They came to warn us about the invasion. It's Erilyn. Remember? The girl who—"

"I know who it is," he said, roughly pulling Aiyanna out of the way. An image of him striking her, an image I'd accidentally pulled from her mind when we were children, flashed in my mind. "She was never one of us." He acted as if he was speaking only to her, but it was clear he meant for everyone to hear. "She's back to exact revenge. A scout. Without her, the upworlders won't know where to find us." He met my eyes, his dark red irises blending seamlessly with his black pupils and looking like congealed blood. "Take them to the pits."

The guards had long, curved blades. One grabbed me while the other took Finn's arm. We didn't fight. It would only assure him that we were guilty.

They hadn't noticed Luna. She'd slunk against the wall and was holding perfectly still. *Stay,* I willed her. *Find us.* I almost felt her affirmation as they pulled us from the room and led us down the stairs, curved blades pressing into her backs.

I heard Aiyanna protesting loudly. Heard her urge him to move the people out of the grotto. For some reason she believed me. The girl I'd harbored hatred for, had run from the memory of, believed me. Knowing that gave me hope, even as they pushed us toward the pits. In the span of three days I would have been jailed by both cities I'd called home.

The two guards stumbled slightly as Luna darted past us, a white blur. They cursed her, unsure of what was she was, but they were charged to stay with us and so they let her go. She was gone, disappeared down the stairs impossibly fast.

The men pushed and pulled us, though we didn't speak or fight back, down through dark corridors. Our guards were both blue-eyed and therefore needed lanterns, which I was thankful for. They grabbed two, shaking them so that the glowworms inside would wake and glow brightly.

My heart leapt strangely at the sight of the dim, green-blue light emanating from behind wavy glass. As a child, the glowworms had been my only friends, and despite the fact that we were being led to prison down in the pits, it felt good to see their cool, lovely light again.

We reached a cavern with a wide opening. Metal bars had been drilled into the rock, and a metal-barred gate opened in the middle. I was shoved in first. The guard nearest us hung a glowworm lantern just beside the wall that cast long, thin shadows from the bars across our skin.

People in the caves rarely raised their voices, and I was sure Finn couldn't hear the guards' whispered conversation. But I could.

"We should stay and watch them," the one who'd held me said, his eyes twitching back and forth between Finn and me, having never seen an upworlder in the flesh.

"Roark will be angry if we leave them here and something happens. She's one of the gifted." He spat the word *gifted* as if it were a disease.

"My family's in the grotto," the other man said. His voice was softer. "My wife and daughter. I have to get to them. Just in case. You heard what the Chief's daughter said."

"Did you not hear me?" the first said. "She's *gifted*. She'll escape and then he'll kill us both."

The second man looked at me and I kept my expression neutral. He knew I'd heard. He sized me up for a moment before shaking his head. "No, I have to go." He put his hand on the first man's shoulder. "The upworlders are coming, whether we have these two or not. I'll not leave my family alone."

He disappeared into the dark alley quickly, only the telltale light of his bobbing lantern giving him away, until that too disappeared around a bend.

The guard who'd dragged me was angry—I could feel it coming off him like steam. He stared at me for a long time and I felt many thoughts pass by me like rapid lightning flashes. He thought I was pretty and he thought upworlders should be ugly. He was afraid. He was lonely. He wanted to go with his friend.

Go. I thought toward him. *Leave us alone.* He shook his head as if a fly were buzzing in his ear.

"I'll be just down the corridor," he said, looking confused. "Don't try anything or I'll gut you both."

Go. I pushed him with my mind.

As he started to walk away, I breathed a sigh of relief, then stumbled and sank to the ground as I heard my name again. *Erilyn!* It was loud, echoing around in my head. I could differentiate between the voices now. There were four or five calling to me, louder than ever. *Erilyn. Come!*

Finn was at my side in a moment. When his palm touched my cheek the voices stopped. I clutched his hand and looked up at him, into his warm blue eyes, and was suddenly overcome with emotion like a sudden rainstorm.

Chapter Thirty-Four
Glowworms

Finn

"Tell me what's going on," Finn said as he held Erilyn's face in his hands. She was on her knees on the ground, breathing hard. She was staring in his eyes as if they were a lifeline, clutching his hands on her face.

Something was happening to her, something he couldn't see, and he was growing tired of just trusting that she'd be OK when he didn't even know what it was she was supposed to be OK from. "Please. Talk to me."

She ducked her head and his hands fell away, then she stood and walked over to where the lantern hung on the wall. Without a word, she squeezed her arm through the bars to her shoulder and grabbed the lantern before bringing it into the cage with them.

The shadows in the room from the small light shifted as Erilyn settled herself against the cave wall on the hard packed earth. She patted the earth next to her and he sat, pressing his leg against hers for his own comfort as well as hers.

Erilyn unscrewed the lid that served as a top and handle. Finn looked closer at the strange green-blue light and realized that there was something moving inside. Erilyn dipped her hand in and a small smile broke out over her face. She carefully scooped up the light and it grew brighter. She opened her hand and held it toward him.

It was a worm, or a grub, really. It was almost as fat, as it was long—shorter than Erilyn's thumb—and it looked like it might be furry, though it was hard to tell because the light it emitted made it difficult to see.

"When I was a little girl, these were my friends." She offered him the grub and he took it, though he didn't really want to. It inched into his palm and he was surprised to find that it was warm and soft. Its little legs were like tiny spongy mushroom caps and he found himself smiling as well.

"I used to think I could hear them singing to me." She laughed lightly as she let a few grubs crawl into her palm. She brought them close to her face and smiled as they glowed brighter. "Now I know I can." Her voice was a bare whisper as her smile faltered and fell away.

Carefully she took the worm from Finn's hand and replaced it, and the ones she held, with the others in the jar. She left the lid off as she sat it next to her on the ground.

"When you killed that man—" Finn winced and she put her hand on his arm. "The Wylden who was going to hurt me," she said more softly, "I *felt* it." Her fingers squeezed and Finn thought he felt a small tremor. "I mean, I really felt it. Felt what it was like to die."

Finn slipped his arm around Erilyn's shoulders and pulled her head to his chest. She sighed against him and pulled back just enough to see his face, as if she needed to see his reaction.

"I thought I was dying. Knew I was." Her soft sigh was sad. "And then I heard you. Here." She pointed to her head. "And I somehow found a way to stay."

Though he'd only known her a matter of weeks, he could tell she wasn't telling him everything. He wouldn't push right now, but he filed it away for later as something to ask. He wanted her to tell him what she would on her own.

"Maybe it was this—" she held up her hand, the one he'd slipped the turquoise ring onto—he'd almost forgotten he'd done that and he blushed seeing it now. "Or maybe it was just that I wanted to hear you. I don't know." Her hand fell back to her lap. "But you pulled me back."

She closed her eyes and took a deep breath. "I left Citadel because I caused an earthquake." She was worrying her hands in her lap, twirling the ring around on her finger absentmindedly. "And after I left, I started hearing things." Her eyes met Finn's, looking haunted.

"I heard my name. Like it was being carried on the wind. A single voice that was so soft, I was sure at first I was imagining it." She sighed, her hands in her lap finally still. The green-blue light from the lantern was steady and dim. "But I kept hearing it, on and off, until I met you."

Finn's arm was still over her shoulders and he pulled her a little closer.

"Being with you blocked it out, somehow." Her eyes were huge as she stared up at him and he nodded when he could find no words. "I didn't hear them at all while we were in Sunnybrook when you were—" she met his eyes then looked way. "When you were gone. But I heard them again when I left." She sighed and bit her lip. "And then, just now, I heard them again. Except it's *not* one voice, it's more than that. And just like I heard you here," she pointed to her temple again, as if afraid to say she was hearing voices in her head, "I heard them—so loud—until you touched me."

She grew quiet then, the glowworm light seeming to dim as she did. It was like she was waiting for Finn to panic, to run away, but just like every other time he'd ever seen her hurting, seen her in need, all he wanted to do was to help her.

"It's like these things I can do are being amplified." She closed her eyes and shook her head. "And I don't know how to stop it except by—"

"Except by being with me. Touching me." His voice was soft and she nodded, eyes closed.

"I'm sorry." She barely breathed the words.

Finn pulled Erilyn to him and wrapped both arms around her. She was limp in his arms as if she had given up.

"After all you've done for me," he said as he kissed her hair, "you think you need to apologize for this?"

Before Erilyn could reply, Luna darted in, a white blur in the shadow. Erilyn's head popped up as soon as she was visible and Luna squeezed through the bars to get to them.

"Good girl," Erilyn said as the cat rubbed against her cheek, her large paw on Erilyn's shoulder.

"She helped me find you." Aiyanna appeared from the darkness, like a ghost taking solid form. Her voice was quiet and a little sad. She held up a large, brass key. "I'm here to get you out."

"The guard?" Erilyn asked as she and Finn scrambled up.

Aiyanna opened the metal gate with the key and smirked. "He'll wake up in a few hours."

"Thank you," Erilyn said, touching Aiyanna's arm. Aiyanna's eyes grew large and she blushed.

"I owe you more than this," she said, in the quiet way of all the people of Citadel.

Erilyn squeezed her arm gently. "We have to get to the grotto."

Aiyanna shook her head. "I sent some people ahead and told them what you told me. They'll believe me. They'll scatter." She looked sure with her chin held high. "If you go, they'll be afraid. They might hurt you."

Something about Aiyanna's tone of voice made Finn uncomfortable. It was the same way he'd felt when Cillian looked at Erilyn with those heated eyes, but he dismissed it and pinched the bridge of his nose.

After a long moment, Erilyn nodded. She looked back at Finn, who nodded as well.

"We have to get you out of here," Aiyanna said, grabbing Erilyn's hand for the first time. Erilyn jerked, but Aiyanna didn't let go. "Do you understand now?" she whispered, and Erilyn nodded again, more slowly.

"Erilyn?" Finn said, but Erilyn's eyes were glued to Aiyanna. He wanted to reach out and grab her, that same jealous feeling heating up inside, but he didn't. After a moment, she let go and turned to him.

"We have to do something first." Erilyn's voice was soft, but forceful. "The voices I told you about," she said, eyes wide and somehow childlike. "They're people here in Citadel. We have to find them."

"How?" he asked, stepping toward her.

Aiyanna stooped to pick up the glowworm lantern. "What are you talking about?" she asked.

"There are people here, children, calling to me." Erilyn looked between Aiyanna and Finn, her expression determined. Finn knew that look—there was no changing her mind. "We're going to go get them and take them with us."

Aiyanna was quiet, her expression angry, but nodded after a moment.

Erilyn took the lantern from her and gingerly poured the grubs into a groove in the rock where they slowly disappeared. Finn was left in darkness. Erilyn's hand slipped into his while Luna pressed against his leg and his sudden surge of panic dissipated.

"Can you see me?" she whispered. Aiyanna's whispered *yes* was more like a passing breeze than a word. "Stay close."

Finn followed Erilyn as she pulled him behind her. Luna was there, too, never getting underfoot but always close. He couldn't hear Aiyanna, but he knew she was there, too, taking Luna's place as vanguard. He felt like a blind man being led into the unknown by some kind of goddess, trailed by an unknown pale devil.

Erilyn squeezed his hand and he squeezed back, feeling his ring on her finger. In that moment, feeling his ring on her hand and a calm assurance that he was sure was intentionally from her, he knew he would follow her anywhere, even into the dark unknown of the underworld.

Chapter Thirty-Five
The Nursery

Erilyn

The voices were silent whenever Finn held my hand, but only if I didn't listen for them. As I led this strange group through the tunnels in the dark, even with Finn's hand in mind, I *listened*. I didn't have to try hard.

Erilyn! They were crying out for me. I started to see images—a wall that shone dark green-blue, drawings on the wall done by a child's hand, by my hand, an old crib, made from scrap pieces of wood, shoved, broken in the corner. I started to see them through each other's eyes— they were children, five of them. We were getting closer. I could feel it. I could hear their individual voices and I moved faster, only slowing when behind me Finn would stumble in the dark.

I pulled us to a stop when I heard voices up ahead— adults, arguing more loudly than they should have. I closed my eyes and let my vision speed ahead until I was seeing through their eyes. The door in front of them—made of thick, old wood—was stuck.

"They're kids. They didn't do this." The woman whose eyes I was borrowing gestured toward the door in front of me. It was strange seeing through her eyes. It was dark—a small flame from a single candle the only light—and yet the room was clear. These were the eyes of someone born to the caves, and I wondered why my eyes weren't like this. Compared to this, I couldn't see at all.

"They're not *just* kids," the man with her said. He was in a guard uniform. "They're gifted. *Freaks*. But Roark wants them in the grotto. And they *are* doing this." He kicked the door and I felt the children behind it huddle together, afraid.

Erilyn. The single voice was a sigh. *You're here?* It was a girl.

I'm here. I felt their collective relief, though I didn't know how I would get them out.

I pulled Finn further from the voices and found an alcove with my hands more than my eyes—the little I could see in the dark now seemed unacceptable after seeing through the eyes of a cave dweller—and I ducked into it, pulling Finn against me to make room for Aiyanna.

"They're children," I whispered just below Finn's ear, knowing Aiyanna would hear either way. "In a room. I think in the room I lived in." My hand was shaking as a sudden realization cascaded over me. "I don't think I was born here." Finn squeezed my hand and I found myself leaning into him, needing his warmth and reassurance as my whole history started to rewrite itself in my mind. "That room was where I lived as a baby. I remember the walls—

they're vitium. And they've put these children in there. Children like me."

As Finn held me closer, lips in my hair, I felt Aiyanna next to us grow sad.

"How do we get to them?" Finn's whisper was louder than mine, but still quiet enough that the men down the hall wouldn't hear.

I took a deep breath, knowing he wouldn't like this. "We don't," I said, squeezing his fingers. "I do."

They both tensed.

"I can get them out. I promise. Please," I whispered, knowing Finn was close enough to feel my breath, to feel my heartbeat against him. "Trust me one more time."

In the dark he found my face with his hand and then brought his forehead to mine. "I do," he said, but the pain in his voice was clear enough without me being able to feel it in my bones.

His heart was racing and for a moment I forgot about Aiyanna, pressed into the space with us, though not touching us. All I could focus on was his warmth, his beating heart, his skin against mine, and I tilted my head and kissed him. It was like being on fire and not burning. When I pulled away, I felt full. Like I could do anything.

"Wait here." I pulled away and darted out into the hall. Luna joined me and I felt stronger.

Down the hall, the guards were still arguing. They were trying to pry the door open with no luck.

Can you help me? I asked the children, knowing they were afraid, knowing that they were small. I felt their assent and took a deep breath. I'd shared my plan with them in my mind and they were ready.

I counted to five in my head before walking, hands outstretched, into the small pool of light the candle made. The two guards turned toward me, startled. The man raised his knife as the door behind him flew open.

The guards were confused and afraid. The children were afraid, too, but they trusted me. I couldn't see them yet. Luna, ever the silent guardian, darted around the guards and into the dark nursery turned prison cell.

"They're coming with me," I said, using the energy inside me to push them. They both stumbled—a small shove. This was one skill I hadn't practiced and I was trusting my instincts and the children to help. I knew I could do it, but like a muscle I rarely used, I wasn't sure exactly how to do it well.

"The hell they are," the man said. He lifted the blade as if to throw it and I *pushed*, the blade flying from his hand as he stumbled back a few paces.

"They are." The woman looked interested in what was happening, but not scared. I focused my attention on the man.

"You're going to go now," I said, trying to force him to believe me, trying to talk to him like I had the dogs that first night I'd met Finn, like I had the guard just a little while ago. *Help me,* I asked the children, who still hid in the dark room behind them. I heard them speak to him. *Go.* The man's eyes went glassy and he started to look around wildly.

He grabbed the woman's hand, his eyes darting all around. "We have to go." He looked at me as if suddenly afraid before he ran down a second corridor.

Luna meowed from the dark, urging the children out. I'd expected darker children, like me, but they were all true cave dwellers with white skin and hair, and they all had red eyes. There were five of them. The oldest was a girl of maybe twelve or thirteen, and she held the youngest, a boy of maybe three. Five sets of eyes locked on me. They were all older than they seemed. I wanted to smile at them, to reassure them, but they could feel my nervousness and to fake anything else would be unfair.

"Follow me." I turned and made my way back to Finn and Aiyanna, the children trailing obediently behind me without making a sound.

Getting back to Finn and Aiyanna had been easy. Getting us all to the surface was proving harder. I let Aiyanna lead, though I knew the children could see in the dark. Aiyanna, though, had the most experience in these caves. And while both the children and I had the ability to see far ahead of where we were, she was the one who knew the guard routes.

I led Finn by the hand, but still felt the children in my mind. Their voices were a familiar presence now that I could pick them apart. I'd heard most of them for almost three years.

We learned each other as we walked in silence. It wasn't talking or even sharing images as much as it was sharing memories or feelings about things. I pieced their history together a little at a time as they did the same with mine.

They were orphans, all of them. With the exception of the youngest, who'd only been there two years, the others had been there the entire four I'd been gone. They had been put there to become like me, to be the beginnings of an army for the citizens of Citadel. They'd been given food laced with vitium, had been forced to live in seclusion in that room, had learned about their powers quickly and painfully.

My heart broke for them. In their time together, they'd learned to function almost as a single individual. The older children cared for the younger, but their minds were synced up in a beautiful, heartbreaking way.

Every so often, Aiyanna would stop us with a raised hand if she needed to check around a bend or in a new cavern. I could barely see her in the dark, but Finn responded quickly to the pressure of my hand on his. Luna stayed with the children, sandwiched between Aiyanna and us.

I felt the air growing cooler as we inched toward the surface and a new tension rose in me. Morrigan and the patrol would be here soon, if they weren't already. If they were already here, they'd be headed for the city center, and then, if she could seek people like I could, the grotto.

I shook my head and tried to pace myself. I needed to get these children to safety. After that, and only after that, would I find her and do everything in my power to stop her.

Chapter Thirty-Six
Surface

Finn

Finn felt strange, moving through the dark, knowing there were people all around, but hearing no one except Erilyn, whose hand was a warm lifeline in his.

Erilyn had brought the children to their alcove, but he hadn't been able to see them. She'd told them in a hushed whisper that she had all five of them and they needed to go. No one had spoken since, but the hairs on the back of his neck were standing up and he wondered if these children were communicating in the way Erilyn could. It made him really uncomfortable.

Aiyanna led, and she would stop them without a sound. Each time, Erilyn would lean back against Finn and he would pull her closer to breathe her in, reassure himself that this was real, that this pitch-black nightmare would end. She would turn sometimes and hug him as if trying to comfort him.

He didn't know how her abilities, her powers, worked, but he would hold her and think, *I'm OK.* She would squeeze his hand or his waist and he could almost *feel* her smile. It was so strange.

Finn felt like they would be walking forever. It had taken a long time, hours, to get down into Citadel, but this seemed longer. It was hard to tell, but they seemed to be taking switchbacks. Part of him worried he would never see the sun again.

At one point, one of the children bumped into him. When they touched him the buzzing came back and he jerked away. It faded as soon as the child wasn't touching him, but he realized as it left that it was a new kind of buzzing—one that he felt on his skin, a tingle–and it didn't hurt. He sighed and Erilyn squeezed his hand in warning. *Too loud.*

He wasn't cut out for this, for darkness and silence. He'd always been kind of introverted, preferring to stay in his home than go out and mingle, but now he knew he was made for the upworld, for the sun, for light. As they turned yet again and he felt the ground slope down, he wondered how Erilyn had lived down here. She was made up of light; she belonged in the woods beneath open skies. She'd been surprised she hadn't been born here, but he wasn't.

He tripped over a rock and she caught him with her other hand. He took that moment to pull her to him for a quick hug and she returned it. Holding her felt like being infused with sunshine and his growing unease and anxiety at being in the dark so long melted away.

Finn had no sense of time, but his calves ached and he was so hungry he could barely stay upright. He felt dizzy and clumsy.

He'd resisted asking to rest, but he was almost to the point where he couldn't go on. He'd opened his mouth and taken a breath when he felt Erilyn's hand grip his painfully tight. He snapped his mouth shut, thinking she'd known what he was about to do. But then her feet slowed and she pressed her shoulder into his side—her sign that they should slow, be cautious. He strained his ears and his eyes but nothing had changed. He wondered what this dark world of dirt and dripping water was like to them, what they could see and hear that he couldn't.

And then, after ages of straining, he did hear something. It was the barest sound, almost like thunder, but not quite. He still couldn't see, but they were moving up now. *Up.* If it hadn't been for the sounds that were becoming more and more clear as they inched forward, he would have taken off running and hoped not to run into wall. Up meant outside.

Erilyn's hand gripped his tighter and tighter. Her body grew more rigid against him. Luna growled low and in the darkness, it was terrifying. She sounded so much bigger than she was.

The thunder that wasn't thunder was a little louder now, though he wasn't sure what it was. The air was colder, though, so he knew they were getting closer to the upworld again.

Erilyn pulled him close. Other bodies closed in around them and he prepared himself for the buzzing. A child-sized hand slipped into his, and for the barest of seconds he felt that tingle along his skin, and then it was gone. Finn gently squeezed the child's hand, surprised at how tiny it was. Until this moment, the children had been figments. The nightcrawlers—*cave dwellers*, he corrected himself—made him uncomfortable with their colorless skin and hair, but feeling this child's hand in his changed something inside him. He'd been too focused on himself, on wanting out. In a way, he was responsible for these five children, following three strangers into the unknown, and he told himself he would focus on them until they were through this. He squeezed the child's hand again and felt the child squeeze back.

He could hear tiny breaths now. They were *all* tired, not just him. They had just been better about hiding it. His cheeks burned in shame and he was, for the first time, glad it was dark.

"We have to keep going," Aiyanna said. Her voice was a mere breath, but they were all close enough that even Finn heard.

"Do you know what those sounds are?" Erilyn asked, her hand in Finn's shaking. "Wylden. Savage people." She spit the words, backed up by Luna's low growl.

"I know about Wylden." Aiyanna's voice was soft, calm.

"No, you don't!" Erilyn's whisper rose to a hiss. "They won't care that we're women, that these are children. They will show no mercy. We don't stand a chance if we keep going."

It was silent for a moment and Finn heard Erilyn's breaths as she tried to calm herself down.

"We can't go back," Aiyanna finally said, her whisper sounding sad. "You heard them behind us, searching." That's why we'd taken so many turns and twists and again I felt shame rise up in me. "We can only keep going up, where our people won't likely follow."

"We have to keep them safe." Erilyn meant the children. The children huddled closer at the same time. One child grabbed his leg while another gripped his arm.

"We will." Aiyanna's voice was firm. "We'll go up, sneak around the fray. The Wylden are busy with the upworlders, they won't see us."

Panic shot through Finn like an icy wind, but Erilyn's posture against him didn't change. She knew. The Wylden were fighting the upworlders. The patrol. Morrigan.

"Everyone's fine so far," Erilyn said, turning to face Finn. He realized, absently, that his sudden fear was something she had most likely felt, and again, his cheeks and neck burned. He shouldn't worry about Morrigan after all she'd done, but he did. She'd been his world for too long to totally disregard her now.

The child gripping his leg nodded against his hip. "There are ten—no, twelve—people. And many more of the *others*." It was a little boy, his voice high pitched and quiet, but steady.

"So far—" came a young girl's voice from a foot or two away, "everyone is OK."

"A few injuries." This third voice came from such a young-sounding boy, Finn wondered how he knew the word.

"We'll go up and around," Aiyanna said firmly. "Two with me," she said and Fin felt the air shift as two children went to her. "Three with Finn and Luna." Finn and Erilyn separated. The loss of Erilyn's touch was disorienting until the little boy grabbed his hand again, and on the other side, a second hand slipped into his. Luna chirped softly and Finn assumed the last child was with her. "Good. Erilyn, it's up to you to get us around."

Aiyanna's faith in Erilyn rang true, even to Finn, who felt deaf and blind here. Erilyn wasn't touching him anymore, but he could still *feel* her, like he could somehow sense her against him. He knew, without knowing how, that they were connected, and he was glad for it. She squeezed his arm once before walking to the front of the group.

"We won't let you fall in the dark," the little boy who held his hand whispered up to him as they started to move. Finn smiled and let the children lead him.

They quickly neared the surface and Finn felt as if he could breathe for the first time in hours as the first bit of light filtered down to them. He could feel the icy wind bouncing off the snow outside as it snaked toward them. The thunder that wasn't thunder was more distinct now, but he still couldn't pick out anything specific. He tried not to think of Morrigan fighting Wylden. One of the children squeezed his hand.

He looked down, directly into the dark eyes of a little boy. His other hand was held by a tiny girl, her gray-white hair hanging long and dirty down her back. Just in front of him, Luna walked next to a little girl who walked slightly bent in order to keep her hand on Luna's back. Aiyanna walked next to the tallest of the children, who held the smallest. This smallest child looked back at Finn with wide eyes that seemed too old for his tiny body. Finn looked past them to where Erilyn stood, barely visible in the almost nonexistent light.

"I'll go scout ahead," Erilyn said. Finn ached to go with her, but knew he shouldn't. He adjusted his grip on the children's hands and they leaned closer to him, strengthening his resolve to stay. "When I've found a way around, I'll call you." She was looking at the oldest girl, who nodded, her spine tall even as she sagged under the weight of the younger child.

Erilyn looked back over everyone's head and focused her gaze on Finn. Even though she wasn't touching him, he felt that same warmth seep into him. "I'll be back as soon as I can."

I nodded at her and she was gone, taking a piece of me with her.

We sat to wait, not knowing if Erilyn would call us in minutes or hours, and we all needed to rest. I sat and three children, the middle three, immediately crawled into my lap. They were small enough but they all barely fit, and I wondered how old they were.

"We don't know," the little girl who'd been holding onto Luna said. "I think I'm—" her face scrunched up as she thought, "six. I'm not sure. I'd have to sit and count all my sleeps."

"It doesn't matter," the oldest girl said, still holding the smallest boy. Aiyanna had offered to give her a break, but the little boy wouldn't let go. The oldest girl was staring in the direction Erilyn had gone, her expression intent. Luna moved between the children, stopping for a moment as tiny fingers petted her fur or hugged her neck, a nursemaid checking on her wards.

"It does," the little boy in Finn's lap said. "I know I'm nine." Finn was shocked. He was so small. "And so is Noah, my sister. We're twins." His voice was quiet, but there was joy there.

"Twins," Noah said, leaning against Finn as if she were about to fall asleep, though her eyes were wide. "Jubal and me."

"Hush," the oldest girl said, still not looking at them.

"What's her name?" Finn whispered and the oldest girl scowled.

Jubal smiled. "Seraphina. But we call her Sera. And that's Asa," he pointed to the little girl who thought she was six. "And that's Galen." The tiny boy, clinging to Seraphina's neck, stared at him without blinking.

"I'm Finn." He looked down at the three children in his lap—one sitting on each leg, the third, smaller girl sitting between them, rigidly upright and alert.

"We know," the twins said—Jubal looking at Finn with a smile, Noah's eyes half closed as she laid on him.

"Right."

"It's been a long time," Aiyanna said. She had been sitting quietly, staring in the direction Erilyn had gone, just like Seraphina. They looked remarkably alike, except Seraphina was much dirtier. She put her hand gently on Seraphina's arm. "Can you—?" she trailed off and the older girl nodded.

"Together," she breathed. All the children, even young Galen, closed their eyes and Finn felt his skin tingle again. It was silent for a long moment, and then the children's eyes opened wide. Asa started to cry and Galen buried his face in Seraphina's long, pale neck.

"What is it?" The hair on Finn's arms and neck were standing at attention.

Seraphina faced him, her sour expression now filled with fear. "Erilyn. They saw her. She's fighting."

One moment Finn was sitting, his blood icy, and the next the children had jumped off of him and he was running as hard as he could toward the battle. His breaths were ragged as he ran uphill, ran toward the light and the noise, ran toward Erilyn.

Chapter Thirty-Seven
Clash

Erilyn

I came to the cave mouth and realized it was the same cave Finn and I had used to enter Citadel. There were more caves, other routes below ground, which meant that Morrigan had tracked us. I'd led her right to Citadel.

Anger at myself welled up in me, but I pushed it away. I needed to focus. I stayed in the shadow, imagining that I was part of the stone, part of the earth—not that anyone out there was looking for me, but I needed to stay hidden. I closed my eyes and let my *sight* go.

I was immediately in the middle of the battle, Wylden and upworlders clashing all around me. Auras mixed as bodies collided—blades flashing, fists and feet flying.

It was dizzying how fast I was moving. I realized I was in the mind of a Wylden. I could feel rage and lust in me as if it were all I knew and I had to fight to remember who I was as I tried to simply observe. It was like holding onto a tree during a windstorm.

The snow beneath our feet was trampled and pink with blood, but I saw no prone bodies. The patrol wore their black uniforms, the Wylden wore their furs and tattered clothes, but it was their auras that caught me. So many colors flaring and blending, but they were all broken somehow, jagged.

In the middle of the fray, I tried to force the Wylden woman whose eyes I was using to look for Morrigan's deep, dark red.

I quickly found her on the fringes, fighting two men much larger than she was. Her high, tight ponytail had come loose and her hair was flying wildly all around. Blood poured from a gash above her eye.

I felt myself being drawn in, lost to the rage of battle, and pulled myself back to my own body, still safe and hidden in the dark cave. The battle was huge. There was no way around.

If we stayed in the caves, whoever won the battle would come through and find us. If we turned and went back toward Citadel, Roark's men would have us. I wouldn't let him have the children, but I couldn't bring them through this, either.

We were trapped.

I was afraid if I *looked* again, I'd be drawn in and wouldn't be able to pull back. There was something about the way my blood had sung with the adrenaline of battle that called to me even as I was repulsed by it. I needed to see with my eyes. Maybe I'd missed something before, distracted by blood lust.

Still imagining that I was stone, hoping no one out there sensed me, I peered around the rock. The battle was all around. Wylden men and women fought black clad patrollers. Off to the right I saw a potential path, hidden by the shadows of the trees cast by the moon and a large pile of crumbled rocks. If we could sneak there, we could make it if I caused a distraction first.

A particularly shrill scream cut through the night and I jumped. A Wylden man had Morrigan pinned beneath his boot, his long, jagged blade lifted above his head, ready to strike.

I darted out into the cold air without a thought as snow began to fall. With a scream of my own, I lunged at the Wylden, knocking him from above Morrigan and tumbling with him into the snow.

Panic set in as soon as my body hit the snow. Why had I done that? I couldn't go back to the children now, to Finn. I'd have to run or fight.

An unseen force knocked the Wylden man from me. I stumbled to my feet, ready to run, when Morrigan's shoulder plowed into my torso. My breath was ripped away as my back slammed into the hard, cold earth.

She leaned back and grabbed my hair before slamming my head into the ground and a colorful array of stars exploded in front of my eyes. With a low growl I shoved her off me. I kept my awareness open—her aura was a mess of jagged lines like broken glass—as my vision cleared.

She found her footing as I did and starting pacing around me, stalking like the big cats had stalked Finn and me. The battle continued around us, the Wylden man who'd attacked Morrigan having been drawn into another skirmish.

"You did this," she snarled. Her hair was stuck to the blood on her face and dirt marred her usually flawless skin. "You brought these monsters."

"What?" I turned a tight circle, always keeping her in my line of sight while trying to keep my awareness open in case someone came up behind me. I could feel her hatred like having my hand directly in a fire. "I didn't do this."

"They met us here!" she screamed, throwing her hands out and knocking me back as air hit me like fists. I scrambled back up and held up my own hands.

"I didn't do this!" I yelled back, drawing the attention of a few Wylden close by. I felt their gazes and then felt their minds probing me. They were intrigued and I shuddered. "I didn't, Morrigan. *You* followed me here. *You* brought them."

"Liar." She spat blood into the dirt.

The battle raged all around us, but for a moment all I could see was Morrigan. I opened up my awareness more and stumbled. The Wylden were ferocious, their auras hazy and shot through with black cracks like spider webs. The patrollers weren't much better, battling inside themselves as well as the Wylden all around. Their auras, like Morrigan's, looked like broken glass, and some were hazed in black like the Wylden they were battling.

I turned my eyes and my awareness back to Morrigan, whose rage had been growing, and gasped. Her deep red aura, broken like glass, was now filled with black spider webs and hazed in black just like the Wylden all around.

"Morrigan," I whispered, suddenly afraid.

And then she was on me, a growl ripping from her throat. I was too shocked to respond. Her fingers clawed at me. My skin tore beneath her nails. She pummeled my body, my face, and I tried to curl into a ball to minimize the pain. I flashed back to being a child in the caves, pummeled by stones, curled around my glowworms to keep them safe. At least this time the ones I needed to protect—the children, Finn, Luna—were far beneath the earth and couldn't be hurt.

As Morrigan beat me, I felt a familiar, terrifying heat well in my belly. I'd tried to stifle it as a child, but now I let it build. Let it start to burn its way through my limbs. I kept my head covered with my arms so I could think clearly. I felt a warm wetness, blood, and I wasn't sure if it was Morrigan's or mine.

It didn't matter. The heat had built to the point where I knew all I needed to do was let go and allow it to rip through me, through her, and this would end.

I was on the brink, but still held on to some transient hope that she would stop on her own.

And then, like a nightmare, I heard Finn's voice cut through the roar of battle, yelling my name.

Morrigan jerked up. I uncovered my face enough to see him. He ran toward us, his face contorted in horror.

The heat in my belly died as I tried to get up, but my whole body protested in pain.

Morrigan looked at him, aghast. I saw her aura shift back toward its normal color. I saw, from the corner of my eye, Wylden notice him and turn.

"No!" I yelled, throwing up my hand. He stopped as if caught by a rope. The Wylden were focusing on the cave. I could feel more than see the children, Aiyanna, and Luna. "No," I whispered as my heart broke.

Morrigan turned to me, her dirty hair swinging in a wild arc. Her eyes flashed once and her aura crackled and was shot through with black once more.

I managed to get to my knees, my chest heaving, my body on fire as bruises bloomed beneath the surface of my skin. The Wylden had seen Finn, knew about the children, and as soon as they could, would go after them.

I got to one knee as Morrigan picked up the long, jagged blade the Wylden man had held above her from where it had fallen to the earth. I looked up into her eyes and saw that she was gone. She snarled, showing all of her teeth, and charged me.

I felt Finn move, released from whatever I'd done to hold him back, as the blade came toward me. Time slowed. I saw the blade's jagged edge move toward me and knew I could stop it, but wasn't sure how—half my attention still on Finn and the children behind me. And then I felt Finn's arm wrap around me as he swung his body around into the path of the blade.

Time sped up and I rolled with him, the blade imbedded in his side. He was smiling up at me until he breathed and then his face contorted as blood seeped from around the metal.

I crouched over Finn in the snow. Morrigan, in front of us, covered her mouth with dirty fingers. She stepped toward us as tears coursed down her face.

The heat in my belly roared forth in a single instant. I looked up at her, crouching over Finn protectively, and she stopped, her face a mask of fear.

The heat inside me became liquid fire. I released it without a second thought, screaming as the fire burned through me, shielding Finn's body with my own.

Morrigan flew back with a grunt and hit the trunk of a snow heavy tree. All around, the Wylden and patrolmen who were fighting were tossed to the ground. The pink-snow covered earth steamed as the snow melted. And for a single moment, there was quiet.

And then, in less than a breath, panic.

The patrollers and Wylden alike were scrambling up, the snow on the clothes and skin having evaporated in the wave of heat I'd blasted them with. Beneath me, Finn wasn't moving. The Wylden were helping their injured before running. The limping patrollers ran back toward Sunnybrook.

Morrigan hadn't moved. I'd thrown her against a tree and there she sat, splayed, blood on the trunk behind where her head had hit. Her foggy eyes were locked on Finn.

Finn. I crouched over him, muscles tense and shaking, daring her with my eyes to come closer.

"Leave," I whispered, my breath rising like fog in the air, which was suddenly icy again as new snow fell and replaced what I'd melted. Her eyes met mine, confused. "Leave!" The word tore through my throat and she jumped as if slapped. Tears had left ragged trails in the dirt and blood on her face. I could feel her anger, her fear, her crushing despair. She turned and followed her patrol into the deep, dark woods.

I looked down at Finn, at his pale skin. My fire was gone and my shaking hands found the handle of the knife. I pulled it out, surprised it came so easily, and covered the wound with my hands.

"Finn. Finn, *please.*" I felt tears, hot on my face, as I tried to staunch the bleeding. "You're going to be OK," I said, my voice a whisper. I leaned over him and pressed my lips to his forehead. He was icy, but his eyes fluttered open.

He stared at me for a long moment, a small smile on his face, before his eyes rolled back in his head and his body went slack.

"No." I breathed. "No, no, no."

I shook all over as I closed my eyes and let my awareness loose. I focused on the green lines of energy that were Finn's essence. I could still see my gold there, threaded lightly through, but his light was starting to dim, to fade. Between my fingers I felt his blood seeping like cold honey.

I didn't know what to do. I was lost, flailing in a sea of blackness as beneath my hands he died.

And then the children were there, their minds joining with mine seamlessly. As one they blended with me, lending me their strength, their knowledge. Suddenly, I knew what to do.

As I thought it I willed it into existence. The torn flesh beneath my hands closed. The veins and blood vessels sealed. Another part of me traveled back to his center, back to the bright forest green light that made him who he was. I dove into it, right to the center, and let my own golden light burn brighter. The brighter I burned, the brighter he burned, until his green was no longer fading. Beneath my hands the bleeding had stopped. The children were still with me, giving me strength.

Still merged with his aura, I opened my eyes. His cheeks were pinker than they had been. His breaths were shallow, but even. I pulled my hands, sticky with blood, from him and gently pulled my aura away. Like removing a bandage, it ached for a moment. With my hands propped on my knees, I looked toward the cave.

The children slowly pulled away, one at a time. They were standing, holding hands, in the snow. Aiyanna was behind them, her tiny hands over her mouth, her eyes sparkling with tears. The children's dark red eyes were on mine and I thanked them with the last of my energy.

The sturdiness of my arms gave way and I fell toward the hard, cold ground. As I fell I saw Luna racing toward me, heard her keening cry as I sank into warm blackness.

Chapter Thirty-Eight
Eye to Eye

Finn

Finn woke under a thick, musty-smelling blanket, curled around Erilyn. He felt groggy, his mouth sticky and dry, and his side hurt. It was dark out, but the sky through the small window was beginning to lighten with sunrise.

"You're awake," came a whisper from beside the softly glowing fireplace. Finn rubbed his eyes and slowly sat, disentangling himself from Erilyn while making sure the blanket stayed over her. Luna was on her other side, stretched along her length.

"Where are we?" Finn stood from the bed and winced. He was in new clothes that fit poorly, but were warm, and thick woolen socks with a hole in the top.

Aiyanna was curled in a wooden chair, a blanket around her, her bright blue eyes almost shining in the darkness.

"A cabin. Our upworld guards used to use it. It's been empty a few years." She held a mug of pine tea in her hands and Finn's stomach growled. "There's more by the fire." She nodded toward it with her chin.

He filled a cup and sat on the hearth. Erilyn still slept, but Luna looked at him from her paws, her eyes sleepy. The children all slept on the other bed on the opposite side of the room.

Aiyanna and Finn sat in awkward silence for a few moments. Finn wanted to thank Aiyanna for bringing them here, for cleaning them up and keeping them warm and safe, but the words wouldn't come. He looked up at her, lit by dark orange firelight, and was struck by her sadness. Her mug was nearly full and her eyes, though unfocused, were on Erilyn.

"I was horrible to her as a child." Her words were soft as she sipped her cooling tea. "Horrible. I made her life miserable."

Finn shifted on the stone hearth and let the warmth of the cup seep into his palms.

"We all do stupid things when we're young," he said, taking a sip and wishing it were stronger.

"No," she said harshly, her gaze landing on him. "You don't understand. I tried—" she took a deep breath, her hands shaking. "I tried to *kill* her. The day she left." She closed her eyes and pursed her lips. "I wanted her to die, because she knew things about me no one was supposed to ever know. And because—" Her head dropped slightly and she shook her head with an angry exhale.

He looked past her anger and saw heartbreak. Suddenly the looks Aiyanna gave him, gave Erilyn, his strange jealousy, all made sense.

"You love her," he said. Her head snapped up, her eyes wide. "Just a guess," he shrugged, sipping his tea. "People often hurt the ones they love." He looked back to Erilyn, watching the gentle rise and fall of her side as she slept, facing away from him. After a long moment of silence, he looked back to Aiyanna. She was still staring at him, afraid. "I love her, too."

Aiyanna squared her jaw and he thought he saw tears well in her eyes. "I know." She sniffed once and sipped her tea again. "And she loves you."

Finn couldn't help the rising warmth in his chest, but he didn't smile. It would only hurt.

"We hurt the ones we love," she parroted back, her tone harsh now, and he looked back to her. "You can't hurt her." Slowly, Finn nodded, and Aiyanna looked away, a tear falling like a drop of silver down her cheek.

It had been two days since Finn woke and Erilyn still slept. Aiyanna wouldn't leave the cabin. The children had found a paste that, when rubbed into the skin, darkened it slightly and made going in the sun safe. Aiyanna, though, didn't use it. Instead she either stoked the fire, tidied up, or sat in her chair and watched Erilyn.

After the first day, Finn had gone out with the children. He and Aiyanna had come to a tenuous understanding, but he still felt awkward around her. So instead of staying with her in the warm cabin, he went out with the children and taught them how to play in the snow. He built a snowman and held Galen on his shoulders most of the time. All the kids had been bundled in clothes made for adults, though Aiyanna had done her best to adjust them. They didn't seem to mind as they played hard out under the sun. Only Seraphina, the oldest, didn't play. Instead, she stood off to the side and watched like an irritated mother. Finn tried to talk with her, but she wouldn't speak to him, and eventually he stopped trying altogether.

During the day the children would help him search for berries and roots buried in the frozen earth—they were remarkably good at finding food. At night he and Aiyanna spoke in short sentences while the children settled and fell into peaceful sleep after their small meals.

By the third day, Finn was worried. Water wouldn't keep her going much longer. He wanted her to wake up.

And yet, a part of him that he was ashamed of was glad she still slept. When she woke, he worried that she would see that Morrigan was still in his mind. He'd seen her injury, seen how angry and broken she looked. Something was wrong with her, and even though he'd just as soon never see her again after all she'd done he still wanted to know she was OK.

When he went back to Sunnybrook for Lucy, he would ask about her, make sure she was OK. After that, he promised himself he'd never think of her again.

A snowball to the chest brought him from his dark thoughts. In front of him, Jubal—one of the twins—stood with a mischievous look on his face. Finn smiled and started to scoop snow to retaliate. Jubal laughed and then jerked toward the cabin. All five of the children did. They all wore smiles. Then Finn felt it—a flush of warmth. *Erilyn.* She was awake.

He started toward the door, his snowball dropped and forgotten, when Seraphina's hand on his arm stopped him.

"Give her a few minutes," she said, wisdom ringing in her young voice. Finn looked down at the young girl and nodded, though he itched to run after her. Her hand fell away and she watched the cabin with him as smoke rose in a hazy spiral from the chimney.

Chapter Thirty-Nine
Tabula Rasa

Erilyn

I woke to the smell of a freshly stoked fire and pine tea. A heavy weight lay across my body. *Luna.* I could feel her purring even through the dense covers I was wrapped in. I let my awareness barely loose and felt Finn right away, outside, happy. Like an injured muscle, it hurt my head to use my awareness, so I pulled it back after a breath.

Body aching, I pushed the covers off. Luna stretched heavily beside me. We were in a cabin. The light from the window told me it was midday. Snow was piled on the sill.

"Erilyn?" Aiyanna's quiet voice startled me. I hadn't noticed her at all, standing off to the side. "I thought you might want some privacy." She handed me fresh clothes. "You can relieve yourself in there." She pointed to a tiny door off to the side.

"Thank you." This felt like a dream. I stumbled into the small room. There was no running water, but there was a space to relieve myself and a basin of freshly warmed water to splash on my face.

From the bruises on my abdomen and arms, I thought I'd been asleep a few days. Gingerly I pulled the new clothes on and folded the others before coming back out.

Aiyanna was sitting in a chair by the fire. When I came out of the bathroom she stood, her hands clenched nervously in front of her.

"How do you feel?" she asked, stepping forward.

I grimaced as I shrugged. "Sore, but OK." I tried to smile, but it hurt. I wondered how black and blue my face was. It didn't feel swollen, but more than one of Morrigan's blows had landed there.

"I'll get you some food." She gathered a shawl to go outside.

I put my hand on her arm and she froze. "You brought us here?"

She looked down at my hand on her arm. She looked delicate and young, not at all like the mean, angry child I'd known. She nodded as she looked up at me.

"Thank you." She blushed and pulled away from my hand.

For some reason, this irritated me. "I don't understand you," I blurted, too tired and sore to be more cautious with my words. Being with Lucy for a few weeks had made me bolder, more honest. It felt good even as it scared me. "You hated me, Aiyanna. You wanted to kill me. And then you saved my life. *Twice*." I threw up my hands and winced as my shoulders ached. "But you act like you don't want me here." I wanted her to look at me, to explain. I had been so relieved that she wasn't dead, that I hadn't killed her, but if we were going to keep moving forward, I needed to understand. "I just don't understand."

She took a deep breath and looked up at me, her crystal blue eyes piercing. "I'm glad you're here," she said, her spine tall, the shawl clutched in her hands. "I'm glad —" she looked up at me and I was struck by a sudden sadness and longing. "I'm glad you're OK."

Icy air wrapped around me as the door opened and a moment later Finn held me in his arms, cold from the snow. He held me tight and it hurt, but I couldn't help but smile. He lifted me off the ground, his arms around my waist, and buried his face in my neck. I breathed him in.

"You're OK," I breathed and he laughed as he sat me down. I heard the door shut as Aiyanna left, Luna with her, but I couldn't take my eyes from Finn's.

"*You're* OK," he said. His hands, still cold, cupped my face delicately. He didn't look surprised by my bruises, which I knew were there by how gentle his fingers were. He looked like he was about to say something, but instead bent down and gently pressed his lips to mine.

Even that gentle pressure hurt, but his lips on mine caused fire to spread through my body. I laced my arms around his neck and deepened the kiss, needing to feel him, to have more proof that he was alive and here with me.

His arms left my face and went back around my waist, lifting me to him so I wouldn't have to crane my neck quite so far. I was torn between kissing him more and breathing, but in the end breathing one. We parted with a gasp. I leaned my forehead against his and reveled in the feel of his breath over my lips.

After a moment of perfect quiet my stomach growled and he sat me down with a laugh.

"You've been asleep for three days," he said, pouring what I knew was pine tea in a mug and handing it to me. I took it in grateful hands and sipped it. "Drink this and then we'll get you some food."

"The children, are they OK?" I didn't want to search for them, not when reaching out for Finn had been so uncomfortable.

"They're fine. Playing outside."

"Outside?" I stood up straight, alarmed "It's daytime. Their skin—"

"They have some kind of ointment to wear. Asa said it would keep them safe for a few weeks before they needed to reapply it."

"Asa?" I asked before a quick sip. I was tired just from standing. Finn sat on the hearth and opened up his arms and pulled me gently onto his knees. His chin rested on my shoulder as his arms held me around the middle.

"I forgot you haven't really met them yet." He smiled. "You will."

It felt strange being in the dark. I hadn't realized how dependent I was on my ability until now.

"They told me you saved my life," he said, his breath tickling the hairs resting against my neck. "You're making a habit of that, you know." I felt him smile against my neck and leaned into him.

"If you would stop making a habit of almost dying, I wouldn't have to."

Finn laughed, big and loud, and pulled me closer him. "I'll try," he said.

Remembering the fight, remembering Finn bleeding out in the snow, I sobered. I put the mug down and turned so that I could see his face. He looked healthy, if a little tired. I shook my head, suddenly angry with him, and his smile fell.

"What you did was stupid, Finn. You could have died." I gripped his thick sweater between my fingers.

His eyes were unapologetic. "If I hadn't, you would have died. I could never let that happen." His voice was soft and his arms around me felt safe. "I know things between us have been strange." His grip around me tightened. "But I need you to know that you're all I want. Just you. And I'll do whatever I can to keep you safe."

The image of my aura mixing with his tangled together like lovers caused me to flush. "Me too," I said, then ducked my head, embarrassed. "I mean this is what I want." I gripped his shirt tighter. "Us."

He smiled and sighed. "Good." He helped me stand and returned my tea to my hands.

With Finn's hand on my back and a blanket around my shoulders, we went outside. The children were playing in the snow, their skin looking slightly darker than it should with whatever ointment they were wearing to protect them from the sun. They all smiled at me as we came out. Aiyanna was standing to the side, the same ointment on her face, a shawl pulled up over her head. She was squinting in the bright midday light reflected from the snow.

"It's peaceful out here," I said as Finn slipped his arm around my shoulders. Everything from the moment we entered Sunnybrook until now, felt like a bad dream. Being out in the woods with Finn at my side—this is what my life was supposed to be like. But even now, standing with only the sounds of the children's laughter around us, I knew that the nightmare wasn't over yet.

"It is." His voice was sad and I knew that he'd realized the same thing.

"But we have to go back to Sunnybrook," I said and he nodded. "We have to find Lucy. And—" I looked away from him, scared of what I would see in his face. "Something was wrong with Morrigan and her patrol." I tensed, but he only sighed. I felt a weight in my chest lift. "Just because the fight ended doesn't mean this is over."

Aiyanna, standing a few feet away, looked up at us with sad eyes. "If I know my father, he'll want to retaliate. Even though the upworlders never made it to us, the battle was evident. He'll attack them before they can attack us. Plus, we have the children." Her quiet voice was somber and I nodded.

"We have to warn Lucy. I think Cillian—" I felt Finn tense at the mention of Cillian's name and I leaned my head on his shoulder—partially to reassure him and partially because I was so tired. "I think he's in on all of it. We'll have to figure out a way to stop our two peoples from killing each other." Suddenly, it felt like too much. It felt hopeless. I sighed.

"We can do this," Finn said and kissed the top of my hair. Aiyanna nodded and joined us on the stoop, standing next to me, not quite close enough to touch.

I stood between them and watched Luna chase after the snowballs the children threw. All five children were smiling, basking in the cold sunlight. If nothing else, we'd saved them from a life of torment under Roark. If that was all that came from this, then it had been worth it.

I breathed in the scent of my cooling pine tea and took strength from Finn's lean form, and from Aiyanna's stoic presence. The only thing I missed was Lucy, but at least she was safe. Luna was safe. The people I loved in this world, the people I cared for, were safe. And in this moment, as I felt Finn's warmth seep into me like sunshine itself, that was all that mattered.

Epilogue

Morrigan

Limping and still dizzy from the fight four days earlier, Morrigan made her way through the woods toward the quarry cliffs. She passed Finley's cabin on the way and considered going in, but she didn't. She hadn't let herself think about his death and being in there, surrounded by his things, his half finished projects, would force her to. She wasn't ready for that yet.

It had been Erilyn's fault. She wouldn't let herself fully accept that he was dead, but she would let herself blame Erilyn. All of this was her fault. If it weren't for her, they'd have the nightcrawlers, they'd have the mines, and she'd have Finley.

She reached the quarry and started down. It was steep, but she'd traveled this path an innumerable number of times. She was prepared for each section of sloping ground that caused her to slide and enjoyed the rush instead of fighting it.

There was a switchback in the path that would lead her outside the wall, but she continued down into the quarry, headed for the very bottom where sunlight only reached late in the evening.

She slowed as she approached and scanned the area with her mind. It was invigorating, knowing what was around you without having to see it first. She found the two people she was looking for, deep in a cave at the bottom, and then she found the third and a cruel smile twisted her face.

As she traveled the last of the steep incline she heard labored breaths. She skidded to the bottom of the incline and stood before the third person, his anger and desperation for her like a drug.

"Hello, Darling."

Before her stood a Wylden man—thin and breathing raggedly through his nose and mouth. His hair was blonde and matted and he looked at Morrigan with a mixture of hatred and lust. As he stared at her, his aura shifted from its original blue until it almost completely matched her own red. He was her first success.

The man was hunched, fists clenched, as if he were holding himself back from coming after her. She smiled and closed the distance, placing her hand on his cheek. He growled, his aura growing brightly, and her smile grew.

"Darling," she said, stroking his hairy, grizzled cheek. She leaned closer to his face. "Know your place," she whispered as she let a tendril of energy—a little pain and a little pleasure—slip through her fingers.

The Wylden keened, his eyes going glassy. She placed a kiss in the corner of his mouth and she stepped around him. He would keep anyone not allowed away as he had for the last few months. He'd even killed another Wylden who'd stumbled too close after being separated from his pack. Morrigan had rewarded her darling for that even as he'd moaned in remorse.

Morrigan picked up a torch that had been left at the entrance and made her way into the deep cavern.

A small fire was burning behind a set of iron bars that had been secured in the stone and earth. A woman with long gray hair, tied back in a silvery braid, was sitting at a table, scribbling into a notebook by candlelight.

"You look like hell," the woman said as Morrigan approached.

Morrigan ignored her and placed the torch in a bracket on the wall. "Any progress?" She directed her question to the second person in the cave—a tall, broad shouldered man with blonde hair that hung in his eyes. He looked up at her from the stones he was inspecting on a tray.

"Not so far. She's doing her best." Cillian rarely came down here, preferring to let Morrigan tend to the vitium research, but he'd come a lot in the last few days.

"That's not good enough." Morrigan turned to the woman who was still pouring over a book and taking notes. "Did you hear me?" The woman grunted in response. "Rosemarie!" she yelled, kicking a metal bar, a twang resounding from the rock and dirt walls.

Rosemarie looked up, her expression tired, her face thin. "What do you expect from me?" she asked, pushing the book away. "You've given me four days to change *everything* about the way you take your precious boost. It took me years to perfect the old way. I need more time."

Rosemarie turned back to her books and sighed, pulling the notebook closer. She shifted her feet, a metal ring around her ankle clanking as she tried to shift it so it wouldn't chafe.

"I expect you to work harder." Morrigan pressed against the bars. She looked back at Cillian and opened her thoughts to him. His eyes grew wide, almost sad, and he shook his head, but Morrigan smiled to show all her teeth. She looked at Rosemarie's aura—bright, pure white, marred with the dark red streaks that let Morrigan know she had some semblance of control. "I expect you to do this in the time you're given or I will kill someone you love."

Rosemarie laughed, an ugly sound, but didn't look up. "There's no one left alive that I love," she said, spinning toward Cillian. "*You* made sure of that." She spat the words. Cillian averted his gaze and cleared his throat.

"Sure there is," Morrigan said, her voice a purr. Rosemarie focused on Morrigan, doubt written across her features. "If you don't do what I need you to, I'm going to kill Erilyn."

Rosemarie froze and Morrigan delighted in the way her aura flared bright before crackling in fear.

"I don't know what you're talking about," Rosemarie said, her voice trembling.

Morrigan laughed. "Did you forget that I own you?" She pointed to her head and smiled. Rosemarie's aura dimmed in defeat. "I know you. And I know where Erilyn is. I'm stronger than her, Rosemarie. All thanks to you. And if you don't do what I say, she dies, and it will be your fault."

Morrigan turned then, smiling at Cillian. His conflicted expression, the sadness that poured off him like smoke, turned her smile into a scowl. She'd had Cillian at one point, too, but Erilyn had stolen him away as surely as she'd stolen Finley.

"You have a week," she said over her shoulder as she retrieved her torch. "If it's not done by then, I'll bring her here to see you and you can watch her die."

Morrigan thought she heard Rosemarie, normally as stoic as stone, inhale as if she might cry. This calmed the anger bubbling inside. She was still in control, still in charge.

Without a word to Cillian, she walked out into the cold day and made her way back toward the city. In a week she'd be healed and she would go after Erilyn, whether Rosemarie had completed the new vitium boost or not. And when she had her, after she hurt her as much as she could, she would kill her.

About the Author

Lindsey S. Frantz was born and raised in Appalachia and earned her MFA from Bluegrass Writers Studio at Eastern Kentucky University. Her stories and poems have previously appeared in numerous literary journals, including *Main Street Rag's Villains Anthology*, *Ruminate Magazine*, and *Emerge Literary Journal*.

She currently lives in sleepy, art-rich Berea, Kentucky with her husband, Vince, and their two young children, James and Sadie.

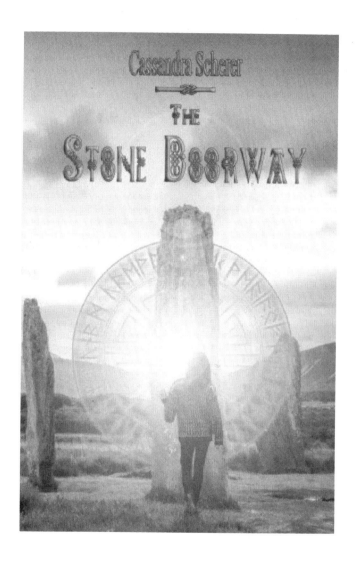

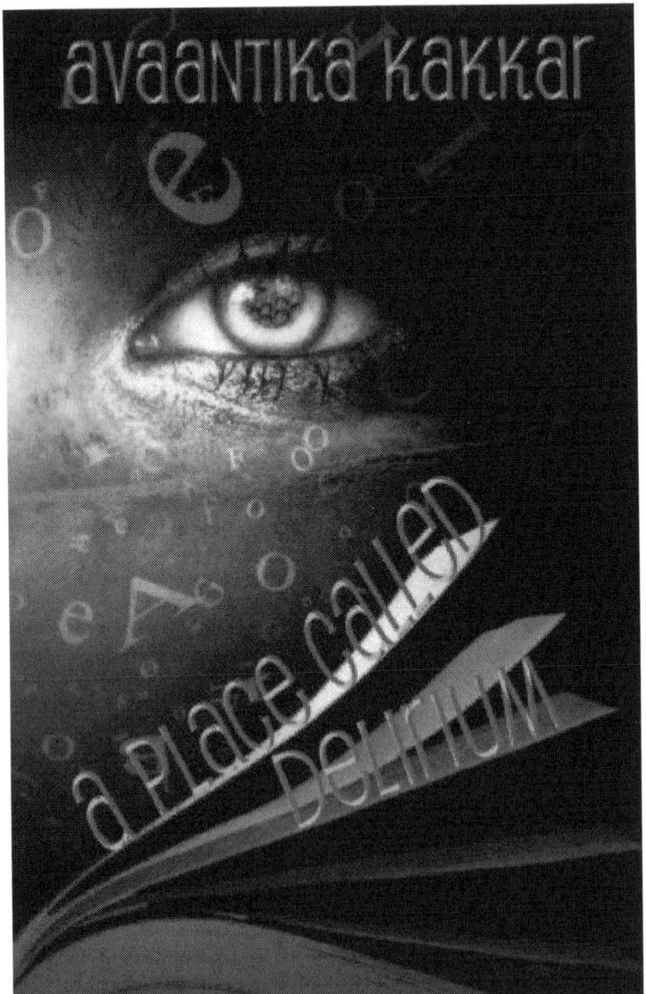
avaantika kakkar
a place called
Delirium

THE CLOCKWORK REPUBLICS SERIES

REVENGE
&ROSES

A STEAMPUNK BEAUTY & THE BEAST

KATINA FRENCH

Printed in Great Britain
by Amazon

45112011R00222